C.J.S. Thompson

I0651008

The Mystery and Romance of Alchemy and Pharmacy

Outlook

C.J.S. Thompson

The Mystery and Romance of Alchemy and Pharmacy

1. Auflage | ISBN: 978-3-73262-933-6

Erscheinungsort: Frankfurt am Main, Deutschland

Erscheinungsjahr: 2018

Outlook Verlag GmbH, Frankfurt.

Reproduction of the original.

THE MYSTERY AND ROMANCE

OF

ALCHEMY AND PHARMACY

THE SCIENTIFIC PRESS, LTD.

THE MYSTERY AND ROMANCE

OF

ALCHEMY AND PHARMACY

BY

C. J. S. THOMPSON

AUTHOR OF "POISON ROMANCE AND POISON MYSTERIES,"
"THE CHEMIST'S COMPENDIUM," "THE CULT OF BEAUTY,"
ETC., ETC.

LONDON

THE SCIENTIFIC PRESS, LIMITED

28 & 29 SOUTHAMPTON STREET, STRAND, W.C.

1897

2

PREFACE.

I⊤ has been my endeavour in the following pages to sketch, however imperfectly, some phases of the romance and mystery that have surrounded the arts of medicine, alchemy, and pharmacy from the earliest period of which we have record down to the close of the eighteenth century. The influence of the past on the present is greater than we commonly suppose. In this age of rapid scientific progress and brilliant research, we are apt to overlook and lose sight of the patient labours of the early pioneers of science, many of whom laid the foundations of discoveries that have since proved of inestimable value to mankind. Hence the history of the past, whether in science or in art, is always worthy of study and attention.

My thanks are due to the Editor of the *Pharmaceutical Journal* for permission to reproduce several illustrations which appeared in its pages together with a portion of this work.

C. J. S. T

LIVERPOOL, 1897.

ALCHEMY AND PHARMACY:

THEIR MYSTERY AND ROMANCE.

PART I.

CHAPTER I

THE DAWN OF THE ART OF HEALING.

T<small>HE</small> birth of the art of healing goes back to a period of great antiquity. The instinct that first led man to utilise the fruits of the earth for his bodily sustenance, may perchance have suggested the herbs which grew around him as a means of alleviating the ills of his flesh.

It is a matter of doubt whether medicine as an art was first practised in Egypt or China; from recent research probably the former, as at the time of the writing of the *Ebers Papyrus*, B.C. 1550, the Egyptians had a considerable knowledge of the use of herbs and other bodies for medicinal purposes.

The art of medicine had two foundations—empiricism and superstition—which have influenced it from its birth down to the present time.

The most ancient record of medicine and pharmacy known was discovered at Kahun in 1889, near the pyramid of Illahun in the ruins of an ancient town, which had apparently been inhabited by the builders of the pyramid. It dates from the twelfth dynasty, B.C. 2700 to 2500, more than a thousand years before the Exodus.

Besides containing instructions for midwives, it includes numerous formulæ for the treatment of various complaints, composed of such very homely articles as beer, cow's milk, honey, oil, onions, herbs, dates, and other fruits.

The *Ebers Papyrus*, which was found reposing between the legs of a mummy, throws a light on ancient Egyptian pharmacy, and was written in the reign of King Amenhotep I., of the eighteenth dynasty. It commences as follows: "Beginning of the chapter of applying medicaments to every part of the patient.

"I have come forth from Heliopolis with the mighty ones of the Temple of the Sun, the wielders of protection, the princes of eternity.

"Rescuing (?) I have come forth from Sais with the Mothers of the Gods, who have given me their protection.

"I have magic formulæ made by the Universal Lord to drive out the stroke of god and goddess, the Male Death and Female Death, *et cetera*,[1] that is in this my head, in this my neck, in this my shoulder, in this my flesh, in these my limbs, to punish the above-named enchanters (?) who introduce disturbance into this my flesh."

Such formulæ, evidently for recitation during the treatment, continue for a page and a half. The book has thus no general title, but plunges at once into the mysteries of the profession.

"Beginning of the mystery of the physician who knows the motion of the heart. There are vessels in it to every limb. When any physician, doctor, or amulet-maker puts his fingers upon the top of the head, upon the occiput, upon the hands, upon the chest, upon the arms, upon the legs, he communicates (?) with the heart, for its vessels extend to every limb, wherefore it is called the starting-point of every limb."

The following may be taken as an example of the recipes given in the manuscript:—

"A remedy for the belly that is painful: Cummin $\frac{1}{64}$ hin, goose-grease $\frac{1}{8}$ hin, milk $\frac{1}{16}$ hekt; cool, strain, and drink". The hin is about 29 cubic inches, and the $\frac{1}{16}$ hekt 18 cubic inches; the prescription is thus roundly $\frac{1}{2}$ cubic inch of cummin, and 4 of goose fat, in half a pint of milk.

This papyrus contains 110 pages, each page consisting of about twenty-two lines of bold Hieratic writing. It may be described as an encyclopædia of medicine as known and practised by the Egyptians of the eighteenth dynasty, and it contains prescriptions of all kinds of diseases—some borrowed from Syrian medical lore, and some of such great antiquity that they are ascribed to the mythological ages, when the gods yet reigned personally on earth. Among others is given the recipe for an application whereby Osiris cured Ra of a headache. In this papyrus is an example of an old Egyptian diagnosis and therapeutics, as follows: "When thou findest any one with a hardness in his re-hit (pit of the stomach), and when, after eating, he feels a pressure on his intestines, his hit is swollen and he feels bad in walking like one who suffers from heat in his back, then observe him when he lies stretched out, and if thou findest his intestines hot and a hardness in his re-hit, say unto thyself, This is a disease of the liver. Then prepare for thyself according to the secrets of the science from the plant pa-che-test and dates, mix them, and give in water."

It also contains numerous recipes for the treatment of diseases, for internal and external use. Most of the drugs mentioned are derived from indigenous plants, and such chemical bodies as alum, salt, nitre, and sulphate of copper are included in some of the prescriptions.

It seems probable that most of the medicines used in these early times were first tried as foods; and those which when taken in large quantities or in special conditions influenced the functions of the body, these and others found to be too strong for dietetic use were relegated to the books of medicine.

As an instance of this, the leaves and seeds of the castor oil plant and the astringent sycamore fig are included in many recipes, but Maspero states that there is little doubt that castor oil was taken regularly in food in the time of the Pharaohs, and at the present time it is a favourite adjunct to the salads of the Egyptian fellaheen. The same writer thinks the Egyptians began by eating every kind of food which the country produced, and so became acquainted with their therapeutic properties.

In another papyrus said to have been written about the time of King Chata of the first dynasty, who reigned B.C. 4000, the following prescription for promoting the growth of the hair is given:—

Pad of a dog's foot	1
Fruit of date palm	1
Ass's hoof	1
Boil together in oil.	

Dr. v. Oefele states of pharmacy before the time of Hippocrates, that although the practice of medicine was not separated from pharmacy among the Greeks and Romans, there was such a separation among the ancient Egyptians, from whom the distinction was handed down to the Copts, and by them to the Arabians; and, in fact, that the term pharmacist is probably of Egyptian origin, being derived from Ph-ar-maki, which signifies the preparation of medicine from drugs. The Egyptian pharmaki who were engaged in that occupation belonged to the higher social ranks of writers or academically-educated persons, comprising also the priests, physicians, statesmen, and military commanders.

The Jews were indebted to Egypt for their primary ideas of medicine, but they cast away the ideas of demonology and magic which clouded what was good in the practice of Egypt. The Talmud recommends onions for worms, and wine, pepper, and asafœtida for flatulency. The Talmudists are responsible for calling the earth, air, fire, and water elementary bodies. In the middle ages the Jews rendered service to the healing art, and had a large share in the scientific work connected with the Arab domination of Spain.

In China the use of drugs goes back to a very remote age, and alchemy was practised by the Chinese long previous to its being known in Europe. For two centuries prior to the Christian era, and for four or more subsequent, the transmutation of the base metals into gold, and the composition of the elixir of immortality, were questions ardently studied by the Chinese. It is, moreover, a matter of history that intercourse between China and Persia was frequent both before and after the Mahomedan conquest of the latter country;

that embassies from Persia as well as from the Arabs, and even from the Greeks in Constantinople, visited the court of the Chinese emperor in Shansi; that Arab traders settled in China, and that there was frequent intercourse by sea between China and the Persian Gulf; and lastly, that China had an extensive alchemical literature anterior to the period when alchemy was studied in the West. All these facts go to prove that the ancient science known as alchemy was originated by the Chinese, and not by the disciples of Mahomed, who only acquired the knowledge at second hand.[2]

It is somewhat curious that while the alchemists of the West were always in doubt as to what constituted the true Philosopher's Stone, the Chinese seemingly had no doubt as to its identity. Cinnabar was regarded by the early alchemists and philosophers of that nation as the wonderful body which was supposed to have the mysterious power of converting other metals into gold, and when used as a medicine would prolong life for an indefinite period. Ko-hung, author of the *Pau-p'uh-tsi p'ian*, a work of the fourth century, and undoubtedly genuine, gives various mineral and vegetable productions possessing in different degrees the properties of an elixir vitæ. In one paragraph of this work he states: "When vegetable matter is burnt it is destroyed, but when the Ian-sha (Cinnabar) is subjected to heat it produces mercury. After passing through other changes it returns to its original form. It differs widely, therefore, from vegetable substances, and hence it has the power of making men live for ever and raising them to the rank of the genii. He who knows the doctrine, is he not far above common men, etc.?"

In *materia medica* the knowledge of the Chinese was much in advance of the nations of the West, and their great herbal, entitled *Pun-Isaun-Kang-Mûh*, written by Le-she-chin in the middle of the sixteenth century, shows the discernment possessed by these curious people. This work consists of forty thin octavo volumes, the first three of which contain woodcuts of many of the minerals, plants, and animals referred to in the text. The woodcuts alone number 1100, and the work itself is divided into fifty-two divisions. The antiquity of the practice of medicine among the Chinese may be gathered from the fact that there exists a work entitled *A Treatise from the Heart on the Small-pox*, which was written during the dynasty of Icheon, B.C. 1122. In this work the eruption is described, and some kind of inoculation is also referred to as a remedy.

But it is to Greece that we have to look for the birth of medical art in the West, its practice by the priests being of great antiquity. The earliest record of a temple of medicine is of one erected in the Peloponnesus in the year B.C. 1130, or about fifty years after the fall of Troy. Other temples or centres of the healing art gradually sprang up, and round each of those clustered a little school of students. There were the temple of Health at Pergamus, the temple of Hygeia at Cytea, and the temples of Æsculapius at Cos and Epidamus, where the famous statue of Æsculapius stood. The father of ancient medicine, Hippocrates, graduated as a student of Cos, and Galen is said to have been at Epidamus.

It was in the temple of Æsculapius at Greece that any record of medicine was first kept, the names of diseases and their cures being registered on tablets of marble. The priests and priestesses, who were the guardians of the temple, prepared the remedies and directed their application, and thus commenced the practice of physic as a regular profession.

These official persons were ambitious to pass as the legitimate descendants of Æsculapius, and therefore assumed the title of the Asclepiades. The writings of Pausanius, Plutarch, and others abound with accounts of the artifices of these early practitioners. Aristophanes mentions the dexterity and promptitude with which they collected and put into their bags the offerings on the altar.

The patients were wont to repose on the skins of sacrificed rams in order to procure celestial visions. As soon as they were supposed to be asleep, a priest, clothed in the dress of Æsculapius, imitating his manner, and accompanied by the daughters of the god (that is, by young actresses well up in their parts), entered and solemnly delivered a medical opinion. The student sat at the feet of the philosopher of his choice, and after a certain period and course of probation, was granted the rights of priest and physician to practise as a teacher and healer.

They had their code and ethics of a standard almost equal to those of to- day, and their knowledge of surgery, and the use of the herbs and plants which grew around them, was not a little.

Entering on their novitiate at their chosen temple or school, they were required to make a protestation or oath, of which the following is the one made by Hippocrates:—

"I, Hippocrates, do now promise and protest to the great god Apollo and his two daughters Hygeia and Panadie, and also to all the gods and goddesses, to observe the contents of this oath or tables wherein the oath is carved, written, or engraved, so far as I can possibly, and so far as my wit or understanding shall be able to direct me, *viz.*, I yield myself tributary and debtor to the master and doctor, who hath instructed me and showed me this science and doctrine, even as much or rather more than to my father who hath begotten me, and that I shall live and communicate with him, and follow him in all necessities which I shall know him to have, so far as my power shall permit and my goods extend. Also that I shall love and cherish his children as my brother's, and his progeny as my own. Further, that I shall teach, show and demonstrate the said science without reward or covenant, and that I shall give all the canons, rules and precepts freely, truly and faithfully to my master, his children as to my own, without hiding or unacting anything, and to all other scholars who shall make the same oath or protestation, and to no others. Also that in practising and using my science towards the sick, I shall use only things necessary, so far as I am able, and as my spirit and good understanding shall give unto me, and that I shall cure the sick as speedily as I may without dilating or prolonging the malady, and that I shall not do anything against equity for hatred, anger, envy or malice to any person whatsoever. Moreover, that I shall minister no poison, neither counsel nor teach poison, nor the composing thereof to any. Also that I shall not give nor cause to be given, nor contend that anything be applied to a woman breeding, to destroy and make her void her fruit. But I shall protest to keep my life and science purely, sincerely and inviolably, without deceit, fraud or guile. And that I shall not cut or incise any person having the stone, but shall leave the same to those who are expert in it. And, furthermore, that I shall not enter into the patient's house lest with purpose to heal him, and that I shall patiently sustain the injuries, reproaches, and loathsomeness of sick men and other base railings, and that I shall eschew, as far as I may, all venereous lasciviousness. Moreover, I protest, be it man, woman, or servant who is my patient, to cure them of all things, that I may see or hear either in mind or manner, and I shall not betray that which should be concealed or hidden, but keep inviolable with silence; neither reveal any creature under pain of death. And therefore I beseech our gods that observing this protestation, promise, and vow entirely and inviolably, all things in my life, in my art, and science, may succeed securely, healthfully, and prosperously to me, and in the end eternal glory.

"And to him that shall violate, transgress, or become perjured, that the contrary may happen unto him, *viz.*, misery, calamities, and continual maladies."

We have here principles laid down which would do honour to any medical body, and which show the highly civilised condition and the excellent moral teaching of the early Greek philosophers and priests.

CHAPTER II.

THE WIZARDS OF EARLY GREECE.

ONE of the earliest magicians or soothsayers of which we have record out of the era of mythology was Tiresias. He lived in the times of Œdipus and the war of the seven chiefs against Thebes. For having offended the gods he was visited with blindness, but being repentant, tradition states they recompensed him for this affliction by endowing him with the gift of prophecy and the act of divination. He is also said to have been able to hold communion with the feathered world, and to have power over the spirits of the dead, whom he could compel to appear and reply to his inquiries. His incantations and spells were supposed to be irresistible, and he could foretell future events by signs from fire, smoke, and other methods of divining.

Abaris, a native of Scythia, was another magician of renown. There is no exact record of the time in which he lived, but he is represented by some as having constructed the Palladium which protected Troy from its enemies for a long time. Other authors declare he was a friend of Pythagoras, who flourished some 600 years later.

According to Herodotus, he travelled over the world with an arrow, eating nothing during his journey. By others it is said the arrow was presented to him by Apollo, and that upon it he rode through the air, and travelled over lands, seas, mountains, and other inaccessible places. But from all accounts his repute as a magician and seer is confirmed. He is said to have foretold earthquakes, allayed storms and pestilence, cured disease by charms and incantations, and was generally revered for his power and command over the dwellers in the unseen world.

Pythagoras, one of the most notable magicians in early history, was born about the year B.C. 586, and lived during the time of Cyrus and Darius Hystaspes, of Crœsus, of Pisistratus, of Polycrates, and Amasis King of Egypt. He was renowned not only as a philosopher but as a leader and politician, and was learned in all branches of science then known. The early part of his life was spent in Egypt, but he also travelled in order to gather experience and knowledge until he reached the age of forty years.

Afterwards he founded a school, where he lectured and instructed a large number of followers who were attracted by his wisdom and learning. He divided his pupils into two classes: the neophytes, to whom were explained the elementary and general principles of his philosophy, while the advanced were admitted into his entire confidence and formed a brotherhood, who threw their property into a common stock and lived together.

During the latter part of his life he is said to have lived in Magna Græcia, where he carried on his studies and made some of his great discoveries. He was a profound geometrician, and two great theorems, one still known as the Pythagorean, are ascribed to him. He propounded the doctrine that the earth is a planet of spherical form, and the sun the centre of the planetary system.

His philosophy prescribed and taught a total abstinence from everything which had animal life, and temperance in all things, together with the subjection of the appetites of the body. By this strict discipline, he seems to have obtained almost complete control over the wills and minds of his followers, from whom he demanded the utmost docility. Preparatory to entering on his novitiate, the pupil was strictly examined by the master as to his principles, habits, and intentions. The tone of his voice, his manner of speaking, his walk, gestures, and the lines of his face and the expression of his eyes, were all carefully observed, and only if all these features were satisfactory was he admitted as a probationer. After this interview the master withdrew from the sight of the pupil, who could then enter on his novitiate of three and five, in all eight years, during which time he was not permitted to look on the master, but only hear him speak from behind a curtain, and he was enjoined to preserve the strictest silence.

To add to his mystery and authority, Pythagoras is said to have hid himself during the day from his pupils, and was only visible to them after the night had come on. He is described as having a most imposing and majestic appearance, with a grave and awe-inspiring countenance. When he came forth he appeared in a long garment of the purest white, with his long beard flowing, and a garland upon his head.

He allowed his followers to believe he was one of the gods, and he is said to have told Abaris that he resumed human form so that he might win the confidence of man.

Doubtless, owing to his great attainments and his superiority to the men of his time, he considered himself more divine than human, and he claimed to have miraculous endowments. Those who were not of his followers ascribed the stories related of him to magic, which probably, like other philosophers, he studied.

Among other stories which tradition has handed down concerning Pythagoras are the following: He professed to have appeared in different ages in various human forms—first as Æthalides, the son of Mercury, and then as Euphorbu, who slew Patroclus at the siege of Troy, and as other individuals also.

He is said to have tamed a bear by whispering in its ear, and prevailed on it to feed on vegetables alone. He called also an eagle down from its flight, causing it to sit on his hand as if quite tame. When Abaris addressed him as one of the heavenly host, he convinced him that he was indeed a celestial being by showing him his thigh of gold, which also he exhibited to sceptical pupils. At another period he absented himself from his associates in Italy for a year: when he re-appeared he stated he had been sojourning in the infernal regions, and gave them wonderful descriptions of the strange things he had seen there.

These and many other fabulous stories are related of this singular man, which prove him to have been as wily as he was wise.

One curious rule by which he bound his pupils is worth mentioning. At the end of their novitiate, if it was discovered that their intellectual faculties were too weak to grapple with the intricacies of his theories and problems, they were expelled the community; the double of the property they had contributed to the common stock was refunded to them; a monument inscribed with their names was placed in the meeting-place of the community, and they were considered as dead by the brotherhood.

It is easy to imagine with what feelings these measures would be regarded by some who were called to submit to them, and so they eventually proved the cause of the break-up of the Pythagorean school.

Cylon, a man of great wealth of Crotona, conceived a great partiality for Pythagoras, and became a novice with Perialus, and submitted to all the severities of the school. They passed through the three years of probation and five years of silence, and were received into the familiarity of the master. But after they had delivered their wealth into the common stock, Pythagoras pronounced them to be deficient in intellectual power, or for some other reason most probably they were expelled. A tablet inscribed with their names was set up, and they were pronounced dead to the school.

Cylon, who was a man of excitable and violent temperament, became highly incensed at this treatment, and resolved on vengeance. Collecting a band of followers, which probably included a large number of rejected students, they surrounded the school of the master and set it on fire. Forty people are said to have perished in the flames, but Pythagoras with two of his pupils escaped to Metapontum, where he took refuge in the Temple of the Muses. The strife fomented by Cylon broke out afresh, and he was closely besieged in the temple by his enemies. The rioting continued, and as no provisions could be conveyed to him, he finally perished with hunger, according to Laertius, after forty days' abstinence.

Thus ended Pythagoras, a man of undoubted genius, and in knowledge much in advance of his time. Although his teachings were mixed up with considerable artifice and deception, he ranks, as one of the greatest of the Greek philosophers.

Epimenides was a native of Crete, and probably lived before the time of Pythagoras. He was credited with marvellous performances from a very early age, and is said when quite a lad to have retired to a cave and slept for fifty-seven years. He then returned to his father's house, which he found in the possession of a new tenant, and the family disappeared. At length he came across his brother, who had grown into an old man, who after some time acknowledged him.

On this story becoming known, he was accounted a favourite of the gods, and he professed to be endowed with supernatural gifts.

He made it known that he was supplied with food by the nymphs, and that he was exempt from the usual necessities imposed on the body by Nature. He boasted that he could separate his soul from his body and recall it as he thought fit. He professed to have dealings with the unseen world, and would exorcise evil spirits or work spells. He had great renown as a seer, and his prophecies were regarded as direct messages from the gods. But the great act of his life was his delivery of Athens from a great pestilence after the rebellion of Cylon. The plague, which had almost decimated the city, could not be stopped, and the Athenian Senate, after much deliberation, resolved to send for Epimenides, who was at that time in Crete. A special vessel was placed under the command of one of the first citizens of the State, who was commissioned to bring the wise magician.

On his arrival at Athens he at once set to work with solemn rites and ceremonials. He commanded that a number of black and white sheep should be led to the Areopagus, then be let loose and allowed to wander whither they wished. Certain persons were instructed to follow them and mark the spot where they lay down, on which place the animal was sacrificed to the local deity. In this manner, it is recorded, the plague was stayed. According to some writers he also sacrificed human victims. Although pressed by the Athenian Senate to take a recompense for his services, Epimenides is said to have refused all gifts, stipulating only that there should be perpetual peace between the Athenians and the people of Gnossus, his native city. He died shortly afterwards, at the reputed age of 157 years.

Empedocles was a distinguished magician, orator, and poet, and was born in Agrigentum, Sicily. He was a follower of Pythagoras, and probably received instruction from his successors. He was credited with miraculous powers, and to have been able to restore the dead to life. He was skilled in medicine and the use of herbs, and was indeed a general benefactor to the citizens of his native place, where he was almost worshipped as a god. Like other philosophers of his time, he was inordinately vain, but was undoubtedly a man of great intelligence, and conferred immense benefits on his fellow-creatures. His belief in the power of magic is shown in the following words he was wont to address to his students: "By my instructions you shall learn medicines that are powerful to cure disease and reanimate old age; you shall be able to calm the savage winds which lay waste the labours of all the husbandmen, and, when you will, shall send forth the tempest again; you shall cause the skies to be fair and serene; or, once more, shall draw down refreshing showers, reanimating the fruits of the earth; nay, you shall recall the strength of the dead man when he has already become the victim of Pluto".

Of himself he said: "I mix with you a god, no longer a mortal, and am everywhere honoured by you, as is just; crowned with fillets and fragrant garlands, adorned with which, when I visit populous cities, I am revered by both men and women, who follow me by ten thousands, inquiring the road to boundless wealth, seeking the gift of prophecy and who would learn the marvellous skill to cure all kinds of diseases".

Of other wizards of early Greece, Herodotus mentions Aristras, a poet of Proconnesus, who is said to have mysteriously disappeared from the earth for 340 years, and then appeared again at Metapontum and commanded the citizens to erect a statue to him. Also Hermotimus, who was reputed to have the power of separating his soul from his body at will. But little is known beyond the merest tradition of these worthies.

CHAPTER III.

THE WIZARDS OF THE ROMAN EMPIRE.

T$_{HE}$ Roman philosophers, like the Greeks, claimed to possess occult powers, and the practitioners of magic and sorcery were numerous during the time of the Empire. We have a graphic description of the incantations of a Roman sorceress in the story of Dido. Deserted by Æneas, she resolves on self-destruction. To delude her sister as to her secret purpose she sends for a priestess from the gardens of the Hesperides, pretending that her object is to effect the return of her lover by means of certain magical incantations. The priestess, who is invested with magical powers, can call up the spirits of the dead, cause the solid earth to rock and quake, and the trees of the forest to descend from the mountains. On the arrival of the sorceress, she commands that a funeral pyre shall be erected in the interior court of the palace, and that the arms of Æneas, what remains of his attire, and the marriage bed in which Dido had received him, shall be placed upon it. The pyre is to be hung round with garlands and branches of cypress, and the whole crowned with a picture of Æneas and his sword.

Altars were placed around, and the priestess, with dishevelled hair, cried aloud with terrible charms upon her three hundred gods, upon Erebus, Chaos, and the three-faced Hecate. The waters of Avernus were then sprinkled about, and certain magical herbs that had been cut by moonlight with a sickle of brass. The priestess had with her the excrescence which is found upon the forehead of a new-cast foal, of the size of a dried fig, a talisman of great power.

Dido is then called upon to approach, and, with her robe drawn up exposing one bare foot, she makes the circle of the altars, embracing them successively, and breaks over each a consecrated cake. The pyre is lit, and the charm is supposed to be complete.

But all the power and the elaborate ritual prescribed by the sorceress were of no avail. Æneas returns not, and the broken-hearted Dido finally stabs herself and dies.

Many prodigies are interspersed throughout the early history of Rome, and most of the acts of these people were surrounded with a halo of superstition natural at the time, and doubtless largely exaggerated. Virgil, Horace, Ovid, and Lucan all allude to the belief in and the practice of sorcery and magic by the Romans.

In the eighth eclogue of Virgil we have a detailed description of a Roman sorceress. She is introduced by the poet as giving directions to her assistant as to the working of certain charms. Her object (a common one apparently at that time) is to recall Daphnis, whom she calls her husband, to return once more to her arms. The assistant is directed to burn vervain and frankincense, and the highest efficacy is ascribed to a solemn chant, which is capable of calling down the moon from its sphere or making the cold-blooded snake burst in the field, and was the means by which Circe turned the companions of Ulysses into beasts. The image of Daphnis is then ordered to be thrice bound round with fillets of three colours, the assistant at the same time repeating the words, "Thus I bind the fillets of Venus," and then paraded about a prepared altar.

An image of clay and one of wax are placed before the same fire; and as the image of clay hardens, so does the heart of Daphnis harden towards his new mistress; and as the figure of wax softens, so is the heart of the ex-lover made tender towards the sorceress. A sacred cake is then broken over the image, and crackling laurels burnt before it. She prays that as the wanton heifer pursues the steer through woods and glens till at length, worn out with fatigue, she lies down on the oozy reeds by the banks of the stream, and the night dew will not even drive her away, so Daphnis may be led on after her for ever with inextinguishable love. The relics of his belongings are then buried beneath the threshold. She bruises poisonous herbs of resistless virtue, which had been gathered in the kingdom of Pontus, herbs which enabled him who gave them to turn himself into a hungry wolf prowling amidst the forests, to call up ghosts from the grave, and to translate the ripened harvest from the field where it grew to the lands of another. The ashes of these herbs are cast over her head into the running stream, while she must not look behind her.

At length the sorceress begins to despair and cries, "Daphnis heeds not my incantations, heeds not the gods". She looks again, and perceives the ashes on the altar are glowing and emitting sparks of fire. Her faithful house dog barks before the door. "Can these things be," she exclaims, "or do lovers dream what they desire? It is not so! The real Daphnis comes; I hear his steps; he has left the deluding town; he hastens to my longing arms!"

In the works of Horace an interesting description of a witches' incantation is also given, the details of which it is instructive to compare with those given by other writers.

Four sorceresses are assembled in conclave, the chief being Canidia, with three assistants, in order to work a charm by means of which a youth named Varus, for whom Canidia had conceived a passion, may be compelled to reciprocate her affections.

Canidia, with the locks of her dishevelled hair twined round with venomous and deadly serpents, orders the wild fig tree and the funeral cypress to be rooted up from the sepulchres on which they grew, and these, together with the egg of a toad smeared with blood, the plumage of the screech owl, various herbs brought from Thessaly and Georgia, and bones torn from the jaws of a famished dog, to be burnt in flames fed with perfumes from Colchis. One assistant, whose hair stands stiff and erect like the quills of the sea- hedgehog or the bristles of a hunted boar, sprinkles the ground with drops from the Avernus, while another, who is reputed to have had the faculty of conjuring the stars and moon down from heaven, assists in other ways.

The fourth witch is busy digging a hole with a spade, in which is to be plunged up to his chin the beardless youth stripped of his purple robe—the emblem of his noble descent—and naked, that from his marrow, already dry, and his liver (when at length his eyeballs, long fixed on the still renovated food which is withheld from his famished jaws, have no longer the power to discern), may be concreted the love potion from which the witches promise themselves the most wonderful results.

Canidia, unmoved by his sufferings, works herself into a great rage, and calls upon the night and the morn to help in her infamous incantation. But her victim manages to evade destruction by means of some magical antidote. She then resolves to prepare a still more powerful charm, exclaiming, "Sooner shall the sky be swallowed up in the sea and the earth be stretched a covering over both, than thou, my enemy, shalt not be wrapped in the flames of love as subtle and tenacious as those of burning pitch".

CHAPTER IV

THE FATHERS OF MEDICINE.

THOUGH Æsculapius is said to have lived so near to the time of the Trojan war, yet the Greeks knew very little about him. The superstition of the time gave him a position among the gods, and as he was adored under the character of the genius of physic, it came at last to be doubted whether he was ever a mortal; consequently his priests were obliged for their own sakes to make themselves masters of all the physic that the master could teach, that they might be qualified to give advice to those who applied to them; their prescriptions passed for the suggestions of the gods, the cures for the miraculous. But both diseases and remedies were carefully recorded. Strabo tells us that from these registers in the temple of Æsculapius at Cos, Hippocrates formed his plan for a proper diet.

Hippocrates, the wise physician and father of medicine, was according to Soranus the son of Heraclides and Phænaretes, descended from Hercules and Æsculapius. He was a Coan by birth, and was first instructed by his father, and then by Herodicus, and Democritus of Abdua, the philosopher. He flourished at the time of the Peloponnesian war, and after being instructed in physic and the arts, left his own country for Thessaly, where his fame soon became known, even as far as Persia. He was sent for by Perdiccás, King of Macedonia, who was then thought to be consumptive, but Hippocrates diagnosed it to be a disease of the mind, and soon cured the king. He is also said to have delivered his own country from a war with the Athenians by prevailing upon the Thessalians to come to their assistance, for which he received great honours from the Coans. He taught his art with great candour and liberality to those who were desirous to learn, and at length died full of honours, it is said, in his ninetieth year, and was buried between Gyrton and Larissa. A quaint old tradition states that at his tomb a swarm of bees settled and made their honey for a long time, with which children troubled with aphthas, anointed by their nurses at the grave, were easily cured.

He was by no means covetous of money, but grave in his behaviour and a lover of Greece, as appears from his curing those of that nation with the utmost diligence, and freeing many of their cities from the plague, for which he acquired great honours.

At first the art of healing was accounted a branch of philosophy, so that the cure of diseases and the study of nature owed their rise to the same persons. Among the many philosophers skilled in the art the most celebrated were Pythagoras, Empedocles, Democritus, and Hippocrates of Cos. After them came Diodes the Carystian, Praxagoras, and Chrysippus, with Hierphilus and Erasistratus, many of whom practised their art in entirely different ways. At this period physic was divided into three schools; the first cured by diet, the second by medicines, the third by manual operations. Those who treated by dietetic methods endeavoured to extend their views farther with the assistance of natural philosophy. Then came Serapion, the apostle of practice and experience, and afterwards Asclepiades, who worked a revolution in medical science as then practised.

The knowledge of both surgery and medicine even in the time of Celsus is very remarkable, and many of the forms of administration of medicine are employed at the present day. The enema was largely used by the ancients, a common one being hydromel, described by Dioscorides as being made by mixing two parts of water to one of honey; sea-water was also employed for the same purpose, and Celsus recommends the copious drinking of hot water as a laxative remedy.

Asclepiades was the originator of massage and friction, and in his book of general remedies describes his treatment, which is similar to that performed to-day. Poultices of meal of various descriptions were commonly employed, linseed or fenugreek being the favourite media.

Asclepiades studied in Alexandria, and after practising in Greece and Asia Minor, finally settled in Rome in the early part of the first century B.C. Here he soon met with success, and established a reputation for great skill. He was the physician and friend of Cicero, and probably also the instructor of Lucretius in the Epicurean philosophy, of which he was an enthusiastic advocate.

He believed the body to be composed of atoms or particles, with spaces between, through which, like a sieve, various atoms of other shapes were continually passing in and out of the body.

In practice he believed in curing his patients with as little discomfort as possible, which doubtless helped to make him popular. He was averse to the employment of violent remedies and the excessive use of emetics and purgatives so much favoured by his fellow-practitioners.

He advocated the use of music as a soothing agent, and was strongly in favour of bathing frequently and of massage.

He strongly believed in wine as a remedial agent, which it has been said may have accounted for his popularity with the Roman ladies, with whom as a physician he was in great demand. He lived to a very advanced age, and died it is stated from the effects of a fall.

Galen, born at Pergamus in the year A.D. 131, studied in the school of Alexandria, which then had a considerable reputation, and there he formulated his system of treatment founded on his knowledge of anatomy and on observation. His fame having spread abroad, he travelled to Rome and became physician to the Emperor Marcus Aurelius. According to Galen, the health of the body depended on an equal and uniform mixture of solids and liquids, and its sickness arose from their inequality; consequently, the physician should foresee illness. He was a profound student of anatomy in his early career, and afterwards turned his attention to physiology. His views as to inflammation, intermittent fevers, and his system of antipathies and sympathies, place him very much above his predecessors.

"In the beginning of the fifth century," says Lacroix, "the practice of medicine, like that of surgery, which was not yet a distinct branch, continued to be free without any authorisation being required. There were even women who, like the Druidesses of the Gauls, treated the sick." Charmers, unconscious, no doubt, of the occult forces which they set to work, attempted to cure neuralgic pains, country bone-setters to mend fractured limbs, while oculists and impostors of the worst kind travelled the country.

It was not until the close of the eighth century that a regular course of medical instruction was founded, the first of the kind being organised at Salerno, in the kingdom of Naples.

Alexander of Tralles, a noted physician, flourished in the middle of the sixth century. No Greek doctor equalled him since the days of Hippocrates in regard to his knowledge of his art in those primitive days. He is said to have possessed to a high degree the art of diagnosis, and he laid down as a principle, that no decision should be arrived at as to the treatment of a case until the specific causes of disease had been carefully considered. His depreciation of violent aperients, his views on melancholia and gout, and his generally common-sense treatment, stamped him as a man of superior attainments and ability. He was the first to resort to bleeding from the jugular vein, and to use iron in certain diseases affecting the blood.

It must not be imagined that the Roman practitioners of medicine were ill-paid, for it is recorded that Stertimus made some £6500 a year, and Canie, a surgeon, is said to have received £2000 for one operation, which contrasts well with fees of modern times. Votive offerings for health to the Roman deities were frequent, and sometimes consisted of land, animals, coin, jewellery, and other articles. Other bribes which have been discovered near ancient shrines are terra-cotta figures of deities, human beings, animals, and also portions of human anatomy, such as the liver or stomach. This superstition still exists, and is practised in many parts of Italy, the peasants making votive offerings similar to those of two thousand years ago.

The object of offering models of various portions of the body to special deities, was doubtless to propitiate the god to heal that special part in which the patient believed his complaint originated.

This custom of making offerings to the gods, called *donaria* by the Romans, originated at a very early period. They often took the form of land, buildings, cattle, tools of trade, jewellery, and cast-off clothes. Thus the temple of Artemis Brauronia was filled with women's clothing. In the temples of the healing gods, instruments of surgery, pharmaceutical appliances, painted tablets representing miraculous healings, and great numbers of models of various parts of the human frame, composed of metal, stone, and terra-cotta, were deposited.

Many of these ancient temples of healing were magnificent buildings with richly-decorated interiors, while others were simply shrines or grottos at the source of some hot spring or mineral water, where hundreds of those afflicted with various ailments flocked to bathe or drink the water. The priests in charge regulated the use of the waters and prescribed for the patients. After completing the course it was customary for the patient to throw an offering into the water, in the form of a silver cup, a coin, or some terra-cotta model of a limb, and then drag himself off, muttering a prayer. Others would hang their gifts on the walls, or deposit them at the feet of the statues of the gods placed around.

Magnificent offerings, such as goblets of valuable metal with votive inscriptions, have been occasionally found, and other ornaments of gold and silver. It is said, however, that *donaria* of precious metals were after a time melted down and disposed of by the priests.

Grateful patients or surgeons sometimes offered surgical instruments as a thanksgiving for a successful surgical operation; thus it is stated Erostratus offered to Apollo in the Temple of Delphus a forceps of lead, to show how little he approved of the fingers as a medium for extracting teeth. Drs. Sambon, Allaire, and others, who have discovered a large number of *donaria* of the Etruscan and Roman period, found among the pottery, invalid feeding-cups and feeding-bottles for infants. Many of the latter were modelled in the form of the female breast, and others in the shapes of animals. These articles were often placed in the tombs of young children who had died in babyhood, instead of the dishes of various foods which were deposited in the tombs of adults.

Among other *donaria* discovered, are models of the limbs and viscera of the human body in clay, showing upon them the marks of the various diseases from which the votaries had suffered. Thus the ancient temples must have presented a curious appearance, festooned on walls and ceilings with these numerous models, all of which told a tale of human suffering.

CHAPTER V.

THE EARLY AGE OF GREEK AND ROMAN PHARMACY.

ROME at an early period gave birth to several philosophers and practitioners in the art of healing. Cornelius Celsus, who is thought to have been a Roman, was a much esteemed writer of the time, and his works on medicine show the advanced state of surgery and medicine during the Roman Empire.

His work on medicine gives a considerable insight into the pharmacy of the Romans in his day. With reference to their weights, he says: "I would have it understood that in an ounce is contained the weight of seven denarii; next, that I divide each denarius into six parts, that is, sextantes, so that I have the same quantity in the sextans of a denarius that the Greeks have in their obolus".

Of the methods of administration employed in early Roman pharmacy, the malagma was commonly used. It was a kind of soft mass composed of herbs and grass beaten up to the consistency of a thick paste, and applied to the skin. Numerous formulæ for malagmas are given, in which pellitory, myrrh, resin, cardamoms, ammoniacum, galbanum, etc., are included. Their malagmas corresponded with our ointments. They also used plasters, of which the basilicon, of galbanum, pitch, resin, and oil, in an improved form, has survived two thousand years. Troches, for healing wounds, were composed of dry medicines held in suspension by some liquid such as wine or oil. Pessaries (vaginal) were originated by the Greeks, who called them pessi. The ingredients were placed in a piece of wool, and thus used. Powders and snuffs were also common methods of administration.

Antidotes for bruises, bites, and poisons were regarded as extremely important. One was called ambrosia, which Zopyrus is said to have compounded for the King Ptolemy; another was the celebrated antidote of King Mithridates.

The Greeks called their embrocations or ointments euchrista. The catapotia was the method used for internal administration in liquid form, for which many recipes are given by Celsus. The following will serve as an example:—

Athenio's Catapotia for a Cough.

Myrrh, pepper, each	p. ℈ i.
Castor, poppy tears, each	p. ℈ i.

which are bruised separately and afterwards mixed.

For venomous bites, the treatment of the ancients, if the wound was severe, was first cupping, or, if slight, the plaster of Diogenes was applied, or a salt fish bound over the wound. A curious remedy practised by the Greeks for hydrophobia was to throw the patient suddenly into a pond, and "if he could not swim let him sink several times, and thus drink; if he can swim, keep him down at times until he may be satiated with water, for thus at once," writes Celsus, "is both the thirst and the dread of water removed".

Their antidote for nearly all poisons was warm oil, given in order to induce vomiting.

The word collyrium, now applied to a lotion for the eyes, was also used by the ancients; but they gave it a greater latitude, and also employed it to describe a composition of powders wrought to a pasty consistence with a liquid, and formed into something like a tent for insertion into cavities.

Of the chemical bodies and drugs known both to the Greeks and the Romans, the number is not a few.

Cinnabar, which seems to have been known from a very remote period, was the name applied to the red sulphide of mercury, and also to dragon's blood. It is doubtless of the latter Pliny says "he believed to be the gore of a dragon crushed by the weight of a dying elephant, with a mixture of the blood of these animals". Copperas, lead, alum, copper, and iron were used as styptics.

Myrrh, frankincense, cardamoms, linseed, isinglass, and cobwebs were used as astringents.

Galbanum, storax, bitumen, are recommended for promoting suppuration, while pennyroyal, sulphur, pellitory, stavesacre, ox-gall, scammony, rue, and opium were all included in their medical recipes.

Dioscorides was the first to attempt to record in anything like a methodical manner the many drugs and chemical substances used by the early Greeks.

Pedacion Dioscorides, born in Anazaba in Cilicia, was a Greek physician, who lived in or about the second century. He gathered a great portion of his information on *materia medica* during his travels with the Roman army, which he accompanied on several expeditions in the capacity of physician. Afterwards he wrote his great work *Peri Hules Iatrikes* (about *materia medica*), which for fifteen centuries or more remained one of the chief authorities on that science. It treats of all the medicines then in use, with their preparations and action as then known. The work of this early physician first appeared in a Latin translation in 1478; the first Greek edition being published in 1499. The work was afterwards translated into Spanish, Italian, French, German, and Arabic.

PEDACION DIOSCORIDES.
From a drawing, 1598.

In describing the *Papaver sativum* and its virtues in this work, he says: "It is not improper to subjoin the method in which the opus or juice of it is collected. Some, then, cutting the poppy heads with the leaves, squeeze them through a press, and rubbing them in a mortar, form them into troches. This is called meconium, and is weaker than the opus. But whoever desires to gather

24

the juice must proceed thus: After the heads are moistened with dew, let him cut round the * (asterisk) with a knife, but not penetrate through them, and from the sides cut straight lines in the surface, and draw off the tear that flows with his finger into a shell. And come again, not long after, for it will be found standing upon it; and the day following it will be found in the same manner." Hence the old name poppy tears. Dioscorides was also learned in the preparation of wool fat, which he calls œsypum, known to modern pharmacists as lanoline. He says: "Œsypum is the oily part collected from sordid wool, thus: The wool was washed in warm water and all its sordes expressed; the fat floated with a froth, and upon throwing in some sea-water it subsided; and when all the œsypum was obtained from it in this manner, it was purified by repeated affusions of water. When pure it had no sharp taste, and was in some degree astringent and appeared white, and was emollient and filled up ulcers."

Recent excavations made at Pompeii and Herculaneum have thrown some further light on various articles of *materia medica* as it existed in the days just preceding the destruction of those cities. Aloe seems to have been held in high esteem by the practitioners of the time, and was employed, we learn from the historian, in twenty-nine diseases. It was prescribed in doses from 1 to 111 drachmas (about 68 grains), and mixed with wine was employed to stimulate the growth of the hair. Aconite, we find, was used in four diseases; and was supposed to be an antidote to any poison which might exist in the system. Other remedies mentioned include gum acacia, colocynth, elaterium, gold, silver, copper, and elecampane. It is further recorded of the latter drug, that Julia Augusta, daughter of Augustus Cæsar, used to eat the root daily.

Of the vegetable remedies about 150 are enumerated, and of these the cabbage seems to have held a prominent place. Other favourite medicines were rye, garlic, anise, mallow, rose, and lily.

In the animal kingdom, the remedies contributed were numerous, being mainly the various parts of man and beast. Among some of the least disgusting, hair, blood, and saliva may be mentioned.

Scrapings from the bodies of athletes, mixed with the oil with which they anointed themselves, were used as a tonic. The hair of a man torn from the cross was used as a remedy for quartan fever. The hyæna was employed as a medicinal agent in seventy-nine diseases; and the crocodile, chameleon, lion, elephant, camel, and the hippopotamus all contributed certain curative agents. Wool fat was held in great esteem.

Of minerals, iron, lead, nitrum, salt, gold, tin, silver, realgar, copper, and misy (a combination of the sulphates of copper and iron) are enumerated. Most of these articles are mentioned by the second Pliny, who was killed during the eruption of Mount Vesuvius which buried Pompeii.

THE ALCHEMISTS.

T$_{HE}$ word chemistry was used for the first time by Suidas, a lexicographer of the tenth century, and at that time meant an alloy of gold and silver. It is alluded to in connection with the Emperor Diocletian, of whom it is said, that irritated by a revolt of the Egyptians against the laws of the empire, he had all their books of chemistry committed to the flames, so as to punish them for their rebellion by preventing them from carrying on the lucrative business arising out of the melting and working of precious metals. There is little doubt the Egyptians and Greeks were acquainted with certain chemical operations, or what was termed the hermetic science, which was afterwards called alchemy in the first century of the Christian era.

The first two great lights that appeared were Al-Chindus, and Geber who discovered the red oxide and bichloride of mercury, nitric acid, hydrochloric acid, and nitrate of silver. Geber's *Summa Perfectionis* and *Liber Philisophorum* embody his researches on the purification and malleability of metals. In the ninth century, the Arab alchemist Rhazes flourished. In his great work entitled *El Hharvi*, he alludes to realgar, orpiment, borax, mixtures of sulphur and iron with copper, and of mercury with acids, and arsenic. He further recommends physicians to use alcoholic preparations and animal oils, etc. He states: "The secret art of chemistry is nearer possible than impossible; the mysteries do not reveal themselves except by force of labour and perseverance. But what a triumph it is when man can raise a corner of the veil which conceals the works of God!" The knowledge displayed of chemistry and its application to the arts at that early period is wonderful, but books were few. The chief evidence of this knowledge is exhibited in the many specimens and art monuments in the museums of Spain, showing the skill of the Saracens and of the Moors.

A little later Mesué states, "certain principles had been recognised as to the analytical classification of the bodies which compose organic matter".

Of the ancient necromancers who have figured in history and romance, Merlin was perhaps the most extraordinary. The earliest mention of his name is in records of the eleventh century, although he appears to have flourished about the time of the Saxon invasion of Britain, in the latter part of the fifth century.

He is first mentioned in connection with the fortune of Vortigern, who is represented by Geoffrey of Monmouth, as at that time King of England. Vortigern having lost all his strongholds in his struggle with the Saxons, at length consulted his magicians as to how he was to defend himself from his troublesome foe. They advised him to build an impregnable tower, and chose a suitable site for its erection. The builders set to work with might and main, but were astonished to find, that as fast as they built in one day, the next morning the earth had swallowed it up, and not a vestige remained. So the king called the wise men together again, when they arrived at the conclusion that the only way to remedy the matter was to cement the walls of the tower with the blood of a human being who was born of no human father.

Vortigern at once sent forth emissaries to scour the country in search of this *rara avis*, and at length by good fortune they came across Merlin, near the town of Caermarthen in Wales, who claimed that his mother was the daughter of a king but his father was an angelic being. The king's emissaries evidently took his word for it, as they speedily carried him before Vortigern. A great meeting of the magicians was called, at which the king presided, and Merlin, instead of being condemned as the victim, confounded the wise men, and told the king the ground they had chosen for his tower had a lake beneath it, at the bottom of which, on being drained, they would find two dragons of inextinguishable hostility. Under the form of dragons he appears to have figured the Britons and Saxons in his speech, "all of which," the historian tells us, "proved to be true".

But the greatest exploit with which Merlin is credited, according to tradition, is the erection of Stonehenge as a lasting monument to the 300 British nobles massacred by the Saxons. It is supposed that these mighty stones had been originally set up in Africa, and from thence were transported to Ireland. Merlin commanded that they should be carried over the sea, and erected on Salisbury Plain; but no workman could be found to move them. He therefore brought his magical power to bear on the huge stones, and by this means they were caused to take the form in which they now stand.

Of the other wonderful stories which romance has woven round the career of this strange individual, we can only say they are interesting, if not exactly true. As 600 years elapsed between the time of Merlin and the earliest known records of his achievements, it is impossible to pronounce on their veracity.

Among the more famous of the early alchemists was St. Dunstan, who flourished in the tenth century; but, if tradition speaks truly, he was anything but a saint in character. He is said to have been a man of distinguished birth, who in his young days lived a life of great self-indulgence, even for that period of peculiar morality. At length, he was seized with a dangerous illness which threatened to terminate his career; but at the last extremity an angel appeared, bringing a medicine which speedily restored him to health. Hastening to the nearest church to return thanks, he was stopped by the devil with a pack of black dogs, whom however he speedily put to flight. In order to expiate his former irregularities, he now secluded himself in the abbey of Glastonbury, where he occupied a cell in which he could neither stand upright nor stretch his limbs in repose, and mortified his flesh exceedingly. Here he studied alchemy and magic, in which arts he soon became well versed. While in this cell, he is said to have had the most extraordinary visitations, and among others the devil was constantly thrusting his head in at the window and taunting the saint, while immersed in his studies. At length, one day, wearied out, Dunstan lost all patience, and seizing his red-hot tongs from the little furnace in which he conducted his chemical operations, caught the devil by the nose, and held him firmly, "while the bellowings of Satan," says the historian, "filled the whole neighbourhood for many miles round". This incident is frequently represented in ancient carvings.

Dunstan was a Benedictine monk, and next came forth and took a prominent part in political and religious matters. He seems to have been the king-maker of his time, and took a prominent part in the ruling of the kingdom during the reigns of Edwy and Edgar.

In the accompanying illustration the alchemist, with uplifted torch, is repeating the specified incantation over the still, under which he has just kindled a fire, having commenced the preparation of the "Elixir of Life".

AN ALCHEMIST.
From an engraving dated 1576.

In the year A.D. 1260, Albertus Magnus, formerly a Dominican monk, was made master of the sacred palace at the court of Rome, and afterwards Bishop of Ratisbon. This great philosophical student was learned in all the then known arts of chemistry, and his manuscripts and works were copied by the thousand. All kinds of extraordinary powers were attributed to him, and it was commonly stated that he could make gold, and that he was a magician. Accused of "having dealings" with the evil one, he resigned his high position and returned to his cloistered cell to carry on his favourite researches and end his days. Next we come to Vincent de Beauvais, often called the Pliny of the middle ages. He, too, was accused of sorcery, and it is said that "at midnight people would creep along the quays of the Seine towards his laboratory in St. Chapelle yard, to see if they could get a glimpse reflected in the river of the magic furnaces in which De Beauvais was supposed to evoke his familiar spirit".

About the same time Raymond Lulli became known to fame. He also was a monk, and born in the island of Majorca, but having a roving disposition he wandered over Europe. He wrote several works on alchemy, among others *Libilli Aliquot Chemici*, etc. Fabulous stories are related of his adventures; and he was cruelly stoned to death by the populace in Tunis, in 1315. He left behind him a following of believers, who called themselves Lullists and spread all over Europe. The genius of the West at this time was Arnauld de Villeneuve, who made several important discoveries in chemistry. His researches were particularly directed to the relation of chemistry to medicine. He is credited with having discovered sulphuric and other acids, and is said to have been the first to distil alcohol or spirit of wine.

Contemporary with these men of learning was our own Roger Bacon, whose love for his art nearly cost him his life, besides many years in prison. The discoverer of gunpowder and the telescope spent most of his life in experimental researches, with the result that he revolutionised the art of war, and gave to astronomers the power of exploring the heavens. He was a man of great ability, never justly appreciated by his contemporaries, and has been rightly named the father of experimental physics. He described most of the laws which regulate matter, and the regular motion of the planets. Although a man of undoubted knowledge and great power of conception, he was bitten with the mania of endeavouring to discover the philosopher's stone, his views respecting which he set forth in his work entitled *Radix Mundi*. Following Bacon came Antonio Quainer, of Pavia, who was the first to manufacture artificial mineral waters.

It has been said by some that the discoveries made by the alchemists were mainly the result of chance, and they were mostly ignorant charlatans; but although they had little method in their research, and a great deal of their knowledge was wrapped up in absurd and superstitious theories, when we look at the result of their discoveries up to the fifteenth century, the most prejudiced must admit that their labours were not spent entirely in vain. They demonstrated the existence of bismuth, liver of sulphur, and regulus of antimony, the distillation of alcohol, volatilisation of mercury, and preparation of aqua regia, sulphuric and other mineral acids, and the purification of alkalies. They had the scarlet dye for cloth, the secret of which has now been lost and cannot be equalled, and their processes of glass-staining cannot be approached by those employed at the present day. It is said that Eck, a German alchemist of Sultzbach, ascertained the existence of oxygen 300 years before it was demonstrated by Priestly. For these and other discoveries we have to thank the early alchemists.

During the fifteenth and sixteenth centuries alchemy began to shake itself free from the wild theories and absurd practices which had impeded its progress. Henry VII. issued a severe edict against alchemical practices, which put a stop to the impositions of a number of charlatans. About this period John Baptist Porta discovered the means of reducing the metallic oxides and of colouring silver, and Isaac and Jean Hollandus made great improvements in enamelling, and demonstrated the manufacture of artificial gems.

From the time of Paracelsus and the introduction of printing, the science received a fresh impetus, and a new order of chemists came into being, whose conflict with the old order for many years is a matter of history.

The old theories of the alchemists were gradually exploded and superseded, and many were driven to the most flagrant quackery to earn a living.

Cornelius Agrippa, who was one of the leaders of the new order, says: "It would take too much time to recount all the follies, the idle secrets, and the enigmas of this trade, of the green lion, the fugitive stag, the flying eagle, the inflated toad, the crow's head of the black blacker than the black, of the seal of Mercury, of the mud of wisdom, and other countless absurdities of the time. Many of them travelled from fair to fair in order to make a little money by the sale of white lead, vermilion, antimony, and other drugs used by women for painting the face, and drugs which the Scripture calls ointments of lust." Meanwhile the efforts of the practical workers were encouraged by administrators and princes, with the result that the application of chemistry and the technical arts became predominant, and metallurgy the leading spirit of the science.

A notable character in the time of Queen Elizabeth was Dr. Dee, alchemist and astrologer. The career of this man, who was more a charlatan than aught else, was one of extraordinary vicissitude. A Welshman by birth, he was educated at Oxford, and then travelled throughout Europe, claiming that he had discovered the elixir of life and the philosopher's stone. He was a man of overweening ambition, and delighted to hear himself called "Most Excellent". In company with a man named Kelly, it is said he discovered a quantity of the elixir in the ruins of Glastonbury Abbey; this they at once annexed and carried off to Poland, accompanied by a nobleman of that country. After travelling from one Court to another, where he is said to have performed wonderful feats with his elixir, he returned to England and settled at Mortlake, where Elizabeth often visited him to consult him on astrology, and he even ventured to predict her death.[3] He was a great favourite at Court in 1595, and the Queen made him Chancellor of Paul's and Warden of Manchester, but he died in great poverty.

AN ALCHEMIST.

From an engraving dated 1576.

The illustration represents an alchemist of the sixteenth century in an ante-room of his laboratory, engaged in fixing a portion of his apparatus. On the table is his luting box and knife. Through one window a view of the laboratory with stills of varied size is obtained, while through the other the sun looks with becoming gravity on the operation.

The Symbols of the Alchemists.

As in modern science chemists write their formulæ and work out their processes by means of symbols, so the alchemists used signs and hieroglyphics to represent the then known elements, metals, and other articles in common use. The so-called elements—fire, air, water, earth—were represented by special symbols, here represented. The metals were supposed to be influenced by the planets to a certain degree, and were represented by their corresponding signs. Various other articles also had their symbols, which served as a means of shorthand at a period when caligraphy was little known or employed.

Fire. Air. Water.

or

Alum. Lead. Tin. Iron. Gold.

Copper. Mercury. Silver. Antimony. Arsenic.

Borax.

Cinnabar. Caput Mortuum. An Oil.

or

Salt petre. A Magnet. Sal Ammoniac. Sulphur.

or

Tartar. A Covered Pot. To Sublime. To Precipitate.

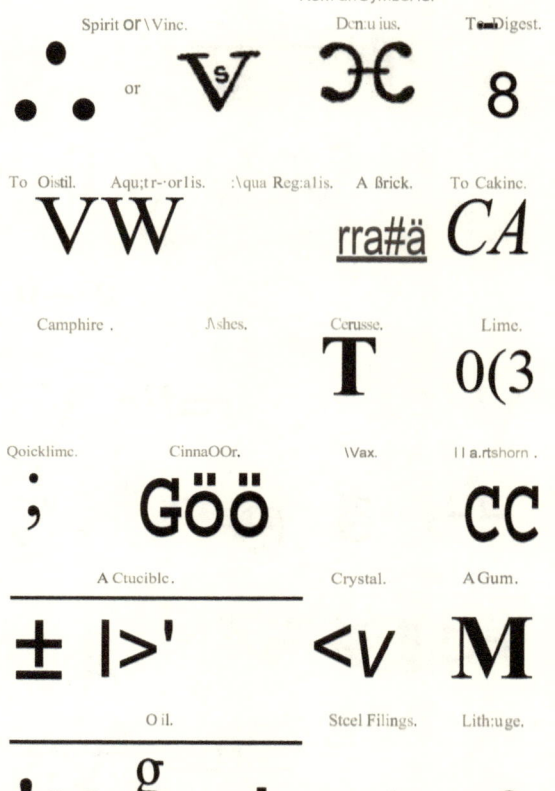

	Rom an Symbol for	
Spirit or Vine.	Den:u ius.	To Digest.
To Oistil.	Aqu;tr--or lis.	:\qua Reg:alis.	A Brick.	To Cakine.
Camphire .	Ashes.	Cerusse.	Lime.
Qoicklime.	CinnaOOr.	Wax.	I I a.rtshorn .
A Ctucible .		Crystal.	A Gum.
O il.		Steel Filings.	Lith:uge.

Spirit or Vine. ∴ or V^s

Den:u ius. ƎC

To Digest. 8

To Oistil. VW

:\qua Reg:alis. / A Brick. rra#ä

To Cakine. CA

Cerusse. T

Lime. 0(3

Qoicklime. ;

CinnaOOr. GÖÖ

Wax. CC

A Ctucible. ± |>'

Crystal. <v

A Gum. M

O il. !oo g

Steel Filings. + ₒ ⟩

Lith:uge. cß

To Lute.   Sublimated Mercury.   Precipitated Mercury.   Nitre.

Realgar.   Sand.   Soap.

Sal Alkali.   Sal Ammoniac.   Salt.   Talc.

Vinegar.   Verdigris.   Vitriol.   Urine.   Day.   Night.

CHAPTER VII.

THE PHILOSOPHER'S STONE.

THE dominating ambition of the early alchemists was to discover the unknown. In the same spirit the modern worker in science gropes onward, and dreams of discovering some contribution towards solving the elixir of life, in the form, it may be, of conquering at least one fell disease. The ancient workers in alchemy confined their researches almost exclusively to metals; they believed that all natural things were composed of four elements, which they termed Fire, Air, Earth, and Water. "When these four elements are conjoined," says Roger Bacon, in his *Radix Mundi*, "they become another thing, whereas it is evident that all things in Nature are composed of the said elements being altered and changed."

But the patient researches of the alchemists were not so much due to a love for scientific investigation as to the overwhelming desire to gain wealth.

A STILL FOR DYSTILLING THE WATER OF LYFE.

1576.

The majority had two fixed objects in view as the goals of their ambition, one being the discovery of some body that would be capable of transmuting the baser metals into gold and silver; and the other, the discovery of an elixir which would prolong the span of human life to an indefinite period. Both these objects seem to have been sought for by man from prehistoric times, and their origin is lost in antiquity. Berthelot remarks that the term "Philosopher's Stone" does not occur in writings earlier than the seventh century, although the central idea is much more ancient.

The philosopher's stone was sought for by the Chinese philosophers at a very remote period, afterwards by the Greeks, Arabs, and others down to the seventeenth century.

Men of undoubted ability and genius wasted both their lives and their fortunes over the search for this illusive chimera, and others condescended to fraud and trickery of the meanest description in its pursuit. Apparently no alchemist of any repute thought it right to die until he had at least claimed to have solved one of these great problems. Thus claimants to the discovery were numerous. The descriptions given of the various processes in ancient manuscripts and works for producing the philosopher's stone are usually of a very elaborate description, and couched in the most fantastic language.

Failure to produce the desired result was invariably accounted for by the omission to carry out some minute detail. Some who professed to have discovered the secret demanded large sums of money to reveal it, and several visited the various courts of Europe to demonstrate it by means of trickery and conjuring.

The notorious Dr. Dee, who flourished in the time of Queen Elizabeth, was one of the last claimants to the discovery, and is said to have received immense sums of money from dupes for imparting the coveted secret, which he demonstrated by means of an ingenious trick.

Realgar, mercury, sulphur, and many other substances were credited with the magical property of transmutation.

In the illustration (p. 65), which is taken from an authentic engraving of the sixteenth century, we have a figure of the apparatus used for distilling the "Water of Life," the process for which is described by Gesnerus in the *Newe Jewell of Health*, printed in 1576. The alchemist, arrayed in his imposing robes, is depicted giving instructions to his assistant as to certain precautions to be taken in conducting the process.

Bacon states that sulphur and mercury are the mineral roots and natural principles upon which Nature herself acts and works in the mines and caverns of the earth; the latter metal he believed to be the true elixir of the philosopher's stone; others, including Rhazes and Merlin, believed it to be an amalgam of gold and mercury, fantastically called the Red man and his White wife.

Concerning the vessels for producing this "Citrine body," as Bacon calls it, the most exact precautions were taken. Special apparatus was used, and a special heat, which was not to exceed the heat of the body. For this purpose horse-dung was employed. Senier, the philosopher, says: "Dig a sepulchre and bury the woman (mercury) with her man (gold) in horse-dung, the fire of the philosopher, until such time as they be conjoined".

Bacon's definition of alchemy was: "Alchymie is the art or science teaching how to make or generate a certain kind of medicine which is called the elixir. It teaches how to transmute all kinds of metals, one with another; and this by a proper medicine." George Ripley, a monk, in 1476, thought that he had discovered the much-coveted stone in pure sulphur. He says: "Let the two sulphurs, *viz.*, the white and the red, be mingled with the oil of the white elixir that they may work the more strongly, and you shall have the highest medicine in the world to heal and cure human bodies, and to transmute the bodies of metals into the most pure fine gold and silver". Berthelot, who has made an exhaustive study of the subject, comes to the conclusion that the doctrines of alchemy concerning the transmutation of metals, did not originate in the philosophical views of the constitution of matter as generally supposed, but in the practical experiments of goldsmiths occupied in making fraudulent substitutes for the precious metals. One cannot but think with pity of the immense labour expended and lost in the attempt made by many of these pioneers of science in their pursuit after this chemical chimera.

Paracelsus, as well as his predecessors, laboured studiously to discover some method for prolonging life. Like Bacon and Verulam, he maintained that the human body could be rejuvenated to a certain extent by a fresh supply of vitality, and it was his aim to find means by which such a supply could be obtained. In one of his works he gives the following reasons for this belief: "Metals may be preserved from rust and wood may be protected against rot. Blood may be preserved a long time if the air is excluded. Egyptian mummies have kept their form for centuries without undergoing putrefaction. Animals awaken from their winter sleep, and flies having become torpid from cold become nimble again when they are warmed. Therefore, if inanimate objects can be kept from destruction, why should there be no possibility to preserve the life-essence of animate forms?" For this purpose he prepared a remedy he called *Primum Ens Melissæ*, which was made by dissolving pure carbonate of potass, and macerating in the liquid the fresh leaves of the *melissa* plant. On this absolute alcohol was poured several times in successive portions to absorb the colouring matter, after which it was collected, distilled, and evaporated to the thickness of a syrup. The second great secret elixir of Paracelsus was his *Primum Ens Sanguinis*. This was prepared by mixing blood from the medium vein of a healthy young person, and digesting it in a warm place with twice its quantity of *alcahest*, after which the red fluid was to be separated from the sediment, filtered, and preserved.

The alcahest was his celebrated universal medicine, and was considered the greatest mystery of all. It was made with freshly prepared caustic lime and absolute alcohol. These were distilled together ten times. The residue left in the retort was mixed with pure carbonate of potass and dried. This was again distilled with alcohol. It was then placed in a dish and set on fire, and the residue that remained was the alcahest.

The following lines were found inscribed on the fly-leaf of an old work on alchemy, printed in 1550, and signed "Philo Veritas":—

ELIXIR VITÆ.

When fire and water, earth and air
In love's true bond united are,
For all diseases then be sure
You have a safe and certain cure.
I will affirm it's here alone

Exists the Philosophic Stone.
This is fair nature's virgin root,
Thrice blest are they who reap the fruit:
But oh! where one true adept's found,
Ten thousand thousand cheats abound.

In an ancient work in the library of York Minster, the writer came across the following in manuscript, signed "Raymund Lulli":—

Remember man that is the most noble creature in composition that ever
    God wrought;
In whom be four elements proportioned by nature,
A neutral mercuriallyte which costeth right naught,
Out of his monie by manie it is bought;
And our monie be not all but our oxtalle towe,
Of the sun and the moon; which Raymund Said So.

CHAPTER VIII.

THE BLACK ART AND OCCULT SCIENCES.

To make a thorough analysis of this interesting subject, and trace the origin of magic, would take much more space than we have at our command; and we can only mention a few of the many forms which may be grouped under the head of the occult sciences, and those especially which had any connection with the alchemists. There is little doubt that most of the alchemists were students, if not practitioners, of magic or some of its branches.

The antiquity of magic is very great; and we have record of magicians and wise men in early Jewish times, as well as the magic formulæ of the Vedas in India, as handed down to us in the religion of the Hindoos. Moreover, magic was practised by the Chaldeans, of whom a certain tribe devoted their energies to studying the occult sciences. Pliny tells us of the dealings in the supernatural in the time of Homer, and other writers record that magic was also known to the Etruscans and Assyrians at a very early period. As time rolled on, the different forms of magic practised became specialised, according to their several natures. For instance, there were Astrology and Oneiromancy, which comprised the various forms of divination; Theurgy and Goetry, the art of evoking good or evil spirits; Necromancy, by means of which communication was held with the dead; and Sorcery, which exercised its power by the influence of dreams.

The longings after the supernatural and unknown felt by the great ignorant masses brought forth individuals in plenty to take advantage of their credulity. During the thirteenth and fourteenth centuries the occult sciences were openly taught in the universities and schools, and 200 years later reached the zenith of their influence; and practitioners of astrology and the black arts abounded and flourished throughout Europe.

The professors of Oneiromancy were those who divined or interpreted dreams, and founded their traditions in the art from its being in accordance with the Scriptures. The explanation of dreams also did not go counter to the doctrines of the Church, and so the cult found many believers among all classes of society. It was denounced by Pope Gregory II. as a detestable practice; but this did not prevent it being largely employed in forecasting the future.

Arnauld de Villeneuve, who wrote a work on the subject in the thirteenth century, gives a certain code by which those who practised it worked.

Whoever dreamt that his hair was thick and carefully curled would soon become wealthy. If anything was wrong with the hair, evil was betokened. It also foreshadowed harm if a wreath was worn composed of flowers that were not in season. Other codes signified that to dream of the eyes, related to children; the head, to a father; the arms, to brothers; the feet, to servants; the right hand, to the mother, to sons, and to friends; and the left hand, to the wife and daughter. Another method was founded on the theory that whatever was dreamt of, the antithesis or opposite would follow in life. From this we have probably the saying common to-day, "dream of a wedding and it is a sign of a funeral". According to many old writers there was scarcely any important event in the middle ages which was not announced by a dream.

The day before Henry II. was struck by the blow of a lance during a tournament, Catherine de Medicis, his wife, dreamt that she saw him lose one of his eyes. Three days before he fell by the knife of Jacques Clément, Henry III. dreamt he saw the royal insignia stained with blood and trodden under foot by monks and people of the lower orders.

Henry IV. also, before he was murdered by Raveillac, it is said, heard during the night his wife Marie de Medicis say to herself as she woke, "Dreams are but falsehoods!" and when he asked her what she had dreamt, she replied, "That you were stabbed upon the steps of the little Louvre!" "Thank God it is but a dream," rejoined the king.

The necromancers, who were supposed to be able to conjure up spirits and raise the dead, were accounted on a somewhat higher plane than the interpreters of dreams. They also based their authority on the Old Testament. The nature of the art was gruesome and awe-inspiring, and there is little doubt many dark deeds were perpetrated by those who practised it. One method of evocation was to kill a child and place its head upon a dish surrounded by lighted candles; the desired spirit was supposed to enter this ghastly object and speak through its mouth. Sometimes the spirit simply consisted of some muttered words from behind a curtain in a dark cellar; another method was to cause the appearance of a sepulchral figure out of smoke or vapour, which would indicate by gesture and reply to questions asked. To evoke a dead man's spirit, it was necessary to go to the grave at midnight with a companion who bore a candle in the left hand and a crystal stone in the right, the conjurer holding a hazel wand with the name of God written on it, and repeating the words:—

"Tetragrammaton + Adonai + Agla + Craton +"

Then striking three times on the ground, with a prayer he commanded the spirit into the stone, when it appeared in the shape of a child.

The conjurer often wore a girdle of lion's skin with the name of God written on it, and the Solomon's circle he described with a bright knife, on the blade of which were written certain mystic words. Necromancy gradually merged into sorcery, which has occasionally come to the surface in comparatively recent years.

Chiromancy, the art of divining or foretelling future events from marks on the palm of the hand, was also practised in antiquity, but in mediæval times it was strongly opposed by the Church. The practice is supposed to have been brought into Europe from the East by the Bohemians in the early part of the fifteenth century. This art eventually merged into astrology, which exerted the greatest influence of all the occult sciences.

The antiquity of astrology is very great, it having been originated by the Chaldeans, and was thought by some of the Jews to have been a method by which the Creator could communicate with His people. The art itself was based on astronomy, and, like alchemy, was the beginning of the study of real natural science. The teller of the stars was not only supposed to foretell forthcoming misfortunes to individuals, but also to forecast the destinies of kings and empires.

The belief in its power was so great that it became the fashion among royal personages of the sixteenth century to keep their own special astrologers, who were lodged easy of access and loaded with honours and wealth. These men were mostly astute Jews well versed in the science of their time, and by means of their supposed powers they often played a very important part in the political affairs of the nation. Thus in the fifteenth century Rovigo, an astrologer of eminence, who is said to have perfected the astrolabe, was attached to the Court of King John II. of Portugal; and Simon Pharès figured at the Court of France in the time of Charles VIII. We must not forget to mention Cosmo Ruggieri, the Florentine astrologer and the confidant of Catherine de Medicis; also the celebrated Nostradamus, astrologer and trusted adviser of Charles IX. This extraordinary man played a prominent part in the history of his time, and was supposed to practise magic and alchemy as well as the healing art. He was consulted by the king in all positions of difficulty, and it is said became immensely wealthy. He died in 1566 at Salon, after having written several notable works.

CHAPTER IX.

THE ART OF FORETELLING.

THE early theory of the art of foretelling by means of the stars, and casting horoscopes, was as follows: The seven planets then known, including the Sun, with the twelve figures of the Zodiac, comprised the astrological system. Each unit or body or nation was supposed to be governed or influenced by a certain star or constellation, and this power extended to all things connected with the person or nation. Thus, Saturn was supposed to influence life, sciences, and buildings; Jupiter—honour, wishes, and wealth; Mars—wars, persons, marriages, and quarrels; the Sun—hope, gain, and happiness; Venus—love and friendship; Mercury—fear, disease, debts, and commerce; the Moon—robberies, wounds, and dreams. The intrinsic quality was denoted by the planet. The Sun was regarded as favourable; Saturn, cold; Jupiter, temperate; Mars, ardent; Venus, fruitful; Mercury, inconstant; the Moon, melancholy. The days, colours, and metals also came under the same influences.

In casting a horoscope, the astronomer had first to observe if the time was propitious, and what planet was dominant in the heavens. Then, by means of calculations and diagrams, he would deduce the consequences from the position and bearing of the stars. The day was divided into four equal parts—the ascendant of the sun, the middle of the sky, the descending of the sun, and the lower part of the sky. These four parts of the day were subdivided into twelve distinct parts, which were called the twelve houses of the sun. It was of the greatest importance in drawing a horoscope to tell exactly in which "house" the star appeared. One can easily trace the connection of the influence attributed to the planets with the old Egyptian and Greek mythologies, and it can hardly be wondered at that the same system should have been brought to bear on medicine.

A favourite method of divination, especially with the sorcerers, was that of gazing into a beryl or crystal. For the proper performance of this ceremony a pure virgin or equally pure youth should be the gazer. The sorcerer, having repeated the necessary charms and adjurations, with the invocation suitable to the spirits he wished to consult, looked into a large beryl or crystal, wherein he saw the answer represented either by types or by figures, and sometimes it is said he might hear the spirit speak to him.

Vallancey states that in the Highlands of Scotland large crystals of somewhat oval shape were kept by the priests to work charms with, and that water poured on them was given to cattle as a preventive of disease. Dr. Dee was a famous conjurer with the crystal in the time of Queen Elizabeth.

Lilly describes these crystals as being the size of an orange, set in silver, surmounted with a cross, and engraved all round with the names of the angels —Raphael, Gabriel, and Uriel.

Among other charms practised was Dactylomancy, which was performed by means of a ring suspended by a thread in the centre of an earthenware or metal pitcher. The ring, which was supposed to have been made under the influence of a certain constellation, was swung from side to side of the vessel, and the sounds it made on touching were taken as predictions and oracles.

The art of divination by fire was called Pyromancy, and was performed by allowing a certain body to burn, the smoke from which, by its density and colour, forecast the future. A favourite medium for consulting this oracle was a donkey's head roasted on hot coals.

Popular belief in mediæval times attributed anything unusual or beyond its understanding, to magic; so most of the early alchemists were believed to be magicians. Both Albertus Magnus and Roger Bacon were accused of dealing in the black arts, one having to resign his bishopric of Cologne and retire to a monastery, and the other to the Franciscan cells in Paris, to free themselves from the charges of their accusers.

CHAPTER X.

BLACK MAGIC.

GEBER, an alchemist of great repute in Arabia, was believed to possess the power of creating gold by magic. He was a man of undoubted learning and a skilful practitioner of his time, yet he was dubbed a sorcerer. He was said to possess all kinds of extraordinary implements; among others, a book of black magic which gave him full power over demons, and a brass idol which spoke oracles. On the day of his death, in 1003, the Evil One is supposed to have carried him off. James Iodoc, an Englishman, achieved considerable notoriety by claiming that he had succeeded in setting the demon in a magic ring. These men should not be confounded with the host of impostors and charlatans who simply preyed on the credulity of the people, but in those days all were judged alike. Most of the great mediæval alchemists dabbled in magic, and all agreed that to obtain the intervention of Satan in human affairs it was necessary to enter into a pact with him. Those who went to this length and became exponents of demonology, or the black art, were initiated with much solemnity.

TAKING THE OATH.

The oath to the demon had to be pronounced in the centre of a circle traced upon the ground, accompanied by the offer of some pledge, such as a garment of the noviciate. The edge of the circle was supposed to establish a mark which the demon could not cross. Heavy perfumes such as vervain, with burning incense and lighted tapers, always formed part of the ceremonial. The smoking brazier, which entered largely into the ritual, was believed to act upon the demons, and was constantly fed with all kinds of mysterious vegetable and animal substances, those that would produce most smoke being preferred. It is said that belladonna and opium were always used as ingredients in the incense, in order to produce a state of semi-stupor and influence the imagination.

The perfumes employed by the professors of the art had each a special significance, and were offered to some planet to form a link with the earth. A mixture of saffron, amber, musk, cloves and incense, together with the brain of an eagle and the blood of a cock, was offered to the Sun.

The white poppy and camphor burnt in the head of a frog, with the eyes of a bull and the blood of a goose, were dedicated to the Moon; while to Mars, sulphur was mixed with hellebore and euphorbium, together with the blood of a black cat and the brain of a crow, and then burnt.

One can imagine the horrible odour that would be caused by burning such articles as these; and, as the columns of smoke ascended, the half-stupefied and scared spectator fancied he saw the forms of writhing demons in the air.

Very curious properties were attributed to certain articles when thrown on live coals. Thus, if thunder and rain were required, the liver of a chameleon was said to produce it; while the gall of a cuttle-fish burnt with roses and aloes-wood was all that was necessary to induce an earthquake.

By burning coriander, parsley, hemlock, liquor of black poppy, giant fennel, red sandal-wood and henbane, almost any number of demons could be raised. Sorcerers of this class were called tempest-raisers.

With the witchcraft practised largely by women in mediæval times, we have not much to do; although belief in its influence was widespread during the middle ages. To bewitch an individual was to cause him gradually to die a mysterious death.

The process commenced at first with great secrecy, by modelling a figure of the intended victim in wax or clay. This having been done, a swallow was killed, and the heart placed under the right arm of the figure and the liver under the left. The effigy was next pricked all over with new needles, each prick being accompanied by the most terrible imprecations against the victim.

Another method was to make the figure of earth taken from a graveyard and mixed with dead bones. Certain mystic signs were then inscribed on it, which were said eventually to cause the death of the victim. So general did the practice of witchcraft become that no class of society was safe from accusation and suspicion, thousands perishing by the faggot and torture.

From the fourteenth to the sixteenth century, supernatural beliefs exerted a great influence on the people. One of the most celebrated trials of the time was that of the Duchess of Gloucester, who was accused of bewitching Henry VI. It transpired at the trial that she had instructed a priest, named Bolingbroke who practised necromancy, to bewitch the king; a sorceress named Marie Gardimain being also implicated. An effigy of the king in wax was discovered half-melted in front of a fire of dry plants, which had been gathered by moonlight in a graveyard. Bolingbroke the necromancer was hanged, Gardimain burnt, and the Duchess of Gloucester condemned to imprisonment for life.

The "evil eye" was another form of witchcraft, mostly practised by women. Visions or apparitions in the sky, foretelling some war or disaster, were firmly believed in by the Church, and caused great consternation. Fiery dragons appearing in the heavens were said to predict civil war; and we also read of pigs bearing royal crowns, and gory stars, all of which were doubtless caused by ordinary phenomena not understood at that time.

The appearance of the devil presiding at a sabbath or meeting of sorcerers is thus described by De Lancre: "He is seated in a black chair with a crown of black horns, two horns in his neck, and one on the forehead, which sheds light on the assembly; the hair bristling, the face pale and exhibiting signs of uneasiness, the eyes round, large, and fully opened, inflamed and hideous, with a goat's beard. The neck and the rest of the body deformed, and in the shape of a man and a goat; the hands and the feet of a human being."

The word witch is thought by some authorities to be derived from *chausaph*, which means a user of pharmaceutic enchantments, or an applier of drugs to magical purposes.

Witches sent storms and barrenness, drowned children, brought on ague, could kill with evil eye, slay with lightning, pass through key-holes, ride through the air on broom-sticks, and perform many other weird and wondrous things.

"They were generally old, blear-eyed, wrinkled dames," says Scott, "ugly and crippled, frequently papists, and sometimes atheists; of cross-grained tempers and cynical dispositions." They were often poisoners, and generally monomaniacs. Epilepsy and all diseases not understood by the physicians were set down to the influence of witches. They were said to make two covenants with the devil, one public and one private. Then the novices were presented to the devil in person, and instructed to renounce the Christian faith, tread on the Cross, break the fasts, joining hands with Satan, paying him homage, and yielding him body and soul. Some witches sold themselves for a term of years, and some for ever; then they kissed the devil, and signed their bond with blood, and a banquet ended the meeting; their dances being accompanied with shouts of "Ha, ha! devil, devil! Dance here, dance here! Play here, play here! Sabbath, sabbath!" Before they departed the devil was said to give them philtres and amulets. These women were usually hypochondriacs, often driven by despair and misfortune to confess any charge made against them.

CHAPTER XI.

SUPERSTITION AND ITS INFLUENCE ON MEDICINE.

SUPERSTITION is a belief in what is wholly opposite to the laws of the physical and moral world, and yet supposed to be attainable by supernatural agency.

The words incantation and charm seem to have been derived from the ancient practice of curing diseases by poetry and music. Democritus says that many diseases are capable of being cured by the sound of a flute when properly played. Marianus Capellus assures us also that fevers may be cured by suitable songs. Galen believed the sound of the flute efficacious in gout and epilepsy. Asclepiades actually employed the trumpet for the relief of sciatica, and tells us it is to be continued until the fibres of the part begin to palpitate, when the pain will vanish. What terrible visions might be conjured up if such remedies were used to-day.

The influence of superstition on medicine may be accounted for by the fact, that from the very first, ideas with regard to the action of drugs must have been combined with those concerning supernatural agencies, for the phenomena of nature in very early times were attributed to spirits. Diseases were supposed to be due to an evil spirit, therefore to cast the disease out was equivalent to curing it, and the methods used for this purpose were by no means always ineffective in curing disease.

Incantations and spells were generally used in addition to a real remedial agent, but the incantations usually got the credit for effecting the cure.

In early times superstition played an important part in the cure of disease, and it prevails to a certain extent to-day. "In the opinion of the ignorant multitude," says Lord Bacon, "witches and impostors have always held a competition with physicians."

There has ever been a peculiar propensity in the human mind to foster a belief in the supernatural, and perhaps more especially in respect to medicine on account of the obscurity and ignorance with which it was once surrounded. In early times almost every disease was attributed to punishment for evil-doing, the working of some demon, or the influence of the stars; hence the use of any article that was strange or rare as a remedy.

"The employment of precious stones for medicinal purposes," writes De Boot, "arises from an Arab superstition which supposed them to be the residence of spirits." They were first used as amulets, and then gradually came to be administered inwardly for various ailments.

"Mystery is the very soul of empiricism," says Paris; "withdraw the veil, and the confidence of the patient instantly languishes." A propensity to attribute every ordinary and natural effect to extraordinary and unnatural causes, is one of the striking characteristics of medical superstition.

The properties that herbs possessed were attributed by the old physicians to the planets which were supposed to influence them, and our medical men to this day head their prescriptions with a sign that originally meant an invocation to Jupiter, which is a surviving relic of this old superstitious practice. Another very curious fact with respect to medical superstition is, that many of the greatest philosophers were firm believers in it. Lord Bacon is said to have believed in the existence of a panacea that would prolong life beyond its natural term. He considered that the principal cause of death was the action of the external air in drying and exhausting the body, which he thought might be prevented by nitre; but although he took three grains of his favourite salt every morning for the last thirty years of his life, he died at the age of sixty-six. We have many customs at the present day which are a survival of the days of superstition, and few have any idea of their origin. The mother, when she hangs round the neck of her child the plaything known as a coral and bells, little imagines she is perpetuating an ancient superstitious practice. The soothsayers attributed many mystic properties to coral, and it was believed to ward off the evil eye, and drive away devils and evil spirits.

For this purpose it was suspended from a child's neck as an amulet. Pliny and Dioscorides greatly esteemed the medicinal properties of coral, and Paracelsus recommends that it should be worn around the necks of infants to keep away fits, sorcery, charms, and to serve as an antidote to poisons. The bells usually suspended to it were originally intended to frighten away evil spirits, and not to amuse the child alone.

Paris mentions a curious circumstance, *viz.*, that the same superstitious belief should exist among the negroes of the West Indies, who affirm that the colour of coral is always affected by the state of health of the wearer, it becoming paler in disease.

But all the remedies that originated in superstition were not entirely useless. Some, whether by accident or not, had a natural power of efficacy, and led to discoveries of importance. In the time of James I., a powder known as the sympathetic powder of Sir Kenelm Digby had a great reputation for healing wounds. Whenever a wound had been inflicted, this powder was applied to the weapon which had caused it, which was also smeared with ointment and dressed two or three times a day. The wound itself was directed to be brought together and carefully bound up with clean linen rags, but above all to be let alone for seven days, at the end of which time it was generally found to be healed. This was, of course, said to be due to the wonderful properties of the sympathetic powder, instead of the fact of excluding the air from the part and not interfering with nature's own healing powers. The mysterious sympathetic healing powder was afterwards said to be simply calcined green vitriol. The rust of the spear of Telephus, alluded to by Homer as a cure for the wounds which that weapon inflicted, was probably verdigris, and led to the discovery of its use as a surgical dressing.

The cures supposed to be performed by royal touch show the power of faith over desire, or mind over matter. The royal surgeons who introduced the patients to be touched for scrofula, doubtless took care to choose those who had a tendency to recover, and who, if left to nature, would probably have gradually recovered. Boswell says that Dr. Johnson, when thirty months old, was taken by his mother to London to be touched by Queen Anne, on the advice of Sir John Floyer, a physician of Lichfield.

From time immemorial the ignorant have had the most unbounded confidence in nauseous remedies, and it would seem as if the nastier and more disgusting the medicines were, the greater faith they had in them. The larger the price asked, the more implicit the faith seemed to be. The Collyrium of Danares, a famous quack eye lotion, was sold at Constantinople for £9 a bottle, and the elixirs sold by Paracelsus and Van Helmont brought extortionate prices. The doctrine of Signatories, as it was called, is of very great antiquity. It implied that every natural substance which possesses any medicinal virtues, indicates, by an obvious and well-marked external character, the disease for which it is a remedy. Thus the bloodstone was used to stop bleeding, on account of its marks resembling drops of blood. The root of the mandrake, on account of its resemblance to the human form, was used as a remedy for sterility. Turmeric was administered for jaundice, and poppies for diseases of the head. Another belief of the ancients was that all poisonous bodies possessed a powerful attraction for one another, and that "like would cure like". The hair of a mad dog was worn as a charm to prevent hydrophobia, and the foot of the ape was used as a remedy for its bite. On the same principle we are solemnly assured that three scruples of the ashes of a witch, after she has been well and carefully burnt at the stake, is a sure protection against the evil effects of witchcraft.

Many ancient superstitions are so deeply rooted that they find believers among the educated at the present day. Take, for instance, the belief that many people have in the efficacy of red flannel. For sore throat, rheumatism, or swelling, they believe it will cure when flannel of no other colour will. This belief may be traced to the colour of the cloth often used in incantations, which was always red.

In some parts of the country a wedding-ring is still believed to be a universal cure for sore eyes.

A curious superstition is still practised in some parts of Wales for the cure of the complaint called shingles. The term for shingles in Welsh means "The Eagle." It was supposed in ancient times that if a person ate of the flesh of the eagle he would never suffer from shingles, and his direct descendants down to the ninth generation could not contract it, and furthermore had the power transmitted to them of curing others so afflicted by blowing on them.

CHAPTER XII

LOVE PHILTRES.

Love Philtres were administered for the purpose of inspiring affection or hatred. In very early times they were frequently used, concocted, and sold by the magicians or sorcerers, who often obtained large sums of money in exchange, from amorously-inclined gallants and maidens. They were composed of various extraordinary ingredients used in medicine at the time, and were either in the form of a powder, which was to be surreptitiously slipped into an article of food to be swallowed, or in a liquid for anointing the clothes or hands, and by things to be held in the mouth.

It is recorded that some sorcerers even used the Host, upon which they traced letters of blood. The following were also used in the preparation of philtres: the entrails of animals, feathers of birds, scales of fishes, parings of nails, powdered loadstones, and human blood.

It is little wonder they excited hatred. The *poculum amatorium* or love philtre of the Romans, and the *philtron* of the Greeks, were venerated with superstitious awe in early times. They became used to such an extent by the former nation under the first emperors, that a decree was promulgated under the Roman criminal law whereby love philtres were deemed as poison, and the punishment inflicted on those using them was very severe. Hairs from a wolf's tail, the bones of the left side of a toad which had been eaten by ants (those of the right side were used to cause hatred), the blood of pigeons, skeletons of snakes, the entrails of animals, and other equally disgusting things, were included as ingredients in Roman love philtres.

Pliny states, that there were also philtres for quenching love. Thus, "if a nest of young swallows is placed in a box and buried, on being dug up after a few days it will be found that some of the birds have died with their beaks closed, while others die as if gasping for breath". The latter were used for exciting love, and the former for producing the opposite effect.

Horace recommends a bone torn from a hungry and voracious dog, and Virgil describes a complete apparatus wherewith a maiden seeks to recover the affections of a faithless lover.

The early Greek and Roman magicians used "hippomanes," which was the lump of flesh found in the head of a colt newly foaled, as an ingredient in their philtres.

About the sixteenth century philtres came to be compounded and sold by the apothecaries, who doubtless derived from them a lucrative profit. Favourite ingredients with these later practitioners were mandragora, cantharides, and vervain, which were supposed to have Satanic properties. They were mixed with other herbs said to have an aphrodisiac effect; also man's gall, the eyes of a black cat, and the blood of a lapwing, bat, or goat.

In Gay's *Shepherds' Week* reference is thus made to love philtres:—

> "Strait to the 'pothecary's shop I went,
> And in love powder all my money spent;
> Behap what will next Sunday after prayers
> When to the alehouse Lubberkin repairs,
> These flies into his mug I'll throw,
> And soon the swain with fervent love shall glow".

"Botanomancy," Ferrand states, "which is done by the noise or crackling that kneeholme, box, or bay leaves make when they are crushed betwixt one's hands or cast into the fire, was of old in use among the pagans, who were wont to bruise poppy flowers betwixt their hands, and by this means thinking to know their loves."

A CHARME OR AN ALLAY FOR LOVE.

> "If so be a toad be laid
> In a sheepskin newly flaid,
> And that ty'd to man 'twill sever
> Him and his affections ever."—Herrick's *Hesperides*.

The winged ant was another favourite ingredient in love philtres, and was first used by Rhazes, who prepared the winged ant in the form of tincture by maceration in alcohol. This tincture, dropped in the homœopathic manner into wine or mixed with food, was supposed to have a wonderful action in producing symptoms of the tender passion in the coldest hearts. The winged ants alone were used in this preparation, which enjoyed a long reputation, and was subsequently known as "Hoffmann's Water of Magnanimity," and largely used in the seventeenth century as an aphrodisiac.

CHAPTER XIII.

THE PIONEERS OF PHARMACY AND BOTANY—PHYSIC GARDENS.

T HE operation of distillation was unknown to the ancient Greeks and Romans, although Dioscorides and Pliny describe a process which may be considered that of distillation in its infancy. The process was not known in England until the time of Henry II. To the Arabs we are indebted for the discovery of manna, cassia, senna, and rhubarb, also aromatics, such as musk, nutmeg, mace, and cloves. Blisters were known and used by the Arabs, who are the first also on record to mention sugar extracted from the cane, and sugar- candy, which they called honey of cane.

Rhazes and Avicenna were the first physicians to introduce improvements in pharmaceutical preparations. The latter was the first to mention the three mineral acids, and distinguish between vegetable and mineral alkalies.

In the year 1226, Roger Bacon, a native of Ilchester, in Somersetshire, and a Franciscan monk, may be said to have laid the foundation of chemical science in Europe. He was excommunicated by Pope Nicholas, and imprisoned for ten years for supposed dealings with the devil. He professed to have discovered an elixir of life, which he affirmed prevented corruption of any constitution and the infirmities of age for many years. Following Bacon, at the end of the thirteenth century, came Arnoldas de Villa Nova, or Villeneuve, who was the first to recommend the distilled spirit of wine impregnated with certain herbs, from which we date our use of tinctures in medicine.

Basil Valentine followed as a pioneer in the administration of metallic medicines; he made volatile alkali from sal-ammoniac, and noticed the production of ether from alcohol.

In the year 1493, Phillipus Theophrastus, Bombast of Hohenheim, afterwards known as Paracelsus, was born near Zurich in Switzerland, a man of extraordinary conceit and boldness, but who wrought a greater change and influence in *materia medica* than any physician since the time of Galen. He travelled all over Europe, and so obtained an extensive knowledge of chemistry and medicine.

This genius of science and quackery, for such Paracelsus must be termed, who scoffed at all the doctrines believed in since the time of Hippocrates, professed to have received his knowledge from the Divine Being Himself. His sheer impudence carried the sympathies of the public with him, and they kissed the skirts of his gown as he passed through the streets, whilst he had among his followers many princes and nobles.

He denounced the apothecaries, who, he said, "could only compose insipid syrups and repulsive concoctions, when they have ready to hand at the bottom of their stills, extracts and dyes derived from the best vegetables and minerals". He disagreed with the doctors also, whose prescriptions he stigmatised as barbarous, and was much against the use of correctives being added to pharmaceutical recipes when they had no natural relation to the preparation itself. He believed in the existence of an active principle in plants, which he termed the "Ether of Aristotle," that could be isolated and used to avert the various disorders of the human body—an idea which is now the leading spirit in pharmaceutical research. His labours did much to stimulate the practical side of chemistry, though his language was mysterious, as, like other alchemists, he wrapped up all his wisdom and his ignorance in the garb of allegory. He was reported to carry about a familiar spirit in the pommel of a long sword that always hung at his side.

Paracelsus is said to have been the first to use mercury internally; he also employed opium, antimony, and lead largely in his treatment; and devised a process for the preparation of red oxide of mercury. He was sent for to many of the European Courts, and by the interest of Erasmus was made Professor of Chemistry at Bale, the first chair that was established in Europe. It was here while seated in his chair, that with arrogant impudence he burnt with great solemnity the writings of Galen and Avicenna, saying that "if God would not impart the secrets of physic, it was not only allowable, but was justifiable, to consult the devil".

He had the greatest contempt for his fellow physicians, and said he had more knowledge in the very down on his bald pate than was in all their writings, and in the buckles of his shoes there was more learning than in Galen and Avicenna, and in his beard more experience than all their universities. The man was a mass of conceit and egotism, yet feared and liked by the people for his boldness.

Latterly he took to drinking heavily, seldom taking off his clothes for many nights together. At length he broke down, and the end came at the age of forty-eight, when this singular man died after a few hours' illness at Saltzburg, in Austria, a bottle of his boasted panacea for all ills being found in his pocket. He believed the human body to be composed of salt, sulphur, and mercury, and that in these "three fast substances" health and disease consist. To give Paracelsus his due, although empiricism and quackery were the chief elements in his career, he exerted an undoubted influence on the medical practice of his time, and with all his egotism did his best to advance the science and art of medicine.

The next pioneer was Van Helmont, who flourished some hundred years later. He was the first to notice the existence of gases, also to use alum in uterine hæmorrhage, through which he acquired a great reputation.

Little was known of *materia medica* by the nations of the West from the eighth to the tenth century. The chief cultivation of medicinal herbs took place in the monasteries, each having its own botanical garden, which contributed much to the progress of medicine. At this time the knowledge of the medicinal value of herbs and roots was much more advanced in the East, and we find that during the reign of Almansour, in the eighth century, a large school was founded at Bagdad, which became a refuge for scientists when exiled from Athens and Alexandria. The works of Aristotle and Galen were translated into Syriac, and the greatest generosity and encouragement were shown to *savants* who settled there. Before this the Arabs had considerable knowledge of the use of plants in medicine, and had made some valuable discoveries. Their physicians recommended the use of senna, tamarinds, and cassia in place of the violent purgatives used by the Greek physicians, and a number of new plants were introduced by Rhazes from India, Persia, and Syria. Mesué wrote his treatise on medicine (*De Remedica*), which, on being translated into Latin, was used as a manual in all the schools up to the Renaissance.

Constantine was the first to introduce the most noted Arabic works into Europe, himself a writer of no little repute. Then several Arab travellers added to the store of knowledge; among these, Ebor-Taitor, a native of Malaga, travelled in Asia to study plants, and eventually became minister of the Caliph at Cairo.

Otho, of Cremona, in a poem of 1500 lines, contributed his knowledge of plants, and John of Milan, in his *Code of the School of Salerno*, compiled the discoveries of a century in medical botany.

Coming to the twelfth century, scientific progress was not so rapid, yet all the investigation that was made originated in the study of medicine. Most of the monasteries and convents besides their botanical gardens, had collections of minerals and animals, which were carefully watched and tended, and the monks and nuns would not only administer to the sick of their own orders, but also to the suffering who claimed their charity. Once lodged there, the treatment was good and wholesome, and consisted mostly of decoctions of simples, backed up by good kitchen medicine, quietness, and rest. One or two monks who had a special knowledge of herbs were usually allotted to this department. It can then hardly be wondered at, that during the thirteenth and fourteenth centuries most of the records we have of medicine are from works by the brethren of the monasteries. An excellent collection of recipes, comprising also a summary of plants, animals, and minerals was compiled by Hildegarde, Abbess of Bingen, and called the *Jardin de Santé*.

This good lady, like many other abbesses of her time, was much interested in the art of healing. She cultivated her own medicinal plants, and carefully noted down their properties for the use of others, and thus left a valuable record.

In the thirteenth century an advance was made in *materia medica* by Gilbert and Hernicus Arviell, two Englishmen who travelled through Asia to study plants and their uses. Simon de Cordo, called Simon of Genoa, also took a botanising exploration into Sicily and the islands of the Archipelago, and afterwards wrote a botanic dictionary.

Another eminent botanist of this period was Peter de Crescenzi, a man of good birth and fortune, who was born at Bologna in 1330, and who greatly interested himself in botany and horticulture. His great work, which was translated into several languages, was called *Opus Rubarium Commodorum*. Contemporary with Peter were three names we must not omit, *viz.*, Vincent de Beauvais, Albertus Magnus, and Arnaud de Villeneuve, who professed a knowledge of alchemy, astrology, and physic. Vincent de Beauvais was a Dominican monk, and his great work, the *Speculum Naturale*, is saturated with the superstition of the time. In this book he states, "the mandragora is of the same shape as the human body; the winged dragon is capable of carrying off an ox, and devouring the same whilst flying". He also describes the scythion lamb, a sort of animal plant which had roots and grew in the ground, and other fearsome creatures, and declared that "in Scotland the fruits of certain trees, when they fall into the water, produce the birds called black divers". Villeneuve wrote many treatises on plants and animals, and eventually became teacher of medicine and botany at the University of Paris. He was undoubtedly a man in advance of his time, and boldly declared "that the most solemn mysteries of the Catholic faith could be explained by the teachings of natural history and experimental physics".

He was therefore accused by the magistrates of sorcery and magic, but escaped through the special protection of Charles of Anjou into Italy, where he settled for a long time.

The fourteenth century saw little advance in the medical art, but it was enriched by one or two great works. One of these, written in Latin by Bartholomew Glanvil, an English monk, was a kind of encyclopædia of immense size, and was called *Liber de Proprietatibus Rerum*, and had a great reputation for centuries afterwards.

The advent of printing about the middle of the fifteenth century rapidly spread the knowledge of more recent discoveries throughout Europe, and many large works on botany and herbalism, illustrated with woodcuts, were published at Mayence and Louvain. At Venice many of the works of the old Arab physicians, Avicenna, Mesué, and others, were printed and eagerly purchased. The discovery of America in 1492 heralded the introduction of numerous fresh additions to *materia medica*, which were brought to this country by explorers and naturalists.

In the sixteenth century, by the labours and researches of George Agricola, a German, and Conrad Gesner, a Swiss, a considerable advance was made in the knowledge of what was called chemical medicine and botany. Agricola, who was the greatest mineralogist the world had then seen, explored and spent much time in the mines of Bohemia and Saxony, and thus obtained a practical knowledge of the then known methods of the working of metals. His contemporary, Conrad Gesner, born at Zurich in 1516, has been called the originator of scientific botany, as he was the first to discover a method of recognising each genus and kind by examining the organs of fructification, and in this way discovered 1800 new varieties. A famous physic garden was planted in Paris in the early part of the seventeenth century by Jacques Gohory, an enthusiastic pharmacist, and this garden eventually became part of the *Jardin des Plantes*. In connection with this garden a school of medicine was founded, the first occupant of the chair of chemistry being William Davisson, a Scotchman, and predecessor to Lefebvre, who afterwards became a chemist at St. James's.

The practice of the teachers of this time was to dictate to their students, and in order to save themselves the trouble of dictating and the students the trouble of writing, which was a very laborious matter in those days, the lecturer would write a book. Thus Jean Beguin wrote a chemical text-book in 1612, which passed through no fewer than fifty-three editions.

We must not omit to mention two other pioneers of this period, who made important discoveries in botany; they were Matthias of Lille, who eventually settled in England, and Andrew Cesalpin, professor of botany at Pisa. The former first formulated the true principles of classification of plants and arrangement into families, such as the orchids, palms, and mosses; and to the latter belongs the honour of having devised the first system of botany. Having compared the process of generation in animals to the seeds of plants, he distinguished male plants by their stamens, and those which yielded seed as female.

The next era is marked by the publication of the first pharmacopœia at Nuremberg in 1542. "For this act," says Paris, "we are indebted to Valerius Cordus, a young student, who, during a transient visit at that place, accidentally produced a collection of medical receipts which he had selected from the works of the past esteemed writers, and with which the physicians of Nuremberg were so highly pleased that they urged him to print it for the benefit of the apothecaries, and obtained the sanction of the Senate to the undertaking." To this slight circumstance we owe the institution of pharmacopœias. The first *London Pharmacopœia* was, however, not published until the reign of James I., in 1618, of which there were twelve subsequent editions, the last being in 1841. The *Dublin Pharmacopœia* first appeared in 1807, the last edition being published in 1850. Until the Medical Act passed in 1858, the right of publishing the *Pharmacopœia* for England, Scotland, and Ireland was vested in the College of Physicians of London, Edinburgh, and Ireland respectively; and as these books contained several preparations similar in name and different in strength, such obvious danger arose for travellers that the *British Pharmacopœia*, published in 1864, became, by Act of Parliament, the standard for Great Britain and Ireland.

The Chelsea Physic Garden is the oldest public botanical garden in Great Britain, but there were private ones of older date, such as that of Gerard, the author of *The Herbal*, which was situated in Holborn, and that of Tradescant, the famous Dutch traveller, gardener to James I., who had an extensive garden of exotic plants in Lambeth.

The founders of the Chelsea Garden were the members of the Society of Apothecaries, who have maintained it for over two centuries entirely for scientific purposes, as was stipulated in the deed of gift, executed by Sir Hans Sloane, in which the growing or cultivation of plants for purely pharmaceutical purposes, or for trade, was strictly forbidden. The origin of this so-called Physic Garden was somewhat amusing, and anything but scientific. The ground was first fixed upon as an eligible spot for building a boathouse for the state barge of the Apothecaries' Company. This ground was walled in about 1674, and planted with trees in 1678, and herbs were grown in it for use in the company's laboratories, some of these plants being from time to time exchanged for others from the University of Leyden. Sir Hans (then Dr.) Sloane bought the estate in 1712; and, as might have been expected of a man of his parts, a pupil of the chemist Stahl and of the botanist Tournefort, and a friend of the great Ray, a new era of usefulness was begun in the Chelsea Garden. In 1722 he handed over the land to the Apothecaries' Society, at a yearly rental of £5, and an undertaking that fifty specimens of fifty species of distinct plants, well dried and mounted as herbarium specimens and properly named, should be handed over to the Royal Society each year until 2000 had been duly delivered. In a catalogue issued in 1730, written by Miller, the head gardener, are enumerated 499 plants, mostly medicinal, so one may judge of the extent of the gardens at that time. Exotics were cultivated in hothouses in 1732, and in 1736 Linnæus paid a visit to the garden.

Thomas Dover, the originator of Dover's powder, was born in England in the year 1660. He settled and practised medicine for a time in Bristol; left there for a period, and returned again. He lived with, and was contemporaneous with Sydenham. He gained much professional reputation on the occasion of a severe epidemic of fever. This may have suggested to him the use of ipecacuanha and opium in a compound.

In Dover's day and time, the apothecaries were in the ascendancy, being the medical practitioners, whilst the physicians were chiefly called in to attend in childbirth and protracted illness. Indeed, it is naïvely stated that the apothecary surgeons rode in their chaises, while the doctors *walked*, and that the former were generally first consulted when the choice of a family physician was to be made. Mercury had at this time an unrestrained use— perhaps *abuse* would be a better word,—and much severe public stricture was made upon the fact. Crude quicksilver was administered, and Dover was a warm advocate of its use—in fact, he was called the *quicksilver doctor*. One Captain Henry Coit, a patient of Dover's, took an ounce and a quarter of crude mercury daily, until he had used more than two pounds weight! Dover professed to believe that mercury freed the patient from all vermicular diseases, opened all obstructions, and made a pure balsam of the blood.

The doctors and apothecaries were at loggerheads. Dover said the best way to affront the latter was to order too little physic—each patient being deemed to be worth a certain sum to the dispenser.

In 1708 Dover joined the company of a group of Bristol merchants in a scheme to fit out two vessels for privateering in the South Seas. Dover, it seems, went as captain, and the voyage was eminently successful in booty. They took in various reprisals from the Spaniards—the hoards of treasure and gold which they in turn had obtained from the native Indians—the principle of *might* applied to *right*. The expedition returned to Britain enriched with spoil, the treasure amounting to £170,000 sterling. It was during this memorable voyage that Dover, landing with some of his crew on the island of Juan Fernandez, discovered the existence of Alexander Selkirk—Robinson Crusoe—in his dreary solitude on this desert shore.

CHAPTER XIV.

AMULETS, TALISMANS AND CHARMS.

From very remote times a somewhat curious link has existed between the art of healing and religion, and those who proposed the cure of the body or the soul have ever sought to work upon that uncanny chord we call superstition, which pervades more or less all classes of mankind. The influence of superstition manifested itself in many ways, and among others the belief in amulets, talismans and charms survives even to-day. Two thousand years ago they were dispensed by the priests, and afterwards by those who practised medicine, alchemy, and astrology, during the middle ages, when medical practice was mainly composed of a mixture of white magic, witchcraft, and religion.

An amulet consisted of an object in wood, stone, or metal, carved or painted; also certain words or signs, written or spoken, which were supposed to possess some mysterious virtue or hidden property, and avert disease and death from the wearer. The word means something that is suspended from the neck, or bound round a part of the body, to strengthen it; to drive off disease or poison, bringing about certain results of a peculiar character, and invested with supernatural virtues. Portions of animals and herbs were also used for this purpose. Talismans were objects, usually of metal or one of the precious stones, worn about the person to ward off danger, ill-luck, or the evil eye, as well as for their supposed medicinal virtues.

By their means it was thought possible to hold commune with the world of spirits. Their origin is lost in antiquity, but they were used by the Assyrians, Egyptians, Persians, and Jews hundreds of years before the Christian era, and afterwards by the Greeks and Romans. It is probable the Jews learned the use of amulets from the Egyptians at the time of the captivity, by whom they were very generally worn. Egyptian amulets were mostly composed of stone or porcelain objects, fashioned in various forms. Some were emblematic of deities, such as the nilometer, which was a symbol of Osiris, while others represented human heads or the figures of animals. Many were engraved with zodiacal symbols which had special significance. The crab was worn to ward off fevers, the bull to guard against the evil-doing of others, fishes kept away gout and kindred diseases, and the scorpion rendered the wearer invulnerable to the bites or stings of venomous reptiles. It was customary with the Egyptians to attach certain amulets to the bodies of the dead to protect them from evil spirits, and they are frequently found suspended from the necks of mummies. Amulets are worn in Egypt to-day, and also in most Mohammedan countries. They usually take the form of a small strip of parchment, on which is written some cabalistic sign or a few lines from the Koran, the whole being enclosed in a small leather or tin case, and hung around the neck. Amulets were also known and much used by the early Greeks. Pliny mentions their virtue, while Galen, Dioscorides, Cardamus, and other ancient writers on medicine, speak of their value in warding off disease. Galen tells us that the Egyptian king, Nechepsus, who lived 630 years B.C., wore a green jasper cut into the form of a dragon, surrounded with rays, which, applied externally to the region of the digestive organs, was said to wonderfully strengthen that part. The Romans were also great believers in the power of the amulet, and in the declining era of the great empire the custom of wearing them became so general that the Emperor Caracalla made a public edict, that no man should wear an amulet about his person, under heavy penalties.

Amulets have been known to that curious nation the Chinese from the earliest period of their history, and are still worn by them. They are sold by the priests in the form of small pieces of metal, chains, or characters written on a piece of skin or parchment, and worn as a charm against accident, sickness, etc.

To enumerate all the extraordinary objects used as amulets in early times, and the wonderful virtues attached to them, would fill a volume, so we must be content to mention a few of the most curious.

The amulets and talismans probably held in the highest esteem were those in the form of precious stones. They were supposed to be influenced in some mysterious way by the planets, and to be the abode of spirits. Five or six hundred years ago a lady would present her knight with a talisman on his departure on some adventurous or warlike expedition; this often took the form of a jewel set in the hilt of his sword. The diamond was thus supposed to endow the wearer with courage, and make him more fearless than careful. A jacinth had the reputation of being able to strengthen the heart, and was often worn close to the region of that organ, fashioned into the form of some animal or saint. The sapphire was supposed to possess a Divine gift of sharpening the intellect, and was also worn as a preventive against the bites of venomous animals. A wearer of this stone was also said to have the power of resisting "necromantick apparitions". The emerald was worn in a ring to prevent giddiness and strengthen the memory. Garcious quaintly states: "It takes away vain and foolish fears as of devils and hobgoblins, folly and anger, and causeth good conditions; if it do so being worn about one, reason will tell him, that being beaten into powder and taken inwardly it will do much more". Great faith was placed in the ruby as an amulet to ward off plagues and pestilences. Cardamus says: "It has the power of making the wearer cheerful, and banishing idle and foolish thoughts". The amethyst was supposed to promote temperance and sobriety, and cause the wearer to abstain from strong drinks and from taking too much sleep. By other writers it is also said to quicken the wit and repel vapours from the head—altogether a very useful kind of amulet to have about. The chrysolite was said to ward off fevers; while the onyx, worn round the neck, was supposed to prevent an attack of epilepsy. The opal was believed to cure weak eyes, and the topaz to cure inflammation and keep the wearer from sleep-walking. Lapis-lazuli, worn as a jewel, was said to make the wearer fortunate and rich, while amulets of jasper resisted fevers and dropsy. Ancient warriors often carried an amulet composed of bloodstone, which was supposed to stop bleeding when applied to a wound. The old Egyptian amulets were mostly carved in stone, porcelain, carnelian, or lapis-lazuli, etc. They were fashioned in many forms, the most common being the heart, the symbolic eye, two fingers, disc and horns, snakes, the tat, and the papyrus sceptre.

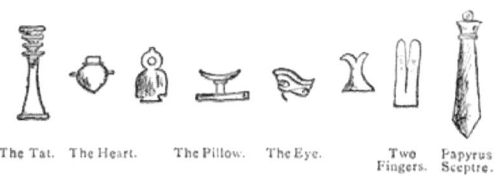

The Tat. The Heart. The Pillow. The Eye. Two Fingers. Papyrus Sceptre.

ANCIENT EGYPTIAN AMULETS OF GOLD AND CLAY FOUND IN MUMMY CASES.

Coming to those fashioned in metal, amulets of gold were also highly esteemed. The precious metal was supposed to strengthen the heart, drive away melancholy, fever, and other infirmities. Silver was attributed with the possession of similar properties, but in a lesser degree. Zoroaster and Paracelsus advocated the use of metallic amulets. Special value was attached to those made from a peculiar metal called *electron*, which was composed of seven metals fused together in fixed proportions. Amulet rings were always worn on the third finger, which was called the medicine-finger by alchemists, through which they believed the heart was most susceptible to influence. Written amulets usually consisted of some cabalistic character, or a few words written on a small piece of skin or parchment. This was either enclosed in a tiny case and suspended from the neck, or bound against the body. It was not uncommon for the physician of the fifteenth century to write his prescription in mysterious characters, and hang it round the neck of the patient, or bind it over the part nearest the seat of the complaint. Of written amulets perhaps the most famous formula was Abracadabra, which, when written on a piece of parchment in the following manner, was said to protect the wearer from most diseases:—

ABRACADABRA
ABRACADABR
ABRACADAB
ABRACADA
ABRACAD
ABRACA
ABRAC
ABRA
ABR
AB
A

Another common formula was the sign A II, which, inscribed on parchment, was worn round the neck to prevent sore eyes. Others were composed of astrological signs and certain numbers. A favourite inscription was A B R A X A S, supposed to ward off fever and pestilence.

The Jews used the fifth and sixth verses of the sixteenth Psalm as an amulet to discover hidden thieves, it being supposed that on repeating these words they would be compelled to come forth from their hiding-places. The modern burglar requires an amulet of a somewhat stronger nature in these prosaic days. A curious charm for warts, used some 400 years ago, was to write on seven little wafers the following words: Maximanus, Walchus, Johannes, Martinianus, Dionysius, Constantius, Serapion, and sing a prescribed incantation first into one ear, then into the other, and then above the patient's poll, after which a virgin was to hang the incantation around the patient's neck, when the warts would disappear. Another amulet to charm away warts was an iron ring made from the chain of a gibbet. The following incantation was supposed to stop bleeding from the nose: Make the sign of the Cross thrice, repeat the Lord's Prayer thrice; then say the *Ave Maria*, and repeat the words Max, Hackx, Lyacx, Iseus, Christus. Among the many strange and curious articles worn as amulets the old philosophers seem to have had the greatest veneration for certain mysterious stones, such as bezoar, the origin of which in most cases is exceedingly doubtful. Dark and weird are the legends relating to the power of the toadstone, that amulet so highly prized by witches and astrologers. Among other properties it was supposed to protect its owner from the bites of venomous animals. Lemnius tells us of "a stone of the bigness of a bean, to be found in the gizzard of an old cock, which makes him that wears it beloved, constant, bold, and valiant in fighting and sports". Such amulets brought big prices, and were eagerly sought after. The toadstone was much esteemed as a charm against the bites of snakes and reptiles; it also had a reputation for curing weak eyes and headache. Orpheus believed that when this amulet was worn by a public speaker he could always compel and hold the attention of his audience. A charm against the evil eye consisted of a quill filled with mercury, sealed at each end, and worn bound to the body. A small portion of the plant called St. John's Wort was carried about the person as a preventive from harm by witches or devils. A toad, well dried in the sun, put into a bag and hung round the neck, low enough to touch the region of the heart, was used to allay hæmorrhage; and a very well salted herring split open and applied to the soles of the feet was a noted remedy for ague. An emerald suspended from the neck was worn as an amulet to ward off the same complaint. *Aqua divina*, a famous remedy, supposed to possess "magnetick power," was prepared by macerating a human body in water and distilling it twice or thrice. Human bones, various parts of a mummy, and other equally gruesome objects, were supposed to be endowed with some mysterious power to ward off accident, disease, and death. In some parts of the country, especially in Cornwall, eel skins were and are still used, tied round the legs to prevent cramp; and two sticks laid crosswise on the bedroom floor were supposed to charm away the same painful complaint. It is still a common custom in other country districts to pass a weakly child through the split branch of a tree in order to make it grow stronger; and a certain class have the strongest belief in a charm of a romantic nature that is worked with the gum called dragon's blood.

A famous amulet, the remarkable history of which inspired Sir Walter Scott to write *The Talisman*, was "The Lee Penny," which we believe is still in existence, and held in veneration in some parts of Scotland. The singular history attached to this coin was as follows: Sir Simon Lockhart, of Lee and Cartland, was a well-known knight in the time of Robert the Bruce and his son David. He was one of the chief Scottish knights who accompanied Lord Douglas on his expedition to the Holy Land with the heart of King Robert Bruce, and was there engaged in the war with the Saracens. Tradition goes on to state that he captured in battle an emir of great rank and wealth, and fixed a price at which he should be ransomed. The aged mother of the prisoner came to the Christian camp to redeem her son, and on pulling out a large purse which contained the ransom, a peculiar pebble inserted in a coin fell to the ground. The old woman, it is said, showed such haste and anxiety to recover it, that it gave the Scottish knight a high idea of its value—on which he refused to set the emir at liberty till the amulet was added to the ransom. This the woman consented to do, and also explained to Sir Simon the use of the talisman, which was of great repute. When dipped in water the liquid assumed the properties of a styptic and a febrifuge, etc. Sir Simon Lockhart, after much experience of its value, brought it home, and left it to his heirs, and it is known as the "Lee penny" from the name of his native place. The coin is said to be of the early Byzantine period. The most remarkable part of its history, as stated in the introduction to *The Talisman*, was, that it escaped condemnation in an extraordinary manner when the Church of Scotland impeached many other cures of the kind which savoured of the miraculous, as occasioned by sorcery, and censured the appeal to them; "excepting only that to the amulet called the 'Lee penny,' to which it had pleased God to annex certain healing virtues which the Church did not presume to condemn". It still exists, and its powers are sometimes yet resorted to.

For epilepsy, a curious custom was to take the sick man by the hand and whisper softly in his ear, "I conjure thee by the sun and moon, and by the Gospel of the day delivered by God to Hubert, Giles, Cornelius, and John, that thou rise and fall no more".

When picking simples for burns the following charm was repeated:—

"Hail to the holy herb,
Growing on the ground,
All in the Mount Calvary,
First wert thou found.

> Thou art good for many a sore,
> And heal'st many a wound;
> In the name of Sweet Jesus, I
> take thee from the ground."

To produce sleep, the following is recommended to be repeated:—

> "In nomine Patris up and down,
> Et filii et spiritus sancte upon my crown,
> Dear Christ upon my breast,
> Sweet Lady, send me eternal rest".

The following was supposed to stop the flux:—

> "In the blood of Adam death was taken,
> In the blood of Christ it was all to slaken,
> And by the same blood I do thee charge
> That thou do run no longer at large".

Singular virtues were supposed to be attached to a "dead man's hand". In a Roman Catholic chapel in Ashton-in-Mackerfield, there is preserved with great care in a white silk bag, a hand, which is still held in veneration, and wonderful cures are said to have been wrought by this ghastly relic.

The hand is said to have been that of one Father Edmund Arrowsmith, who was executed at Lancaster in 1628, for apparently no greater offence than that of being true to his faith. After his execution one of his friends cut off his right hand, which was preserved for many years at Bryn Hall, in Lancashire, and afterwards removed to Ashton.

This "Holy hand" was formerly held in great esteem in Lancashire, and pilgrims came from all parts of the country to receive its touch, which was reputed to cure various diseases. It was believed to remove tumours when rubbed over the part, and restore health to the paralysed.

There is a curious superstition still prevalent in some parts of Lancashire, that when cat's hair gets into the stomach it causes sickness, which may be cured by eating a piece of egg-shell once a day.

Consumption was believed by the ignorant to be produced by drinking water which had been boiled too long. The cure was to dig a hole in the earth, lie in it face downwards, and breathe into the soil. This extraordinary remedy was also largely used for coughs, asthma, and those suffering from hysteria.

A curious charm is still practised in Devonshire as a cure for the complaint called a white swelling or white leg. Bandages are used to tie round the afflicted limb, over which the following charm is repeated nine times, and each time followed by the Lord's Prayer:—

"As Christ was walking, He saw the Virgin Mary sitting on a cold marble stone. He said unto her, 'If it is a white ill thing, or a red ill thing, or a black ill thing, or a sticking, crackling, pricking, stabbing, bone ill thing, or a sore ill thing, or a swelling ill thing, or a rotten ill thing, or a cold creeping ill thing, or a smarting ill thing, let it fall from thee to the earth in My name, and the name of the Father, Son, and Holy Ghost. Amen.'"

This comprehensive charm would seem to cover a multitude of ills indeed.

The following charms are taken from a MS. of the year 1475:—

A Charme to Staunch Blood.

"Jesus, that was in Bethlehem born, and baptyzed was in the flumen Jordane, as stente the water at hys comyng, so stente the blood of thys man N, thy serwaunt, throw the virtu of thy holy name + Jesu + and of thy Cosyn swete Sent Jon. And sey thys Charme fyve tymes with fyve Pater nostirs, in the worshep of the fyve woundys."

For Fever.

"Wryt thys wordys on a lorell lef + Ysmael + Ysmael + adjuro vos per angelum ut soporetetur iste Homo N. and ley thys lef under hys head that he wote not thereof, and let hym ete Letuse oft and drynk Ip'e seed small grounden in a morter, and temper yt with ale."

It is said that the inhabitants of Colonsay had an ancient custom of fanning the face of the sick with the leaves of the Bible.

Many and varied are the charms for curing warts. "For warts," says Sir Thomas Brown, "we rub our hands before the moon and commit any maculated part to the touch of the dead." Grose tells us to "steal a piece of beef from a butcher's shop and rub your warts with it; then throw it down the 'necessary house,' or bury it; and as the beef rots your warts will decay".

The leaf of the castor-oil plant worn round the neck was believed to ward away devils, because the leaf is like an open hand.

In Bale's *Interlude* the following charms are given:—

"For the coughe take Judas Eare
With the parynge of a Peare,
And drynke them without feare
        If ye will have remedy:
Thre syppes are for the hyckocke,
And six more for the chyckocke;
Thus my pretty pyckocke
        Recover by and by.
If ye cannot slepe but slumber,
Geve Otes unto Saynt Uncumber,
And Beanes in a certen number
        Unto Saynt Blase and Saynt Blythe.
Give Onyons to Saynt Cutlake
And Garlycke to Saynt Cyoyake,
If ye wyll spurne the heade ake.
        Ye shall have them at Quene hyth."

Amulet rings were made from various metals, and worn to ward off disease and misfortune.

In Berkshire there is a popular superstition that a ring made from a piece of silver collected at the communion is a cure for convulsions and fits.

Rings were also made from coffin-nails dug out of a grave, and coffin-hinges, and used to cure cramp. Boorde, in his *Introduction to Knowledge* (1542), says: "The kynges of Englande doth halowe every yere Crampe Rynges, ye which Rynges worne on one's Fynger doth helpe them whych hath the crampe".

One of the favourite charms of the early Britons was the *anguineum*, or snake's egg, which was supposed to be produced from the saliva of serpents, and besides its healing properties it got the credit of being able to float against the current.

Many of the ancient writers believed that all charms were impotent without the repetition of certain words. Thus the following words are recommended by Barrett to be repeated as a charm against flux of blood:—

"In the blood of Adam arose death,
In the blood of Christ death is extinguished.
In the name of Christ I command thee, O blood,
        That thou stop fluxing."

A piece of clean new vellum bearing the letters

יהרה

was considered a powerful amulet against ague.

Pliny makes several allusions to the poison of toads, and Juvenal tells us of the lady

"Who squeezed a toad into her husband's wine".

66

The life of James VI. of Scotland was once attempted by a woman named Agnes Sampson, who confessed on her trial, that in order to compass the king's death, she had hung up a black toad for nine days and collected the juice that fell from it. The toadstone was greatly valued as an amulet against a great variety of diseases. It was often set in valuable rings, which were handed down from generation to generation. Some are said to have borne a figure resembling a toad on their surface. They varied in colour, some being dark-grey, and others of a brownish fawn colour. These stones were supposed to grow only in very old toads, and to be extracted when they were dying. In reality, they were manufactured of fused borax and many other materials.

The toadstone was supposed to be specially powerful against witchcraft and poison. When placed in proximity to the latter, or applied to one bewitched, the stone was believed to sweat or change colour. It was sometimes given internally as a remedy for fever or the bites of reptiles. The toad itself was also credited with medicinal virtues, and was given in plague and small-pox. Aubrey gives a process for preparing the toad for internal use, in which "twenty great fatt toads are directed to be stewed slowly, while alive, in a pipkin on the fire. The calcined remains are again heated, and then finely powdered." Sir Kenhelm Digby speaks of their virtues, and recommends toads for quinsy, bleeding at the nose, and, above all, a most valuable remedy in king's evil and scrofula. Within the last fifty years "toad doctors" visited most country fairs, often selling bags containing the legs torn from the body of a living toad for six or seven shillings each.

Among other curious charms used by the Romans to prolong life, especially among the aged, was the singular practice of being breathed upon by young girls. This custom is frequently mentioned by ancient writers, and was believed to be efficacious also in prolonging life in certain diseases. A reference to this singular charm is recorded by Kohansen in an inscription which was discovered at Rome, cut in a marble tablet, and which ran as follow

"To Æsculapius and Health,
this is erected by
L. Clodius Hermippus,
who by the breath of young girls lived 115 years and 5
days
at which physicians were no little surprised.

———

Successive generations lead such a life."

———

In later times amulets in civilised countries merged into the wearing of images of saints, or consecrated objects, and the use of scapularies by Roman

Catholics at the present time. There is little doubt that the custom of wearing precious stones in rings, and the charms worn as pendants to watch chains, originated in the amulet and talisman. Who can say that the belief in such charms has even yet died out? How many people are there at the present day who do not carry about them some coin, token, or object, to which they would probably be ashamed to confess, they attach some mysterious virtue? The belief in keeping a crooked sixpence or a broken ring is evidence of that peculiar vein of superstition that runs through most of us, which, strange though it may seem, the advance of science and education has not altogether dispelled.

CHAPTER XV.

MONK PHYSICIANS—ITINERANT DOCTORS—SURGERY IN THE MIDDLE AGES.

THE treatment prescribed by the monks, who were ready to cure the body as well as the soul, consisted mainly of holy water, prayer, the touching of relics, and a number of decoctions of herbs, the properties of which they were acquainted with. Many of these physician monks wandered about the country devoting themselves to the wants of the sick.

During the eleventh century hospitals began to spring up in various parts of the country and over Europe. They seem to have originated at the time of the crusades. Lacroix says: "The Johannists, and the brotherhoods of St. Mary and St. Lazarus devoted themselves to missions of charity in the East; in France, there were the brothers of St. Antony and of the Holy Ghost; and throughout the world the heroic chevaliers of St. John of Jerusalem or of the Templars, whose countless establishments combined the triple character of conventual church, almshouse, and fortress, and who, attired in a dress both military and monastic, wore a mantle similar to that seen in the statues of Æsculapius, as a sign of the double mission—beneficent and warlike—which they had sworn to fulfil".

Each of these orders had a special form of treatment, and took charge of specific diseases. Thus, the Templars paid special attention to those pilgrim soldiers and travellers particularly troubled with ophthalmia, scurvy, or those suffering from wounds. The Johannists professed the cure of epidemical disease and pestilence. The order of St. Antony looked after those stricken with dysenteries and those complaints known as St. Anthony's fire, while the Lazarists treated leprosy, small-pox, and pustular fevers. The first school of nurses of which we have record, is one organised by Hildegarde, Abbess of Rupertsberg, who died 1180. These nuns gave great assistance in the hospitals. Thus the monks about the twelfth century tended the bodies as well as the souls, and even accompanied armies on military expeditions in that capacity.

In the thirteenth century faculties were established at Montpellier, Salerno, and Paris, by the order of papal bulls, to grant degrees in medicine. In order to obtain the title of master physician, the candidate had first to become a clerk, then pass an examination before masters or doctors selected from the staff of the college by the Bishop of Maguelonne.

The barbers at this time came to occupy an important position in medicine, and were promoted to the rank of subordinate surgeons, chiefly for blood-letting and minor accidents.

In the fourteenth century medicine had rapidly progressed in Europe, and the celebrated physician and surgeon Lanfranc founded the St. Cosmo College at Paris, the examinations of which all surgeons were obliged to pass. A decree was also passed by the King of France in 1352 prohibiting any one who was not an apothecary, student, or mendicant monk from practising medicine. The king, we find, also exempted the master barbers from doing duty as watchmen, as "the barbers being nearly all of them in the habit of practising surgery, great inconvenience might arise if they were absent from their houses when sent for during the night".

In France, the little barbers, as they were called, travelled about on foot from village to village with a bag containing their drugs and remedies, while the great barbers, or sworn surgeons, astride their hacks with tinkling bells to announce their approach, wore long robes trimmed with fur, and other rich apparel. They were usually accompanied by an assistant and several servants, who carried their cases of instruments, which always included scissors, nippers, a probe or *éprouvette*, razors, lances, and needles. He also carried five kinds of ointments, *viz.*, basilicon, apostles' ointment, the white ointment, yellow ointment, and the dialtœa ointment for subduing local pain.

Guy de Chauliac, who was physician to three successive popes, stated "he never went out on his visits without taking several clysters and plain remedies, besides gathering herbs in the field, so as to treat diseases in a proper manner".

Even at that early time the credulity of the public became imposed upon by quacks, and Lacroix tells us of an English surgeon, one Goddesden, who had two sorts of prescriptions, one for the rich and another for the poor; he sold at a high price to the barbers a so-called panacea, which the latter sold at a large profit, and this was simply a mixture of frogs pounded in a mortar. In one of his books there is a short chapter on *disagreeable* diseases, as he terms them, "which work their own cure, and bring no grist to the doctor's mill".

In the fifteenth century the practice of medicine became more and more influenced and dominated by the occult sciences, and especially astrology. All mankind was ruled by the stars, and the cause of various diseases was attributed to the conjunction of certain planets. "They believed the blood rose during the daytime towards the sun, and descended into the lower extremities at night; that at the third hour the bile subsided, so that its acid properties might not be mixed with the course of the blood; and that at the second hour the atrabilis, and in the evening the phlegm, subsided." Such illusions and erroneous beliefs stopped the progress of science, and threatened to turn a noble art into mere charlatanry. In this country the surgeons mostly practised as apothecaries; and we are told that when Henry V. invaded France in 1415, the only surgeon he had in his camp was one Thomas Morstede, who was with difficulty induced to accompany the army, bringing with him twelve assistants.

The sixteenth century saw an effort to throw off some of these errors which had grown round the art. The invention of printing helped largely in disseminating knowledge throughout Europe, and the followers of medicine assumed a higher position.

AN APOTHECARY'S SHOP. FIFTEENTH CENTURY.

Towards the end of the fifteenth century Tachenius wrote: "There is no new thing under the sun whatsoever, therefore the followers of Hippocrates have handed out, and as it were midwifed into the world, the same was from the beginning though our eyes were not so clear-sighted as to discern it". To which Stephen Pasquier replied in the following rhyme:—

> "Some Paracelse of novelty implead,
> For which, judged crime, he erst was banished,
> So Hippocrates, Chrysippus, and at Rome
> Asclepiade, too, were new. They'd all one doom.
> They who condemn new things condemn the old,
> Or else do both misjudge and are o'er bold."

During the crusades the surgeons naturally acquired a very large experience in the treatment of wounds—incised, lacerated, and contused. Baldwin was severely wounded before Jerusalem, having received a spear-thrust "through the thigh and the loins". He fell fainting from his horse, but the most skilful leeches were summoned, "by whose art and skill the king and valiant athlete

71

was enabled to recover from this deadly wound". Baldwin was also wounded in the foot before Antioch, and the surgical talent available was baffled by the injury to such a degree that it was proposed to kill a Saracen after wounding him in the same part, so as to learn the proper course to pursue. Baldwin, however, refused to allow this crude attempt at experimental surgery to be made. There seem to be no medical records of the second crusade. In the third, the French king, Philippe Auguste, and our own Cœur de Lion suffered grievously from a disease, the symptomatology of which included extensive exfoliation of the skin, shedding of the nails, and loss of the hair. The disease is called *Arnoldia* by the chroniclers, and is variously conjectured to have been leprosy or syphilis. It could hardly have been leprosy, for both the royal sufferers recovered, Cœur de Lion being killed eight years later at the siege of Chalus, and Philippe Auguste dying of quartan ague twenty-four years after Richard. Of the fourth crusade we have no medical details. In the fifth, St. Louis of France was accompanied by his private physician Dudon and other leeches; among them was a lady doctor or *phisicienne* named Hernandis, who probably attended the queen in her confinement, which took place at Damietta. The expedition suffered terribly from scurvy, typhus, and other pestilences. The part played by water in the diffusion of disease would seem to have been recognised, though the methods of water examination would hardly satisfy a modern chemist. A piece of white linen was dipped in the water to be tested, and then dried; if there were any stains on the linen the water was condemned, but if not it was pronounced pure. The addition of four crushed almonds or beans was believed to make the water of the Nile safe for drinking. The method of disinfection adopted for the king's tent was to fumigate it with a mixture of amber, chick peas, or lupine, which were macerated in wine, and then placed on live charcoal. In the sixth crusade, which took place twenty-two years later, vast numbers, including St. Louis himself, fell victims to ignorance of the elements of sanitation.

CHAPTER XVI.

PLANT LORE, DRUG CHARMS, AND FOLK MEDICINE.

A CURIOUS survival of the age of superstition and romance attaches to the red resin known as dragon's blood, and is still largely practised by a certain class of uneducated women in many parts of the country. The resin is the product of the *Pterocarpus Indicus* growing in the East Indies, and now chiefly used as a colouring agent in varnishes and stains, etc. It was formerly employed in medicine for its astringent properties, but has now entirely gone out of use for that purpose.[4]

The secret of its use as a charm is shrouded in some mystery, and those who use it are very reticent in giving particulars; but it has been gathered, that several charms of a romantic nature are worked with this otherwise very commonplace article of commerce. The most common of these seems to be practised by young girls who are jealous of their lovers and seek to win back their affection. A small quantity of dragon's blood is procured, wrapped in paper, and thrown on the fire whilst the following couplet or incantation is repeated:—

> "May he no pleasure or profit see,
> Till he comes back again to me".

Another method much believed in by women of a certain class, and used by them to attract the opposite sex, is to mix dragon's blood, quicksilver, saltpetre, and sulphur, and throw them on the fire, repeating a similar incantation.

A chemist in the north of England, giving his experience on the sale of dragon's blood, says: "I have had great difficulty in finding out for what purpose it was used. It was not for medicine, but for a kind of witchcraft. The women burn it upon a bright fire, while wishing for their affection to be returned by some one of the opposite sex; also those who have quarrelled with their husbands and desire to be friends again; girls who have fallen out with their young men, and want to win them back; as well as young women wanting sweethearts. A working man recently came to me for a small quantity, and I inquired for what purpose it was required. He was very reluctant to mention anything about it, but at length said, a man had made him lose three sovereigns, and he wished, as he had been swindled out of the money, to have his revenge, and make him suffer for it. He was going to turn the dragon's blood on a clear fire, and he believed that the ill wishes of the person thus burning it would have a dire effect on the individual thought of."

Another charm said to be worked with this drug, in which an inverted teacup plays a prominent part, has reference to the sex of expected offspring.

Altogether, considerable romantic properties seem to be associated with this resin, but there seems to be no authentic record of the same, the only probable explanation being, that it was used and sold, like other innocent articles, by those who were supposed to have dealings in the black art, for working charms, which have thus been handed down from mediæval times. Coles states: "The early Greeks called dragon's blood *Cinnabaris*, not knowing whether it was of vegetable or mineral origin; and that Pliny, Solinus, and Monardus have set it down for truth that it was the blood of a dragon or serpent, crushed to death by the weight of the dying elephant falling upon him; but he thinks it was certainly so called from the bloody colour that it is of, being nothing else but a mere gum". It was used medicinally as an emmenagogue, and in the arts 300 years ago by goldsmiths and painters in glass, by the former as a base for enamel to set a foil under precious stones to give them greater lustre, and the latter by fire, to strike a crimson colour into glass for stained windows.

That a belief in charms and witchcraft is still fostered by ignorant people in some parts of the country, is manifest from cases reported in the newspapers from time to time. Two practitioners of the occult sciences were haled before the magistrates but recently. One, an old crone, who confessed to using dragon's blood in working her love charms, was rewarded with seven days with hard labour.

The other, which came to light in Cornwall, was a middle-aged individual who practised as a wizard. His treatment consisted of writing an amulet to be worn near the body. Money was then required to remove the spell from the bewitched patient to some one else. To this victim was to be lent neither "cock, pin, or pan," and by the aid of the planets the patient would be cured. But these are hard times truly for the wizard and magician, and this professor was rewarded with seven months' incarceration in one of her Majesty's gaols.

Singular superstitious properties are attributed to certain plants. The walnut was formerly employed in medicine as an application to wounds and an antidote to poisons; and the following old riddle, says William Coles in 1657, "almost every one knows":—

> "As high as a house,
> As little as a mouse,
> As round as a ball,
> As bitter as gall,
> As white as milk,
> As soft as silk".

There is an old tradition that the more the branches are beaten, the more prolific the fruit will be. There is a fable in Æsop of a woman who asked the walnut tree growing by the wayside, which was pelted at with stones and sticks by them that passed by, why it was so foolish as to bring forth fruit seeing that it was so beaten for its pains, to which the tree rehearsed these two proverbial verses:—

> "Nux, Asinus, Mulier, Simili suret lege legati,
> Haes tria nil recte faciunt si verbera cessent".

"The English whereof," the chronicler quaintly continues, "I could tell you, but that I fear the women of this preposterous age would be angry." True it is that this tree, the more it is beaten the more nuts it bears. The walnut was one of the chief ingredients in the celebrated antidote against poison which was attributed to the wise king Mithridates. The formula ran as follows: "Two (wall) nuttes and two figges and twenty rewe beans, stamped together with a little suet and eaten fasting, doth defende a man from poison and pestilence that day".[5]

Sage was much esteemed by the housewife for simple ailments, and its properties are embodied in the following lines, which are of great antiquity:—

> "Sage helpes the nerves, and by its powerfull might
> Palsies and Feavers, sharp it puts to flight".[6]

An old writer says, "Be sure you wash your sage for fear the Toades, who as I conceive come to it to discharge their poyson, should leave some of their venom upon the Leaves".

Of rue, which was largely used as a carminative, the following couplet has been handed down:—

> "Rue maketh chast, and eke preserveth sight,
> Infuseth wit, and Fleas doth put to flight".

Tradition says that a weasel, going to fight with a serpent, eateth rue, and rubbeth herself therewith to avoid his poison. Crollius states: "The sign of the cross upon the seed of the rue, drives away all phantoms and evil spirits by signature".

Henbane, the Latins called Apollinaris, either from Apollo, the inventor of physic, or because it makes men mad like unto Apollo's creatures when they deliver his oracles. "It was called in English henbane, because the seeds are hurtful to hens," says William Coles. "The fumes of the dryed herb when burnt, will make Hens fall from their roosting place as though they were dead."

Of the moonwort, a simple used to allay bleeding and applied to fractures, an old tradition says that it can be used to open locks, fetters, and shoes from those horses feet that go on the places where it groweth, and of this opinion was Culpepper, who, though he railed against superstition in others, tells a story of a troop of horse of the Earl of Essex, which being drawn up in a body, many of them lost their shoes upon White Downe in Devonshire, near Tiverton, because moonwort grows upon the heaths.

The root of the *Polygonatum angulosum*, commonly called Solomon's Seal, has a popular reputation for removing the congealed blood from a bruise after a blow or fall, for which property it appears to have been used 800 years ago. Coles states: "The bruised roots soddereth and gleweth together broken bones very speedily and strangely, the roots being stamped and outwardly applied as a pultis. The same also is available for outward bruises, falls, or blowes, both to dispel the congealed blood and to take away the paines, and the black and blew markes that abide after the hurt." The origin of the name Solomon's Seal is doubtless due to the dark marks seen on cutting the root transversely, which somewhat resemble an ancient seal engraved with characters.

Of Solomon's Seal, Dioscorides says that "the root pounded and laid on fresh wounds heals and seals them up"; and it is on this account that Gerard considers its name to have originated.

An old author quaintly remarks with respect to its properties: "The roots of Solomon's Seale stamped while it is fresh and greene and applied, taketh away in one night, or two at the most, any bruse, blacke or blew spots gotten by fals, or woman's wilfulness in stumbling upon their hastie husband's fists or such like".

The anemone was regarded by the ancients as an emblem of sickness, and Pliny tells us that the physicians and wise men ordered every person to gather the first anemone he saw in the year, repeating at the same time, "I gather thee for a remedy against disease". It was then devoutly placed in scarlet cloth and kept undisturbed unless the gatherer became unwell, when it was tied either around the neck or the arm of the patient.

The trefoil, vervain, St. John's wort, and dill were supposed to possess the power of protecting the wearer from the evil eye or witchcraft, hence the old rhyme called Saint Colme's charm:—

> "Trefoil, vervain, John's wort, dill,
> Hinders witches of their will;
> Well is them, that well may
> Fast upon St. Andrew's Day.
>
> Saint Bride and her brat,
> Saint Colme and his cat,
> Saint Michael and his spear,
> Keep the home frae reif and wear."

There is an old tradition that the white veins of the variety of thistle known as the *Carduus Marianus* was caused originally by a drop of the milk of the Virgin Mary having fallen thereon, and for this cause the plant was in early times much revered.

The house leek, with its pretty rose-coloured flowers, often seen growing along the tops of walls and on the roofs of cottages in country places, was formerly known by the imposing name of the thunder plant, from the power it was supposed to possess of averting lightning from the house or building on which it was planted. Hence the custom of planting it on the roof.

St. John's wort was a noted herb in magical arts, and was also esteemed as a repellant of spectres and to drive away demons, and was called *Fuga Dæmonum* by the old botanists. French and German peasants still gather the plant with great ceremony on St. John's Day.

That charming little wild flower the scarlet pimpernell, which grows in our fields and hedges, ranked among the simples of ancient times. It was used as a remedy against the plague, and an antidote against the bites and stings of venomous insects, and to stop bleeding. This latter attribute was doubtless more mythical than correct, being founded on what the ancients called having the signature, which meant that if a substance was of blood colour it signified it would stop bleeding because of the same. Hung over the door or porch of a house, it was believed to defend the inmates from witchcraft.

Josephus states in his *History of the Jews*[7] that Solomon discovered a plant efficacious in the cure of epilepsy, and that he employed the aid of a charm or spell for the purpose of assisting its virtues. The root of the herb was concealed in a ring, which was applied to the nostrils of the demoniac; and Josephus himself declares that he saw a Jewish priest practice the art of Solomon, with complete success, in the presence of Vespasian, his sons, and the tribune of the Roman army.

From this art, exhibited through the medium of a ring or seal, we have the Eastern stories which celebrate the seal of Solomon and record its wonderful sway over the various orders of genii, who were supposed to be the invisible tormentors or benefactors of the human race.

"Vervain," says Coles, "was reported to be effectual against all poisons and the venom of dangerous beasts and serpents, and also against bewitched drinks and the like, so that it is not only used in, but against witchcraft. That this herb is used by witches may appear from the story of Anne Bodenham, the witch of Salisbury, who sent her ruffian-like spirits to gather vervain and dill, which was to be given to one whom she desired to bewitch."

The magi of the ancient Elamites or Persians made use of vervain in their worship or adoration of the sun, always carrying branches of it in their hands when they approached the altar.

They also believed that by smearing the body over with the juice of this plant, the individual could have whatever he wished, be able to reconcile his most inveterate enemies, cure diseases, and perform other magical operations. They always gathered the plant when neither sun nor moon was visible, and poured honey and honeycomb on the earth as an atonement for robbing it of this precious herb.

The Greeks called it the Sacred Herb, and used it to cleanse the festival table of Jupiter before any great ceremony took place.

The Romans also employed it in the performance of their religious rites, for cleansing their altars, and sprinkling holy water.

It was hung in their dwellings to ward off evil spirits.

Vervain was also one of the sacred plants of the Druids, both in Gaul and Britain. They cut it with much ceremony in the spring of the year, and made offerings to the earth for so doing. They also used it to anoint the body to cure disease.

The ancient Greeks and Romans dedicated it to the god of war, and in Scandinavia it was deemed sacred to Thor. The eye anointed with an ointment of vervain was supposed to possess second sight. Its influence over Venus has doubtless to do with its use as a love token. It is said that the custom is still practised in Germany of presenting a bride with a wreath of vervain.

Other magic wreaths worn by lovers when they wished to see their fate, were composed of rue, crane's bill, and willow.

The hawkweed commonly seen in our fields was regarded by the Greeks as the emblem of quick-sightedness, believing that the hawk, a bird renowned for its bright eye and quick sight, sharpened its visual organs with the juice of this plant. Thus it became famed in early medical practice as a remedy for dimness of sight, and was employed to feed the hawks used in the old art of falconry.

In Scotland, a twig of the rowan tree or mountain ash is often sewed up in the cow's tail, to protect the animal from witches and warlocks.

The squill was used by the Egyptians for dropsy, under the mystic name of the "Eye of Typhon".

An old name for the fruit of the mandrake was "love apples". They were frequently used in ancient times in philtres and love potions. This plant belongs to the natural order *Solanaceæ*, which also includes the potato and the tobacco plant. Its leaves spring directly from the root similarly to those of the lettuce, before it shoots into flower, and its purple-coloured blossoms are succeeded by a yellow berry or "apple," which still ripens in Palestine at the time of the wheat harvest. An overdose of the fruit is said to produce a sort of temporary insanity. From the earliest times it has been credited with magical virtues, and supposed to confer superhuman powers on its possessor. The most valued specimens were those which grew under a gibbet where a malefactor hung in chains. It was believed that on being torn from the earth the mandrake uttered a groan, and that whosoever heard it, dropped dead on the spot. The approved method of gathering it was to fasten the plant to a dog's tail, and beat the animal till his struggles pulled the root up. The dog heard the groan and died, but those who directed the proceedings escaped by having their ears stopped with pitch or wax.

It was customary in Germany in mediæval times to form or carve small figures out of the mandrake root, which were called *abrunes*. "These images," says Phillips, "they dressed regularly every day, consulted as oracles, and their repute was such that they were manufactured in great numbers and sold in cases."

They appear to have been brought over to England in the time of Henry VIII., and met with ready purchasers, it being pretended that they would, with the assistance of certain mystic words, be able to increase whatever money was placed near them. These roots were said to have been taken from plants which had grown underneath gibbets, and had been influenced by the flesh of the criminals hung thereon.

It is singular how the willow has ever been associated with sorrow and sadness, even from the time the daughters of Israel hung their harps on its branches. Among heathen nations the tree was regarded as an evil omen, and was used as torches at funerals. "The early poets," says Johns, "made the willow of despairing woe," and Shakespeare frequently alludes to it as being used to weave garlands for jilted and sorrow-stricken lovers. Benedick says:—

"I offered him my company to a willow tree, either to make him a garland, as being forsaken, or to bind him up a rod as being worthy to be whipped".

And Bona, in *Henry VI.*, remarks:—

"Tell him, in hope he'll prove a widower shortly,
I'll wear the willow garland for his sake".

It seems to have been customary to wear it twined round the head as a symbol of sorrow and mourning, but the origin of the custom is unknown.

A peculiar virtue was supposed to be attached to the eating of almonds, which is still believed in some parts of the country, *viz.*, that it protects the eater from drunkenness.

Gerard says, "Five or six being taken fasting keepe a man from being drunke".

The pretty flower called the bachelor's button, which is common in our hedgerows, is said to possess the following peculiar property of divination. "When carried in the pocket by men, and under the apron by women, it will retain or lose its freshness according to the good or bad success of the wearer's amatory prospects."

A considerable amount of romantic lore lingers about the bean and nut. The bean was regarded with veneration by both the Greeks and Romans, and on account of its sacred associations became the instrument for voting by ballot in early times. Nuts of various kinds have long been associated with certain love charms, and some of these old customs, such as the cracking of nuts, still survive and are practised on All Hallow Eve. An old charm for nut-testing runs as follows:—

> "Two hazel nuts I threw into the flame,
> And to each nut I gave a sweetheart's name;
> *This* with the loudest bounce me sore amazed,
> *That* in a flame of brightest colour blazed;
> As blazed the nut, so may thy passion glow,
> For 'twas *thy* nut that did so brightly glow".

There is an old tradition that the white hawthorn was used to plait the sacred crown of thorns, and that from that time the tree was endowed with special virtues.

An old writer says: "He that beareth a branch on hym thereof, no thundre, ne, no maner of tempest may dere hym; ne, in the howse that it is ynne may none evil ghost enter".

A great amount of superstition was associated with various ferns in mediæval times, and fern seed was supposed to possess the wonderful property of rendering those who swallowed it invisible.

According to the doctrine of Signatures, various shaped leaves were used for special diseases. A liver-shaped leaf was used to cure complaints of that organ, and a heart-shaped leaf was used for diseases of the heart, and so on.

The black hellebore was employed by the ancients to purify their dwellings, and they believed that its presence in their rooms drove away evil spirits. It was also customary to bless the cattle with hellebore to keep them free from spells wrought by the wicked.

When dug up for these purposes, certain religious ceremonies were observed. First a circle was drawn round the plant with a sword, and then, turning to the east, a humble prayer was made by the devotee to Apollo and Æsculapius, for permission to dig up the root. If an eagle approached the spot during the performance of the rites, it was supposed to predict the certain death of the person who took up the plant in the course of the year.

It is related by Dioscorides that Carneades, the Cyrenaic philosopher who undertook to answer the books of Zeno, sharpened his wit and quickened his spirit by purging his head with powdered hellebore.

The peony owes its name to Pæon, a famous physician of ancient Greece, who is said to have cured, by the aid of this plant, the wounds which the Greeks received during the Trojan war. It was largely used as an amulet, and demons were supposed to fly from the spot where it was planted. A small piece was worn round the neck to protect the wearer from enchantment.

There is a curious tradition connected with that charming little flower the forget-me-not. It is, that the juice, or decoction of the plant, has the peculiar property of hardening steel, and that if edged tools of that metal be made red hot and then quenched in the juice or decoction, and this be repeated several times, the steel will become so hard as to cut iron without turning the edge.

The elder had a great reputation as an amulet. An old writer states, "if one ride with two little sticks of elder in his pockets he shall not fret nor pant let the horse go never so hard".

According to the *Anatomie of the Elder* (1655), "The common people keep as a great secret in curing wounds the leaves of the elder, which they have gathered the last day of April, which, to disappoint the charms of witches, they had applied to their doors and windows".

A piece cut out between two knots was worn as an amulet against erysipelas.

Lupton says: "Make powder of the flowers of elder gathered on Midsummer Day, being before well dryed, and use a spoonful thereof in a good draught of Borage water, morning and evening, first and last, for the space of a month, and it will make you seem young a great while".

The elder is still believed in the south of Germany to drive away evil spirits, and in Denmark and Norway it is held in the same veneration. It is customary in the Tyrol to plant an elder bush in the form of a cross on a new grave, and if it blossoms, the soul of the body interred beneath is supposed to be in Paradise.

CHAPTER XVII.

MUMMIES AND THEIR USE IN MEDICINE—THE UNICORN.

WHO first introduced mummies as medicinal agents is not known, but there is something particularly weird and gruesome in the idea of the ancient physician dosing a sick patient, with the remains of a predeceased fellowman, in order to restore him to health. The art of embalming was practised thousands of years before the Christian era, and was regarded as the greatest token of esteem that could be paid by the living to the dead. Pomet says there were two kinds of embalming practised by the ancient Egyptians. The first and most costly was used to none but persons of the highest class, and was valued at a talent of silver, or about £500. Three people were employed in the operation; one was a kind of designer or overseer, who marked out such parts of the body as were to be opened. The next was a dissector, who with a knife of Ethiopian stone cut the flesh as much as necessary, and as the law would permit, and immediately afterwards fled away with all the expedition possible, because it was the custom of the relatives and domestics to pursue the dissector with stones and do him all the injuries they could, treating him as an impious wretch and the worst of men.

After this operation the embalmers, who were accounted holy men, entered to perform their offices, which consisted in removing the internal organs, cleansing with palm wine and other aromatical liquor, and during the space of thirty days they filled the cavity with powdered myrrh, aloes, Indian spikenard, bitumen, and other aromatics. In the process of embalming used by the middle class, which cost about £250, the body was syringed with a decoction of herbs and oil of cedar, then put into salt for seventy days, after which it was enveloped in bandages of fine linen, which had been dipped in myrrh and asphaltum, and the designer, who was called the scribe, covered the wrapping with a painted cloth, on which were represented the rites of their religion in hieroglyphics, and the animals which the dead loved most. There was a third process of embalming used by the poorer people, in which a mixture of pitch and bitumen was used. The bodies were first dried with lime, and then coated with a mixture of nitre, salt, honey, and wax to protect them from the air. Mummies of deceased persons were held in the greatest reverence by their relatives. The faces were sometimes gilded and painted and adorned with head-cloths, they were then placed in elaborate cases according to the position and rank of the person, and deposited in the highest part of their houses. An old writer states: "They reckoned their deceased as such a valuable token and pledge of their faith, that if any of them happened to want money he could not give a better security than the embalmed body of his relation; and that which made it esteemed so was, that they would spare no pains to pay the money again; for if by mischance the debtor could not redeem this pledge, he was reckoned unworthy of civil society, which engaged him indispensably to find out ways to recover his kinsman in the time limited, otherwise he was blamed by all the world".

Some 300 years ago a large trade was carried on, mostly by Jews, who imported mummies for medicinal purposes, as they were much used by the ancient physicians; but there is little doubt that a great deal of fraud was practised by the mummy merchants, and that many were specially manufactured for the purpose. Pomet, alluding to this in his *History of Druggs*, writes: "We may daily see the Jews carrying on their rogueries as to these mummies, and after them the Christians; for the mummies that were brought from Alexandria, Egypt, Venice, and Lyons are nothing else but the bodies of people that die several ways. Those from Africa called white mummies, are nothing else but bodies that have been drowned at sea, which, being cast upon the African coast, are buried and dried in the sands, which are very hot." When the ancient physician prescribed mummy for a bad headache, he rarely got what he imagined. "For," the writer continues: "I am not able to stop the abuses committed by those who use this commodity. I shall only advise such as buy to choose what is of a fine shining black, not full of bones and dirt, of a good smell, and which being burnt does not stink of pitch. Such is reckoned proper for contusions, and to hinder blood from coagulating in the body. It is also given in epilepsies, vertigoes, and palsies. The dose is two drachms in powder, or the same made into a bolus. It also stops mortifications, heals wounds, and is an ingredient in many compositions." In a price list, dated 1685, mummy is quoted at 5s. 4d. per lb.

Of the mummies used in medicine five kinds were known.

Factitious.—Those in which bitumen and pitch were largely used in the process of embalming.

Those bodies dried by the sun in the country of the Hammonians between Cyrene and Alexandria, being mostly the bodies of passengers buried in the quicksands.

True Egyptian.

The Arabian, being those bodies embalmed with myrrh, aloes, and other aromatic gums.

Artificial mummies. Crollius in his *Royal Chemist* gives the following process for preparing artificial mummy:—

"Take the carcass of a young man (some say red haired), not dying of a disease but killed, let it lie twenty-four hours in clear water in the air, cut the flesh in pieces, to which add powder of myrrh and a little aloes, imbibe it twenty-four hours in spirit of wine and turpentine, take it out and hang it up for twelve hours, then imbibe it again, twenty-four hours in fresh spirit, then hang up the pieces in a dry air and a shady place." A rather cheerful operation for the apothecary. It would possibly account for many a mysterious disappearance in those days.

Mummy entered into a large number of preparations which we come across in the old dispensatories. There was the balsam, which is described by an old writer as "having such a piercing quality that it pierceth all parts and restores wasted limbs, consumption, and cures all ulcers and corruptions". Beside mummies, the apothecaries stocked human fat, respecting which gruesome material Pomet says: "Everybody knows in Paris the public executioner sells it, the druggists and apothecaries a little; nevertheless, they vend a sort of it prepared with aromatic herbs, and which is without comparison much better than that which comes from the hands of the hangman". Human fat was much esteemed for rubbing, in cases of rheumatism and kindred complaints.

Another part of the body used in ancient medicine was the human skull; also a growth called the moss from the human skull, probably of fungoid origin, that appeared on the bone on keeping. An old writer in the seventeenth century says: "You may see in the druggist shops of London some skulls entirely covered with moss, and some that only have the moss growing on some parts. They send these skulls especially to Germany, to put into the composition of the sympathetic ointment which Crollius describes in his *Royal Chemist*, and which is used for the falling sickness."

Special virtue was attributed to skulls taken from gibbets. Referring to these, Pomet states: "The English druggists, especially those of London, sell skulls of the dead upon which there is a little greenish moss called usnea, because of its near resemblance to the moss which grows on the oak. These skulls mostly come from Ireland, where they frequently let the bodies of criminals hang on the gibbet till they fall to pieces." The human skulls were sold at 8s., 9s., 10s., and 11s. each. They were given in the form of powder, or one of the preparations, such as the oil or tincture. Besides the skull, other human bones, calcined and powdered were used. An oil and a tincture of skulls, an extract of the gall and the heart of man made with rectified spirit, was dropped into the ear as a remedy for deafness, and also given internally for epilepsy. Human hair was used for jaundice, finger-nails as an emetic (which one can hardly wonder at), and blood drawn from a healthy man, drunk hot, was used to prevent fits coming on. The brains of various birds and animals were highly esteemed. The latter were roasted and rubbed on children's gums when teething. The livers of ducks and frogs, and a dead mouse dried and beaten into powder, were given to relieve kidney disease.

Another extraordinary article used in medicine was the horn of that fabulous animal the unicorn. Concerning its origin we have recourse again to Pomet, who states, "the unicorn is an animal which our naturalists describe under the figure of a horse, having in the middle of his head a spiral horn of two or three feet long, but we know not the real truth of this matter to this day". This horn was formerly held in high esteem because of the great virtues attributed to it by the ancients, especially against poisons, "which is the reason that so many great persons are fond of it, so that it has been valued at its weight in gold".

Ambrose Paraens, in a treatise which he wrote on the unicorn, says that in the deserts of Arabia he found wild asses carrying a horn in the front, which they used to fight against the bulls. That there *was* an animal with one horn, most of the old writers agree, but whether it was a goat, or an ox, or a hart, or an ass, no one could say. The horn was probably collected from any of these animals, and as long as the horn was there it doubtless answered the purpose. The *true* unicorn, if you dare believe Ludovicus Vertomanus, who says he saw two of them in Mecca which were kept within the precincts of Mahomet's sepulchre, is of a weasel colour, "with the head like that of a hart, the neck not long, and the mane growing all on one side, the legs slender and lean like the legs of a hind, hoofs cloven like a goat's feet, and the hinder legs all hairy and shaggy on the outside. His horn was wreathed in spires of an ivory colour." There is little doubt that most of the horn used medicinally, was that obtained from the narwhal or sea unicorn. In the year 1553 a great unicorn's horn was brought to the King of France, and valued at £20,000 sterling. That which was presented to Charles I. of England is supposed to have been one of the largest ever seen in the world. "It was seven feet long, weighed thirteen pounds, and was in the shape of a wax candle, but wreathed within itself in spires, hollow about a foot from its root, growing taper little by little towards the point of polished smoothness, and the colour not perfectly white." Ancient authors ascribe wonderful properties to the horn of the unicorn. It was supposed to resist all kinds of poisons, cure the plague, all manner of fevers, the biting of serpents, mad dogs, etc., and was chiefly used as a cordial, for which purpose a jelly was made of it.

CHAPTER XVIII.

THE ORIGIN OF THE SOCIETY OF APOTHECARIES—APOTHECARIES AND THEIR PRACTICE—APOTHECARIES AND THEIR BILLS—CURIOUS REMEDIES—A DRUG PRICE LIST OF 1685.

T_{HE} earliest record of the apothecary in England seems to be of one Richard Fitznigel, who acted in that capacity to Henry II. This individual subsequently rose in degree at Court, and exchanging the pestle for the crozier, eventually became Bishop of London. In 1345 we hear of one Coursus de Gangland receiving for his services as apothecary to Edward III., and for taking care of and attending his Majesty during his illness in Scotland, a pension of sixpence a day.

Those who practised medicine, surgery, and pharmacy were called physicians, while their assistants were known as apothecaries. Many of the latter, as they began to learn the secrets and habits of their employers, began business on their own account, also dealing in drugs and other commodities, until they became a powerful body.

When the College of Physicians was established in 1518, they were soon empowered "to search, view, and see the apothecaries' wares, drugs and stuffs, and destroy such as they found unfit for use".

In the latter part of the century a distinct separation took place, and we find that in 1600 there were physicians, surgeons, apothecaries, barber surgeons, druggists or distillers and sellers of waters and oils, and preparers of chemical medicines. It was not until the year 1617 that the Apothecaries' Society had a separate existence, when it was enacted that no grocer should keep an apothecary's shop, and that no surgeon should sell medicines.

In 1623 the Society of Apothecaries established a dispensary, for the purpose of making some of the most important medicines then used in a uniform manner, and in May, 1618, the first *Pharmacopœia* was published by the College of Physicians. We are told that it was so imperfect that they brought out an improved edition in December of the same year. This was published in Latin, and it was through making and publishing his translation of this work that Nicholas Culpepper (who was a man of common-sense in his time) got into disgrace with the College of Physicians, who in consequence refused him a licence to practise.

A PHYSICIAN.

From a drawing, dated 1490.

The history of the Society of Apothecaries of London is an interesting one. It is a mystery or guild which has retained its original function of a trading corporation. It arose as an offshoot of the Grocers' Company, which descended from the pepperers and the spicers, who amalgamated in 1345 under the name of the Fraternity of St. Anthony. The Grocers' Company is one of the most powerful and wealthy of the twelve great Livery Companies of London which have survived from mediæval times.

King James I. appears to have interested himself in the separation of the two bodies about the year 1614, and in spite of vigorous opposition by the grocers, a charter was granted on 6th December, 1617, making the apothecaries a distinct mystery, under the title of the Society of Apothecaries. This charter restrained the grocers and all other persons from keeping an apothecary's shop in or near London, and it gave the Society a right which had been inherent in the Grocers' Company, of paying domiciliary visits to the apothecaries' shops to search for, to seize, and destroy bad drugs and medicines, a power at first limited to London and seven miles round, but afterwards extended throughout England and Wales. This was discontinued shortly after 1833.

The first hall or council-house of the society consisted of a house and grounds known as Cobham House, in Water Lane, Blackfriars, immediately behind what is now the Ludgate Hill Station. It was purchased in 1633, mainly through the instrumentality of Gideon Delaune, chief apothecary to Anne of Denmark, who was one of the retinue sent to attend her from Norway when she became the wife of James I. This hall was destroyed by the great fire of London in 1666, and its site lay vacant for ten years before it was rebuilt. The second hall was enlarged and improved in 1786, and it still stands.

In the reign of Queen Anne, Prince George of Denmark, who was then Lord High Admiral, applied to the society to know if they would undertake to supply the navy with drugs, as it was very badly served at that time. This the society agreed to do, and for so doing was drawn into a long series of quarrels with the College of Physicians, whose members thought it was the duty of an apothecary "to remember his office is only to be the physician's cooke".

A knowledge of herbs and simples was soon found necessary to these early compounders of medicine, and as a means of instruction, botanical excursions or herborisings, as they were called in those days, soon formed a prominent feature of the society. This led eventually to the decision to rent a physic garden, for which purpose the gardens available near the hall were unsuitable, and in 1673 the Botanic Garden at Chelsea was leased to the apothecaries for a term of sixty-one years, by Charles Cheyne, Esq., lord of the manor.

The custom of examination grew up within the society very gradually, the first examinations being found necessary to ascertain whether the apprentices could decipher the very illegible handwriting in which the physicians wrote their prescriptions or bills, an accomplishment for which apparently they have been ever famous.

INTERIOR OF AN APOTHECARY'S SHOP.
From a drawing by Drapentier, 1670.

Then came the division of the apothecaries from the druggists, the former in the process of time becoming a subordinate class of practitioners who attended an individual afflicted with some internal disease not requiring external or manual aid, and who prescribed for the cure of such complaint and supplied the medicine; while the latter were supposed to confine themselves to the dealing in and preparation of drugs for the apothecary.

The apothecary was paid for the medicine which he supplied, which was not by any means in small quantities, and so was supposed not to encroach ostensibly upon the province of the physician, who received his remuneration for advice only, and did not provide medicine.

In 1812 a tax was put upon glass which increased the price of bottles greatly, much to the chagrin of the apothecaries, who were paid according to the number of draughts and potions which they could induce their patients to swallow. It was customary to place each dose of medicine in a separate bottle, and charge it at the rate of one or two shillings a dose, so the apothecary naturally felt aggrieved at the glass tax, which, however, was soon afterwards repealed.

The following excellent rules and regulations were laid down by William Bulleyn for the guidance of apothecaries of his time:—

THE APOTICARYE.

1. Must first serve God, foresee the end, be cleanly, pity the poor.

2. Must not be suborned for money to hurt mankind.

3. His place of dwelling and shop to be cleanly, to please the senses withal.

4. His garden must be at hand, with plenty of herbs, seeds, and roots.

5. To sow, set, plant, gather, preserve, and keep them in due time.

6. To read Dioscorides; to know the nature of plants and herbs.

7. To invent medicines; to choose by colour, taste, odour, figure, etc.

8. To have his mortars, stills, pots, filters, glasses, and boxes clean and sweet.

9. To have charcoals at hand to make decoctions, syrups, etc.

10. To keep his clean ware close, and cast away the baggage.

11. To have two places in his shop—one most clean for the physic, and a baser place for the chirurgic stuff.

12. That he neither increase nor diminish the physician's bill (*i.e.*, prescription), and keep it for his own discharge.

13. That he neither buy nor sell rotten drugs.

14. That he peruse often his wares that they corrupt not.

15. That he put not in *quid pro quo* without advisement.

16. That he may open well a vein for to help pleurisy.

17. That he meddle only in his vocation.

18. That he delight to read Nicolaus, Myrepsus, Valerius, Cordus, Johannes Placaton, the Lubri, etc.

19. That he do remember his office is only to be the physician's cook.

20. That he use true measure and weight.

21. To remember his end and the judgment of God; and thus do I commend him to God, if he be not covetous or crafty, seeking his own lucre before other men's help, succour and comfort.

In Glasgow the sale of drugs and poisons was carefully restricted and regulated as far back as 1599. Under the terms of a charter granted to the Faculty by King James VI., and dated November, 1599, visitors were appointed, and they were given

"Full power to call, sumonnd, and convene before thame, within the said burgh of Glasgow, or onie otheris of ouir said burrowis, or publict places of the foirsaids boundis, all personis professing or using the said airt of Chirurgie, to examine thame upon thair literature, knawledge and practize; gif they be fund wordie, to admit, allow, and approve thame, give them testimonial according to the airt and knawledge that they sal be fund wordie to exercise thareftir, resave thair aithis, and authorize thame as accordis, and to discharge thame to use onie farder nor they have knawledge passing their capacity, laist our subjectis be abusit".

It was further provided by "James, be the Grace of God, King of Scottis," in his fatherly solicitude for his subjects, that

"The saidis visitouris sall visit everie hurt, murtherit, poisonit, or onie other persoun tane awa extraordinarily, and to report to the Magistrate of the fact as it is".

The visitors were also empowered, with the advice of their brethren, to make regulations for the common weal anent the art of surgery, and to inflict punishment upon those infringing them. With regard to the sale of drugs, it was provided that—

"Na manir of personis sell onie droggis within the Citie of Glasgow, except the sam be sichtit be the saidis visitouris, and be William Spang, apothecar, under the pane of confiscatioune of the droggis".

The responsibility of the seller is clearly defined in a clause which further stipulates that—

"Nane sell retoun poison, asenick, or sublemate, under the pane of ane hundred merkis, excep onlie the apothecaries quha sall be bund to take cautioun of the byaris, for coist, skaith, and damage".

These powers were confirmed by Charles, "King of Great Britain, France, and Ireland".

The ancient apothecary believed in the administration of physic in quantities which, in these advanced days of infinitesimal doses and concentrated preparations, would be considered something alarming.

The following interesting extract is from the diary of William Blundell, a celebrated cavalier of Lancashire, who took an active part in many of the conflicts in Cromwell's time. On being taken ill, we are told, he sent for his medical man, one Dr. Worthington, of Wigan. The doctor's bill, together with some quaint remarks thereon, are entered in the cavalier's diary by his man, Master Thelwall, as follows:—

1681. "After my master had been long ill of a violent cold, Dr. Worthington came first unto him on 8th January. He staid two nights, and received for his pains £1 10s. He brought along with him, a lohoch, ten pills, with a bottle of spirits somewhat bigger than one's thumb, and a paper of lozenges, with

French barley and several ingredients for making the water thereof. On the eleventh day he sent a glister, with a large pint bottle of a cordial julep, and a small bottle of syrups, to be sucked up with a liquorice stick, also some small quantity of sal prunella.

A PHYSICIAN.

From a drawing by Amman, Sixteenth Century.

"The doctor was with my master the second time, on 17th January, and received for his pains 15s."

Then comes the copy of Dr. Worthington's bill, dated 24th October, 1681:—

	£	s.	d.
Spirits	0	4	6
An ointment	0	1	4
January 8.			
Spirits	0	4	6
Ten pills	0	2	0
A lohoch	0	2	0
Lozenges	0	4	0
Jujubes and sibertines	0	0	8
French barley	0	1	0
Ingredients	0	1	6
Syrups	0	3	0

A cordial julep	0	10	6
A glister	0	2	6
January 11.			
Syrups	0	3	0
White powder	0	0	4
Five pills	0	1	3
The oiled sugar	0	7	0
Syrups	0	5	6
Oil of sweet almonds	0	1	8
Spirits of ptisanne	0	7	6
For a messenger	0	1	6
	£3	5	3

Master Thelwall then goes on to say: "My master's opinion of these several things in particular, is here to be inserted for further use, *viz.*, that the spirits first named, of which twenty-six drops were put into one small cup of barley water and beer, had no apparent effect, although he doth not much doubt but the secret effect might be good. That the like might be said of the pills, mentioned in two places, although it seemed that they did somewhat assuage his cough, which was extremely violent. The lohoch, a liquor like syrup, did apparently bring up phlegm, and was well liked. The lozenges were pleasant, and did sometimes stop the cough. Barley water with the ingredients was cooling and pleasant. Syrups twice mentioned, although of much different prices, seemed to be the same.

"The cordial julep, of which there was a large pint bottle, was pleasant, but the effect not apparent. The glister extraordinary effective and good. White powder, supposed to be sal prunella, assuaged the thirst. The oiled sugar, with the spirits ptisanne, besides the extreme dearness, was almost wholly useless, in regard that the patient being much in the mending hand when they were sent unto him. He sent back to the doctor about seven-eighths of the oiled sugar, and yet he paid for the whole. The oil of sweet almonds, of which seven or eight drops were taken in a bolus of white sugar-candy, frequently helped the breast made very sore by coughing."

AN APOTHECARY.

From a drawing, 1641.

We subsequently learn that the good old cavalier was at length cured of his ailments, which he certainly ought to have been from the multiplicity of the remedies employed. Many of the forms in which medicine was administered in those days have entirely gone out of use, and others we have still with us.

Another example of the apothecary's bill appears in the appendix to the *Eleventh Report of the Historical Manuscripts' Commission*, among the transcripts of the manuscripts of the Marquess Townshend. There is one, dated 24th June, 1619, of a paper endorsed "The Apothycarie's bill," Sir Roger Townshend's account, which contains the following items:—

	s.	d.
"Grene ginger"	7	0
Tabacco	2	0
Grene ginger	8	0
A masse of pills	5	0
An electuarye	3	6

Under the name of Mr. Stanhope Townshend, 12th September, 1618, are:—

	s.	d.
"A clyster"	3	4

A julep	3	0
A cordiall with behoardston	3	0
The cordiall julep	3	0
Hearbs for brothe	0	4
Rose water	0	6
A suppositorye	0	6
Another suppositorye	0	6
An unguent	0	3
A purge	3	0
Purgeing pills	2	6

The lohoch, the base of which consisted of honey or thick syrup, was a very favourite form of medicine for a cough, such as the lohoch demulcent, lohoch of fox's lungs, and lohoch expectorant.

The julep was another ancient form of administration much in vogue. Balsams, of divers compositions, had great repute as expectorants. William Blundell in his diary (1681) mentions: "The Elder Lady Bradshaw sent a bottle containing, as we guess, about one ounce of balsam, which in her letter she calls 'Balsam of Sulphur'. That it must be taken morning and night, three or four drops, naked and alone in a spoon; that it must be warmed before it will drop at all, by reason its thick and clammy." The sugared oils were simply made by triturating various essential oils with white sugar, and usually given for their carminative action.

Another favourite vehicle was broth, generally composed of many and strange ingredients. We have come across the broth of calves' lungs, broth of the bones of lizards, and broths made from snails, tortoises, woodlice, crabs, and vipers.

The recipe for the broth of viper we have taken from an old black-letter book, and is rather curious:—

> " ℞ Living viper   j.
>
> Remove his head, tail and viscera, excepting his heart and liver, cut it into little pieces and mix it with the blood, and add—
>
> Well water   12 ounces
>
> in a close vessel, boil for two hours and strain, and the broth will be made."

The *materia medica* of the old apothecary was largely drawn from the animal kingdom, the greater part of it being, no doubt, handed down from a very early period, when witchcraft and superstition exerted a powerful influence on the minds of the people.

Among the many curious things used, we find that the liver of a mad dog, or a wolf, washed in wine and dried in a stove, was employed as a remedy for hydrophobia. The nimble lizard had a reputation as a sudorific and antisyphilitic. Dried toads and the cast-off skins of snakes and adders, were administered in dropsy as a diuretic.

The horn of rhinoceros was used in epilepsy, and goat's blood and eel's liver as a cure for dysentery. The oil of frog's spawn was celebrated as an application for chilblains. The jawbone of a pike and the spine of a lamprey in powder, were prescribed for leucorrhœa. Pepys mentions in his diary, that he wore a hare's foot as a sovereign remedy against the plague, in which charm he seemed to place more faith than in the various plague waters that were recommended to him as unfailing antidotes for that terrible disease.

In the time of Edward I. there was a list of drugs recorded by the king's physician, one Nicholas de Tyngewyke, in 1307, which throws an interesting light on the pharmacy of that period. The list includes distilled oil of turpentine, aromatic flowers for baths, carminative electuaries, plasters and ointments of various kinds, the oils of wheat, ash, and bay, water of the roses of Damascus, wine of pomegranates, remedies prepared from pearls, jacinths, and coral, and many other drugs. The king was taken ill at Carlisle, and the cost of conveying these remedies from London to that city amounted to £159 11s. 10d., the apothecary's bill for the medicines being £134 16s. 4d.

In 1596 Sir Henry Winton, who was sent as ambassador by Elizabeth to Henry IV. of France, met with an accident while on his mission. According to the records "he was physicked with *confectio alcarmas*, which was composed of musk, amber, gold, pearl, and unicorn's horn, and with pigeons applied to his side, and all other means that art could devise sufficient to expel the strongest poison, and he be not bewitcht withall".

The apothecaries of the seventeenth century were not overburdened with the estimable virtue of modesty, as instanced in the following quaint announcement:—

"Cornelius Tilbury, sworn chirurgeon-in-ordinary to K. Charles II., to his late Sovereign K. William, as also to her present Majesty Queen Anne—address at the Blue Flower Pot, in Great Lincoln's Inn Fields, at Holbourn Row (where you see at night a light over the door); and for the convenience of those that desire privacy, they may come through the Red Lyon Inn in Holbourn, between the two turnstiles, which is directly against my back door, where you will see the sign of the Blue Ball hung over the door.

"I dispose of my famous Orvietan, either liquid or in powder, what quantity or price you please. This is that Orvietan that expelled that vast quantity of poison I took before K. Charles II., for which his Majesty presented me with a gold medal and a chain."

AN APOTHECARY.
From an engraving, 1517.

The physician's fees were by no means small in the time of the Commonwealth, as may be judged from the following extract from the *Memoirs of the Verney Family*:—

"Sir Theodore Mayerne is buryed," writes Dr. Denton, "and died worth £140,000." Sir Ralph thought £30 too small a fee to pay Dr. Denton for his attendance on his wife during her confinement, but for his pressing poverty he would have sent him £50, equal to about £200 of our present money. Dr. Radcliffe's regular fees were estimated to bring him in an income of at least £4000 a year; Dr. Mead's were valued at between £5000 and £6000. Sir George Wheler's sickness, after a Christmas dinner at Dr. Denton's, cost him "the best part of £100". He had caught a chill after dancing, which turned to "a spotted feavour"; Sir George Ent was called in: he had all sorts of "Applications of Blisters and Loudanums". "My Apothecary's … bill came to £28. He was a good man, and told me if I fell into a feavour again, Sage Possit would do me as much good as all the Physitians Prescriptions."

In Sir Daniel Fleming's account books we have record of the amount paid to medical practitioners in 1659, as follows:—

To Doctor Dykes for comeing and laying plasters unto Will	£0	10	0
For his plaisters and paines contributed towards the cure of Will, the sum of	5	0	0

A further entry also shows the value of the midwife's services at the same period. Under date

July 30th, 1659. Given unto Daniel Harrison's wife for being my wife's midwife, 5/-.

In the household books of Lord William Howard we learn that on 25th September, 1612, he paid one Mr. Adamson, an apothecary of Keswick, "for xxii dayes and his physick, £xiii. vi,s. viii,d".

Some of the early preparations used in pharmacy were as elaborate as they were mysterious. The Treacle of Andromachus the elder, a recipe of great antiquity, contained sixty-three ingredients; and the celebrated Mithridate of Damocratis contained forty-eight.

The origin of the formula for "Mithridates" is ascribed to Mithridates, King of Pontus, whose recipe Pompey brought to Rome, where Damocratis sang its praises and proclaimed its virtues. It was considered by the ancients a panacea for every ill. Of the historic preparation known as the Treacle of Andromachus, its invention is attributed to that worthy. Pliny says that the formula of a similar composition was inscribed in verse 300 years before the Christian era upon the temple of Æsculapius, and that Andromachus merely imitated, by order of Nero, the composition of the Mithridate, which had then been known for a considerable time.

Of the forms of administration there were a great variety in the sixteenth century, and many, such as the Rob which consisted of the juice of fruits boiled down to two-thirds, the lohoch, and the treacle, have quite gone out of use.

But notwithstanding modern research and scientific advance, some of the ancient formulæ still survive and are employed to-day.

It may not be generally known that the preparation known as hiera picra was originated by Galen, on the properties of which he placed high value on account of its excessively bitter taste. Charas states that the great physician gave it the name of hiera picra or holy bitter.

In the *pil. aloes. et myrrh.* of the *British Pharmacopœia*, commonly known by the old name of *Pil. Ruffi.*, we have a formula handed down intact for over a thousand years.

In mediæval times ladies were not above using preparations to beautify their complexions, and among others for this purpose, we find the formula of a cerate composed of white wax, spermaceti, oil of cole seed, bismuth, borax, and alum, which was spread on a cloth to cover the face at night, and worn as a mask.

Among the parts of the body used as medicine was human blood, on which some early physicians set great value for the cure of epilepsy and diseases of the brain.

Charas, in his *Royal Pharmacopœia*, says: "In the month of May take a considerable quantity of healthy young men's blood, let blood in that season who are *not red haired*. This blood is to be distilled twice, or spread on plates and dried in the sun or an oven. All writers extol the volatile salt of man's blood, for the cure of epilepsy, it being also very proper to suppress vapours that arise from the stomach and spleen."

In a Celtic leech-book preserved in the University of Leyden, which is said to have been written in the ninth century, there are the following curious recipes:—

"1. To prevent wrinkles. Smear the face with a mixture of water and the pounded root of wild cucumber. Wash with cold water. 'Hóc sí triduo face*re* uolueris mirabile*m* effectu*m* uidebis.'

"2. To remove freckles. Rub a bull's gall on the face.

"3. To cure headaches. Gather plantain-root before sunrise, and tie it on the head. Use also the juice of the seed of the elder-tree, a cow's brain, goat's dung dissolved in vinegar; swallows' nests mixed with water, and applied to the forehead; water out of which an ass or an ox has drunk.

"4. To purge the head. Pour the juice of cabbage (*brassica*) into the nostrils.

"5. For dimness of the eyes. Pound fennel-roots, mix with honey, and boil over a slow fire; add cistern-water or woman's milk. Smear the eyes with the fat of a fox (*adipe volpis*).

"6. Another remedy. Mix a child's urine (*lotium infantis*) with the best honey; add a decoction of fennel-roots ('omnem caliginem mirabiliter discutiet').

"7. The beginning of this paragraph has been cut off. The remedies prescribed are butter and *cram occifæth* (garlic...?), mixed with ram's fat ('per aruinam ariætis').

"14. To cure the bite of a dog. Apply two or three onions calcined and boiled with lard and honey.

"15. To extract a straw from the eye. Chant the psalm *Qui habitat* (Ps. 90) thrice over water, with which then douche the eye, *et sanus ærit.*"

Among the various remedies fish play a prominent part. For gravel it is recommended that the head of a pike be boiled in a newly-glazed earthen pot, then reduced to powder and drunk in a glass of white wine. A sure means of curing gout is to wear continually three or four moles' feet tied to one's garters. For nose-bleeding, the sufferer is advised to blow up the nose the powder of a stone found in the head of a carp, or to plug up the nostrils with hare's fur. A certain remedy for curing a drunkard of his evil way is to give him as many eggs of the screech owl, boiled hard, as he can possibly eat, when we are assured he will ever after be a total abstainer.

In the first book of the *Secretes of the reverent Maister Alexis of Piemont*,

1562, which is a kind of general receipt-book for the apothecaries of the time, there occur some curious formulæ, which may be taken as a fair example of the pharmacy of those days. The process of making the oil of red dog is given with elaborate detail.

"To make an oile of a redde dogge," says the chronicler, "by the meane whereof (beside other infinit vertues that it hathe) I have healed a Fryer of Saint Onostres, who had by the space of twelve years a lame and drye withered arme, lyke I styche so that nature gave it no more nouryshement—

"Take a yonge dogge of redde heare and keep him three days without meate, and then strangle him with a corde, and let him lie dead a quarter of an houre, and in the meane time boyle a kettell of ayle up by the fire, and putte the dogge in whole, or in pieces, it maketh no matter howe, so that he be all there with the skynne and heare; make him seethe so untyl he be almost sodden to pieces, keepying always the kettell close covered: In the meane tyme take scorpions to the number of four score or a hundred, and put them in a basyn on the fyre untyll they be thoroughly bruised. Then putte them in the sayde kettell with the ayle and the dogge, puttinge to it a good dishful of great grounde wormes, well washed, a good handful of Saint John's Worte, a handful of wylde marshe mallowes, and a handful of wallworte, with an once of saffron. Seethe all these things well to-gether, and then let it ware colde." The liquid being strained off and certain aromatic gums added, the preparation was complete.

The belief that carrying a piece of camphor will ward off infectious diseases, is a relic of the old days of amulets and charms. In 1547 Alexis recommended compounds to carry against the plague and fever, and we find that aromatics were used to perfume clothes in the time of the early Jews, long before the birth of Christ.

Among other secrets of Alexis, there is a curious recipe to "*cause mervelous dreames*".

"Take the bloode of a lampwink or black plover, and rubbe your temples with it and so goe to bedde, and you shall see mervelous thinges in your sleepe; or else if you eate at nighte a little of the herbe Solani or Visicaria, or some Mandragora, or elles of the herbe called in Greek Hyoscymus, in Latin hath these names, Altercum, Appolinaris, and Symphonia, and in the English some call it Henbane, and you shall see in the nighte goodly things in your dreame."

The apothecary apparently omits to mention that a heavy meal of very ordinary cheese, combined with the succulent fruit of the cucumber, before you go to bed, will also make you see marvellous and weird things in your sleep.

The gifts and wisdom of the apothecaries were according to their writings very wonderful, but none perhaps is more remarkable than the following recipe on a matter which would baffle the scientists of the present day.

The chronicler writes: "To make a woman that beareth alwaies daughters to beare also sonnes, it is a thing very easy, and hath good succes, and hathe been divers times proved. Let her eate an herbe in English called mercurie, which hath only two seedes; also the skrapings of an elephant's tooth."

The name of the originator of the "everlasting pill" has not been handed down to posterity, but whoever he was, he was certainly an economist, and could not be charged with inventing it for his own gain. It consisted of a small globule of metallic antimony, which was believed to have the property of purging as often as it was swallowed.

A single pill of this kind would serve a whole family during their lives, and was doubtless, transmitted as an heirloom to posterity.

Paris says, "we have heard of a lady who, having swallowed one of these pills, became seriously alarmed at its not passing through". "Madam," said her physician, "fear not; it has already passed through a hundred patients without any difficulty."

It is said to have been the constant custom of Cardinal Wolsey to carry in his hand an orange deprived of its contents and filled with a sponge soaked in vinegar, impregnated with various spices, in order to protect him from infection when passing through the crowds of people which his splendour of office attracted.

An old writer, one James Penrose of the middle ages, questions if Cleopatra applied the asp to her breast as is commonly supposed, because, as he remarks, "the veines are so very slender".

"Petrus Victorius blames the painters who depict the Egyptian queen applying the asp to her breast, seeing it is manifest out of Plutarch in the life of Antonius, and out of Plinie likewise, that she applied it to her arme."

"Zonares relates, that there appeared no signe of death upon her, save two blew spots on her arme."

"Cæsar also in her statue, which he carryed in tryumph, applyed the asp to her arme; for in the armes there are great veines and arteries which doe quickly and in a straight way convey the venom to the heart, whereas in the papps the vessels are slender."

Gesnerus gives a method used by the apothecaries for changing the colour of the hair which is somewhat singular. It is by means of one of the many waters of the philosophers, and is made as follows, in the language of the text: "Take a moule which serveth unto the dying or coloring of heares whyte, eyther of man or beast; let the moule be artely brought to powder with Brimstone, adde to it the juice of celandine which orderly be myxed, let to stande for certaine dayes, after dystill the whole according to taste. The virtue of this water is in such wise, that if a beast wholy blacke of heare shall be washed all over with this water, the heare shall in that time became so whyte as snowe."

The aloe mentioned in the Bible, usually in connection with myrrh and frankincense, is not the same drug as that used in medicine to-day, and is even without its bitterness. It is the product of the *Aquilaria Agallocha*, a tree of large size growing in the Laos country and Assam. The wood is light in colour and inodorous, but under certain conditions a change takes place in it, and it becomes charged with a dark aromatic juice. It was formerly used as a spice in embalming, and is employed in China and the East as incense in the temples.

A curious little work, entitled *The House Apothecary* written by Dr. Gideon Harvey, physician-in-ordinary to his Majesty, and printed in 1670, affords a further interesting glimpse at pharmacy 200 years ago. It would appear that the apothecaries then, like some of their descendants of the present day, excited a considerable amount of jealousy among the physicians by prescribing in certain cases, and meddling generally "in matters which they did not understand".

The worthy doctor begins by recommending people to prepare their medicine at their own homes, it being a far safer and easier way than sending it to the apothecary to be made, and as a further inducement states: "And you shall also save nineteen shillings in twenty shillings, according to the extravagant rates charged by many apothecaries, in so doing. I must tell you, I have oft seen bills of apothecaries rise to twenty, and sometimes thirty pounds in the time of a fortnight; and what is more, I have known an apothecary's bill so extravagant that the sum at the bottom of his account amounted to fifty pounds in the space of thirty days, when the ingredients of the whole course could not be computed to stand him in forty shillings." A severe indictment indeed.

The doctor then goes on to inform us that "in preparing medicines at home you may be certain the ingredients are sound and fresh, and you can have your medicines without attending the apothecary's leisure or having the trouble of sending three or four times to his shop for them; and, most important of all, you may be assured in so doing you shall save nine pounds in ten, and sometimes forty-eight pounds in fifty".

Another treatise written to denounce the excessive charges of the apothecaries was *The Accomplished Physician, the Honest Apothecary, and the Skilful Surgeon*, published and sold at the "Angel" in Duck Lane, in 1656. It attacked the unfortunate apothecary on all sides. It states that "if the apothecary finds you costive he sends you a clyster, at the price of half a crown, which by consulting *The Accomplished Physician*, etc., you may learn how to make yourself for three half-pence. If he apprehends your stomach to be oppressed, he orders his man to boil a little cardamoms in water, strain it, and put to it three or four spoonsful of rank oil of sweet almonds, to cause you to vomit and carry off a little phlegm, and for this he charges you half a crown, which you can make yourself for two-pence."

The author finally confides to the public "that it is fortunate that the little apothecaries and prescribing surgeons have not much knowledge of the great medicines, such as mercury and antimony, as they would at most times do great mischief with them, using them at unseemly times, as if you laid hold of a club to knock down a louse; such great medicines should only be used by the physicians, who should reserve them in secret".

Most of the herbs and roots in common use were brought to the town markets and vended by the physical herb-women, who would bring them in baskets to Newgate Market, Gutter Lane, or Covent Garden, and there sell them by the handful, a dozen for a groat. The measures in use were of a very primitive description, chiefly the fascicle and the pugil.

In 1656 a quart white glass bottle cost 1s. 6d., and a green glass retort 8d. Plague water at certain times was in great demand, and was usually sold at the apothecaries for 3s. 6d. a pint. The price of most conserves was 2d. an ounce, and ointments retailed at 8d. an ounce. An ointment that was much in vogue and very popular among the people was *Unguentum Ægyptiacum*, similar to the ointment of the great Felix Wurtz. Its composition is somewhat interesting and quaint. "Take of verdigriese 12 drachms ground very fine in a brass mortar, observing while you are powdering to hold your head back from the mortar and keep your mouth and nose stopped, to prevent those venomous steams from getting up into your brain. Then take 3 ounces of honey and 12 drachms of sharpest vinegar, place them in a broad brass pipkin, put in the verdigriese, stir and boil them on a gentle fire unto the thickness of an oyntment of a purple colour." Of the waters in common use the *Accomplished Physician* gives directions for the preparation of several. The London treacle water, *aqua mirabilis* and *aqua raphani composita*, were noted for scurvy. The London snail water was recommended as an invaluable remedy in consumption, which, "owing to the cool, clammy, and glutinous substance of the snail, facilitated the expectoration and repaired the parts consumed". Gascon's powder, or *pulvis é chelis cancrorum*, was regarded as a valuable medicament, and much esteemed and ordered by the great physicians. It was an expensive mixture, and contained equal parts, in powder, of crab's eyes, the oriental pearl, red coral, white amber, oriental bezoar, and the black tops of crab's claws. It was sometimes ordered and taken in the form of pills mixed with hartshorn jelly. The apothecary's price for this powder was 40s. an ounce, or one penny per grain. We are told that if made at home the cost would only be 13s. 1¼d. Another preparation exceedingly popular in the seventeenth century was the emplastrum opodeldock of Feliz Wurtz, "so much cried up among surgeons beyond the sea". It was a red plaster, composed of wax, Venice turpentine, juice of celandine, oak leaves, ammoniacum, galbanum, and vinegar. Then some powdered magnets, and such mysterious compounds as *Crocus Martis*, *Crocus Veneris*, and prepared tutria, were thrown in, and all boiled together. The following is extracted from an old price list of the seventeenth century, which gives a good idea of some of the extraordinary articles kept in the old apothecaries' shops, and the prices charged. It is headed "Rates and prices currant of Druggs and other commodities, belonging to physick, as they are commonly sold at the Apothecaries and Druggists in London, 1685":—

Mother of Pearl	6d. per oz.
Crab's eyes	5s. 4d. per lb.
Crab's claws	1s. 6d. ,,
Fox's lungs	2s. ,,
A mummy	5s. 4d. ,,
Bone of stag's heart	1s. 6d. ,,
Borax	4s. ,,
Saltpetre	10d. ,,
Jalap	3s. 4d. ,,
Rhubarb	14s. ,,
Liquorice	1s. ,,
A boar's tooth	1s. each.
A dead man's skull (cranium humanum) according to size	8s. to 11s. each.
Musk	5s. per drachm.
Bloodstone	2s. 8d. per lb.
Opium	12s. ,,
Elaterium	36s. per oz.
Lac Sulphur	3s. ,,
Red coral	4s. per lb.
Oleum Copaibæ	2s. per oz.
Gum acacia	10s. per lb.
Turmerick	8d. per lb.
Elicampane	1s. 4d. per lb.
Galingal	4s. ,,
Gentian	8d. ,,
Spanish Liquorice	6d. ,,
Hellebore, white	1s. ,,
Hellebore, black	1s. per lb.
Pyrethrum	1s. ,,
Sarsaparil, according to its goodness, from	4s. to 5s. per lb.
Squills	6d. ,,
Winter's Bark	2s. ,,
Lig. Aloes.	9d. per oz.
,, Guaici	2d. per lb.
Senna Alex., the best	4s.
Cubebs	2s. 4d. per lb.
Nucis Vomicæ	1s. 4d. ,,
Cardamom	4s. ,,
Aloes Succot, according to its goodness	4s. to 6s. per lb.
Scammony	12s. ,,
Cantharides	4s. ,,
Civet	5s. 6d. per dram.

Ising-glass	5s. 4d. per lb.
Sea-horse tooth	4d. per oz.
Sea-horse pizzle	4d. ”
Skink, a piece	1s. 4d.
Spermaceti	3s. per ounce.
Stag's pizzle	6d. ”
Elk's claw	2s. a piece.
White wax	2s. per lb.
Yellow wax	1s. 4d. per lb.
Cinnabar	3s. per oz.
Mercury Sublimate	5s. 8d., or 6s. per lb.
Seed Pearls	4s. to 8s. per oz.
Mother of Pearl	6d. per oz.
Mithridate	6s. per lb.
Aqua Fortis	5s. 4d. per lb.
Ol. Cinnamon	£1 12s. per oz.
Ol. Vitrioli	5s. 4d. per lb.

Besides the above, precious stones in powder, and diamond powder, which was regarded as a powerful poison, commanded very high prices.

CHAPTER XIX.

PHARMACY IN THE TIME OF QUEEN ELIZABETH.

To obtain a clear conception of the great advance that has been made in medicine and pharmacy, it is necessary to look back through the vista of centuries at the Elizabethan apothecary. In doing so, we should note how the influence of superstition and charlatanry, with which the art of healing was surrounded and intermixed, has been gradually dispersed under the searching light of science. One can picture the apothecary's shop in the days of "good Queen Bess". Up a narrow winding street, paved with round cobble stones, and no pathway to protect you from the jostling and nudges of the passing chair-bearers, French pages, and watermen who throng the thoroughfares, his abode may be denoted perhaps by the gilded crocodile which hangs over the doorway, accompanied by a pole from which depends a pair of brightly- burnished metal pans, denoting the practice of the chirurgical art. The overhanging gables of the half-timbered houses darken the low-roofed shop, through whose small windows filled with little panes of bottle glass, a very dim light penetrates. A mysterious odour permeates the interior and strange things are seen hanging from the rafters,—flying fish, tortoises, and a long alligator float mid-air. Strings of poppy-heads, bunches of chamomile and centaury, also glass jars containing adders and worms adorn the counter. On one shelf an array of bright brass mortars, and round about on others, a great collection of quaint bottles and earthen pots, containing electuaries, unguents, and lohochs; syrup bottles with long curved spouts, and bladders full of seeds and wax. In the corner stands the great iron mortar, whose heavy pestle is suspended from a spring beam, and another is filled with little drawers to hold the gums and spices.

AN APOTHECARY.
From an engraving, 1517.

Away at the back a red glow appears from the furnace, and alembics, big and little, lie about. At night the shop is crowded with poor women buying worm-seed for their children or treacle to drive out the measles, and with country people who have come for drugs and drenches for their sick cattle. "There are serving-men waiting for their masters' purgatives and electuaries, or the fops' facewashes of oil of tartar, *lac virginis*, and camphor dissolved in verjuice. Smart maids are buying conserves and sackets for their mistresses, or perfumes for my lady's chamber. Here desperadoes and rakish gallants could purchase poisons, and blushing maidens would buy their love charms and philtres, or antidotes to counteract the same. Some apothecaries kept a little room for taking tobacco, furnished with silver trays, and a maple block for cutting it, where the gallants met and gossiped, or learned tricks in smoking from fashionable professors, for nearly all the apothecaries sold tobacco—real Timidado—nicotine cane, and pudding, as it was called." The old apothecary's prescriptions were composed of strange ingredients, sometimes crab's eyes and boar's teeth, or powdered pearls, and viper broth.

106

He would recommend you a toad, well dried in the sun, put in a bag, and hung round the neck by a string low enough to touch the region of the heart, to allay hæmorrhage. A preparation of garlic and honey smeared on the person was a certain charm against the bites of vicious dogs and reptiles, or the stings of venomous insects. Toothache could be charmed away by a few leaves of the "shepherd's purse" placed in the sole of the shoe. An excellent recipe for sore eyes was the expressed juice of the calyx of the red honeysuckle, provided always that the flowers were gathered kneeling and repeating nine Pater nosters in honour of the Trinity, nine more "to greet our Ladye," and a creed. My Ladye Falkenbrydge's recipe for eye-water was much esteemed, and ran thus: "Corne-flowers gathered with their cuppes and bruyse them; macerate them in snowe or snowe water for twentye-foure houres, then dystyl in a moderate sandebath and applye it night and morning". This was prescribed in 1553. A favourite cure for rickety children was to pass them through the split stem of a tree. For ague, a very well salted herring, split open, was applied hot to the soles of the feet; or an emerald worn round the neck formed a potent charm against the same complaint. The learned Boorde, in his *Breviary of Health*, says: "The medical treatment of the day was a mixture of religious theories, superstition, and white magic". He recommends for a bad rheum the application of oil of scorpions and fox fat; for a bruised skin, washing it with white wine and plastering with an oak leaf; and he quaintly states "the best remedy for itching is long nails and scratching," which, at any rate, is common-sense. To preserve the health and a good complexion, he recommends young maids to wipe their faces daily with a scarlet cloth, and only wash them once a week.

Another peculiar phase of pharmacy in those early days was the instructions of the various apothecaries' guilds to their members as to prayer. The compounder of prescriptions was directed to go down on his knees and supplicate before he commenced his labours. Many old herbals and works on pharmacy, especially in Germany, contain curious wood-cut illustrations of the apothecary at his devotional exercises. Cyriacus Schnaus, an apothecary of Nuremberg, published a book in 1565, wherein he, in person, is represented as kneeling on a large mortar before a sacred picture. This custom may have been originated by the monks, many of whom followed the art of healing.

A PHYSICIAN FORECASTING FROM THE URINE.
From an engraving, 1517.

A writer of the time states that the itinerant dentist was also a well-known figure at the street corner. For 100 marks he would put out both your eyes, and quite cure your inflammation with one drop of his *aqua mirabilis*, at twelve-pence a drop. He offered you an antidote from stab or bullet for five marks, and by his side waved a banner stuck all over with horses' teeth, to show his skill.

He cured your toothache by charms, sometimes writing mysterious words on a paper, and burning it under your nose; or he would sear your teeth with hot wires, most effectively; or make you inhale the hot vapour of henbane seeds, and then show you the worms that he had conjured out, which are certes now wriggling in the water. He wore a chain of molar teeth around his neck, and shook them from time to time as he held up a bottle of liquid and called out: "These are the spirits that pass with the blood into the rheum, to vex the teeth of men". His descendants may still be seen at the present day working wondrous cures, decked out in similar fantastic garb, or extracting teeth gratis, and by sheer bold impudence reaping a golden harvest.

Having thus shown how the now almost forgotten pioneers of science laid the foundation of the arts of medicine and pharmacy, and how much we owe to their patience and diligence, a brief reference may be made to the class of medicaments in use in the days of Queen Elizabeth, immediately prior to the differentiation in England of the first pharmacists—the apothecaries—and the beginnings of pharmacy as a separate art.

AN ITINERANT DRUG SELLER.
From a fifteenth century drawing.

"A few simples," says Burton, "well prepared and understood, are better than such a heap of nonsense, confused compounds, which are in apothecaries' shops ordinarily sold."

For madness and melancholy, wormwood was used. Another remedy was clarified whey, with borage, bugloss, endive, succory, etc., a good draught of which was taken in the morning, fasting. For the spleen and liver, syrups were prescribed composed of borage, thyme, epithyme, hops, scolopendra, fumitory, maiden-hair, and bizantine. These syrups were mixed with distilled water by the apothecaries, or stirred into juleps.

Of conserves there were innumerable varieties, and ointments of oil and wax, as well as liniments and plasters of herbs and flowers, well boiled with oil or spirits.

Cataplasms and salves were frequently made of green herbs sodden, pounded, and applied externally.

Gradually, as the years have rolled on, and as the science of chemistry has unlocked the marvellous resources and products of nature, most of these old relics of the days of superstition and witchcraft have been left behind and forgotten, and it remains only for some old black-lettered tome to tell the story and for us to fill in the background to the picture.

CHAPTER XX.

FAMOUS EMPIRICS AND THEIR NOSTRUMS.

In the early part of the eighteenth century, the enterprising empiric seems to have hit on a new method of lining his pockets at the expense of the public, and we have the advent of the so-called proprietary or quack nostrum, which has developed into such gigantic proportions in later years. To bring some special drug into notoriety in those days it was first necessary to spread some tale abroad as to its extraordinary virtues, then by means of a pamphlet (for there were few other advertising media) recount the marvellous cures it had performed, and back them up by mentioning a few great names. In this way the quack medicines originated.

In a similar manner, some drugs that have since proved of great use to humanity were brought into note. Peruvian bark was first imported into Spain by the Jesuits, where it remained seven years before a trial was given to it. It was first administered to a Spanish priest in 1639, and but for the supreme power of the Church of Rome it would in all probability have sunk into oblivion. Pope Innocent X., however, at the intercession of Cardinal de Lugo, ordered the bark to be duly examined by the best experts of the time, and on a favourable report being presented, it at once rose high in favour.

The "Elixirs of Life" made by the early alchemists may be said to have been the forerunners of quack medicines, and for these concoctions fabulous prices were demanded. Those made by Paracelsus and Van Helmont were known throughout Europe, and must have brought considerable grist to the mill of their proprietors. The Collyrium of Danares, which enjoyed a wide reputation in the seventeenth century, was sold at £9 per bottle. Then there was the Sympathetic Powder of Sir Kenelm Digby, noted for healing wounds, and Hoffman's Water of Magnanimity. Another famous nostrum made by Paracelsus was called *Præcipitatus Diaphoreticus Paracelsi*, and warranted to cure a fever in four days.

"Dutch drops," which were originally sold for half a guinea a bottle, are said to have brought the proprietors £2000 in one year.

The *Eau Médicinale de Husson*, another well-known quack nostrum, was introduced by an officer of that name in the service of Louis XVI. It is said to have been simply a decoction of meadow saffron. Dr. James' celebrated fever powder, which enjoyed a great reputation in this country, is stated to have been the invention of an Italian named Lisle, and a recipe for its preparation was published in Colborne's *English Dispensary* in 1756. Oliver Goldsmith believed this to be a remedy for all ills and took it regularly up to his death.

The Count St. Germain, a Frenchman, realised large sums by vending an artificial tea, which he affirmed would prolong life. It is said to have been composed chiefly of senna and fennel leaves. The Chevalier d'Ailhoud was another adventurer who introduced a powder which met with such a sale that he soon saved enough to buy a whole county. That prince of empirics the Count Cagliostro sold his Balm of Life, or stomach elixir, at an exorbitant price. He asserted that he had lived 200 years by its use, and was rendered invulnerable against poison of every description.

During his residence in Strasburg, while boasting and expounding the virtues of his nostrum and antidote to a large assembly of the townsfolk, a physician who was present, and who had not taken part in the conversation, quitting the room quietly, went to an apothecary's shop and ordered two pills to be made of equal size. Taking them with him, he made his way back to the room, and walking up to the loquacious quack he said, "Here, my worthy Count, are two pills. The one contains a deadly poison, and the other is perfectly innocent. Choose one and swallow it, and I will take the one you leave."

The Count took alarm, and after making all kinds of apologies and excuses, at last refused to swallow the pill. The physician, smiling, then took his place on the platform, and in view of the company swallowed both, and then, to the discomfort of Cagliostro, announced that both pills were simply composed of bread. The Count beat a speedy retreat.

In 1794 considerable sensation was excited by the account of some wonderful cures made by a Count Thün of Leipzig, who professed to cure gout, hypochondria, and hysteria by laying his hands on the head of the patient.

The early part of the present century saw a great increase in the number of these nostrums, the usual method adopted by their proprietors being to set up in great style in a fashionable part of the town, and by lavish display and various eccentricities, to attract general attention.

Among the foremost in London was a German Jew who called himself Doctor Brodum. This individual, who, it is said, started life as a footman, took a large house in a fashionable square in the west-end, and drove a pair of horses in a gorgeous chariot. He called his nostrum "Nervous Cordial," its properties being set forth in a pamphlet entitled *A Guide to Old Age*. He is said to have amassed a fortune in a very short time.

Another notorious quack was Doctor Solomon, who eventually settled in Liverpool. He originally sold blacking in Newcastle, but finding it did not pay, came to Liverpool, where he tried to establish a newspaper. This effort also proved a failure, and Solomon at length turned his attention to quack doctoring, and brought out a nostrum called "The Balm of Gilead". This proved successful, and he soon made enough money to build himself a substantial house in Kensington, which was at that time a fashionable suburban district. To advertise his preparation he wrote a pamphlet called *The Guide to Health*, extolling the virtues of the "Balm of Gilead and Anti- Impetigines". This treatise, the cover of which was adorned with an engraving of his mansion at Kensington, stated "the most learned physicians have been unable to discover in the cordial Balm of Gilead the least particle of mercury, antimony, or any other mineral except *pure virgin gold* and the balm of Mecca".

The Doctor was a well-known character in the streets of Liverpool in the early part of this century, and in his daily promenade always carried an elaborate gold-headed cane. The celebrated "balm" is said to have been simply brandy flavoured with some aromatic oil, and although sold at a guinea a bottle, was in great demand.

A story is told of a prominent tradesman of the time, who discovered that his wife was consuming considerable quantities of the invigorating balm. Being further informed that this had become a common habit with many of her friends, he took counsel with the husbands of these ladies, with the result that they determined to punish the doctor by carrying out the following plot. On a certain dark night, a messenger was despatched to the doctor's house, asking him to come at once and see a patient a little way out in the country, and to be sure and bring with him several bottles of his Balm of Gilead. The unsuspecting victim soon set out on foot along the country lanes, and on getting to a very lonely part, was pounced upon by four men disguised in cowskins, who, with long horns and tails, looked like fiends incarnate. The poor doctor thought his last hour had come, and went down on his knees and invoked all the prophets he could think of; but his tormentors dragged him off to a field close by, where they made him swallow bottle after bottle of his own nostrum, then ducked him in a pond and tossed him in a blanket.

Solomon was so incensed at this outrage he determined to leave Liverpool and settle in Birmingham, but in a short time returned to the former city, where he died, and was buried, according to his directions, in his own garden.

The following verse, referring to these empirics, is extracted from an old ballad:—

> "Brodum or Solomon with physic,
> Like death, despatch the wretch that's sick,
> Pursue a sure and thriving trade;
> Though patients die, the doctor's paid!
> Licensed to kill, he gains a palace
> For what another mounts a gallows!"

The electropathic girdles of our own time had their anti-type in Perkin's far-famed tractors for preserving health, for which the proprietor demanded the sum of five guineas a set. The wonderful properties attributed to them were set forth in a small book, entitled *The Influence of the Metallic Tractors on the Body*.

Among the nostrums that enjoyed popularity in the early part of this century were De Velno's Vegetable Syrup, Dr. Senate's Lozenges of Steel to prolong life, Leake's Patent Pills, Dr. Burton's Vital Wine, Beddoe's Volatile Cordial Oxygen Gas for preserving life, Dr. Squirrel's Tonic Drops and Powders, Godbold's Vegetable Balsam, and many others.

The foibles of many of the most prominent empirics of the period are well hit off in the following old ballad:—

"We can boast of a Beddoe's whose oxygen gas
Can render immortal the ape and the ass;
While Swainson the botanist, son of Apollo,
Swears we ne'er shall be sick if his syrup we swallow.
                                        Derry down.

"While Solomon flies on the wings of the wind,
His magical Balm of Mount Gilead to find,
Little Brodum stands stewing his herbs in a copper,
And to vend his decoction for gold he thinks proper.
                                        Derry down.

"Dull Gardner, destroyer of worms and of men,
Like Leake, sells his pills to rouse death from his den;
And Perkins stands brandishing two-pointed tractors,
To heal the contusions of girls, beaux, and actors.
                                        Derry down.

"There's the lotion of Gowland that flays ladies' faces,
Distorting the features of our modern Graces;
There, Lignum's dire pills—but of quackery enough!
Let John Bull take his pipe and contentedly puff.
                                        Derry down."

CHAPTER XXI.

THE ANTIQUITY AND HISTORY OF THE MORTAR.

The mortar is the most ancient of pharmaceutical implements, its earliest use carrying us back to prehistoric times, when the early Briton bruised his grain in the hollow of a granite boulder. There is little doubt indeed that mortars were employed for the purpose of bruising and reducing hard bodies to powder, centuries before medicine as an art was thought of or known.

The name is derived from the Latin word *mortarium*, which is probably from the root *mordeo*, to bite, akin to the Sanscrit *mrid*, to grind or to pound; the literal meaning of the word being a vessel in which substances may be pounded with a pestle.

The origin of the mortar appears to have been identical with that of the mill or quern as it was called in ancient times. The primitive implement used by prehistoric nations for the purpose of crushing their grain, was simply made by hollowing out a cup-shaped hole in a block of stone or granite, and pounding the grain placed in this receptacle with a smaller stone of suitable form. These grain-crushers, together with stone rollers and pounders, have been found in the circular huts of the Britons in several parts of North Wales.

This method was also used by the early Jews before the Christian era for crushing their spices and gums, the knowledge of which they doubtless gathered from the Egyptians during the captivity.

ANCIENT EGYPTIAN MORTAR.

In many of the ancient Egyptian papyri we find directions given to bruise certain herbs and roots, but no mention is made of the implement used for that purpose; carvings in stone, however, are extant which show the mortars used by the Egyptians were similar in form to those employed several centuries later.

It is interesting to note that the mortar has also been known to several Oriental and savage races from time immemorial; and in the mortar employed by the pharmacist to-day we have an implement that links us not only with prehistoric man, but also with the savage races of the world. In Africa, mortars and pestles of wood have been used from a period of unknown antiquity for the purpose of crushing grain. The one illustrated in Fig. 1 is composed of wood, and was brought from Central Africa. In India, stone mortars with wooden pestles have for centuries been used for shelling and pounding rice. Fig. 2 represents a Cingalese mortar of stone, from two to three feet in height, taken from a drawing of the seventeenth century.

FIG. 1.

Coming to the time of the Roman Empire, we have the first real evidence of the use of the mortar for pharmaceutical purposes. Medicine and pharmacy allied, in the time of Celsus, had become practical arts; and we know from the preparations described by that author that practical appliances were necessary. Thus the *malagma* used as an application to the skin was a kind of soft mass directed to be beaten up to the consistency of a

FIG. 2.

thick paste; and the ingredients of the catapotia were often ordered to be bruised before being mixed.

Roman mortaria composed of earthenware are very commonly found, and many examples may be seen in most of our museums among other Roman remains. They were chiefly made for domestic

FIG. 3.

use, and although they vary very little in pattern, the sizes are numerous. The larger ones are, as a rule, very strongly made, and all have a thick divided rim with a rounded moulding. The inside was roughened with splinters of flint or hard stone, or hard-burnt earthenware, which was fixed on with a kind of "slip" or liquid clay with

which the Romans finished their ware. A wooden pestle was used with these mortaria, which were no doubt chiefly employed for triturating and mixing various condiments for domestic use. The Roman mortarium shown in Fig. 3 is twenty-eight inches in breadth, and bears the stamp of the maker's name, showing it to be the work of one Publius Raso.

Some of the smaller mortaria found are composed of a very white clay of a vitreous character burnt hard like porcelain, and are nonabsorbent. These were probably used for mixing more delicate condiments.

There were large manufactories for mortaria in Britain, situated chiefly in the south of England, at the mouth of the Thames, and in Essex and Staffordshire. From these factories there was a considerable export trade to Rome and Gaul.

Roman mortars of stone are much rarer, and the one depicted in Fig. 4 is a unique specimen, and was with little doubt at one time used for pharmaceutical purposes. Composed of stone, with a solid square base, it stands about twelve inches high, and is about eight inches broad. The notches at the corners are evidently intended for fixing it down on a wooden table or slab, to keep it steady when being used for pounding or breaking up hard substances. Closely akin to mortars were the

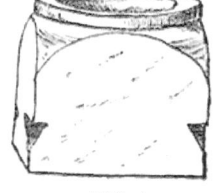
FIG. 4.

querns or small mills used for grinding purposes from the Roman period. In shape they somewhat resembled the mortar, but were covered in at the top, having a hole in the centre through which the pestle was worked. They were made of stone and wood. A beautiful example of a wooden quern is depicted in Fig. 5.[8] It stands thirteen inches high, and is made of very hard wood. It is an exquisite specimen of the turner's art, some of the side mouldings being of great delicacy, no thicker than a fine needle, yet perfectly true in every particular. The pestle was worked through the hole in the centre of the cover. These wooden querns were used during the sixteenth and seventeenth centuries.

There is little doubt that marble succeeded stone as a material for making mortars, and this brings us down to mediæval times, when the apothecaries,

combining the practice of medicine and pharmacy, became wielders of the pestle.

The value of the mortar as a pharmaceutical implement was recognised by these early practitioners, and was given the most prominent position in their shops, and so the pestle and mortar became a symbol or trade sign of pharmacy.

The great bell-shaped mortar, which was of considerable capacity, usually stood, mounted on a solid block of wood, near the centre of the shop, the

FIG. 5.

huge pestle, three feet or more in length, being suspended from a long wooden spring beam by a chain and ring. One can readily picture the youthful apprentice, clad in jerkin and trunk hose, exercising his muscles with the ponderous pestle, and with what mingled feelings he would essay the task of pounding half a hundred-weight of aloes to begin his day's work and give him an appetite for his midday meal. These large mortars were usually bell-shaped in form, as illustrated in Fig. 6, and composed of iron or bell-metal. The smaller mortars of this period were made of brass, copper, and bell-metal, and were occasionally ornamented with some symbol or device. Many were very elegant in form, and they usually stood in bright array on the counter. The pestles were made flat, top and bottom, so that either end could be used for pounding.

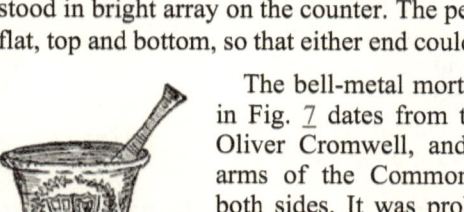

FIG. 6.

The bell-metal mortar depicted in Fig. 7 dates from the time of Oliver Cromwell, and bears the arms of the Commonwealth on both sides. It was probably once the property of an official State apothecary. The brass mortar

FIG. 7.

shown in Fig. 8 is peculiar in shape, and is supported by four

FIG. 8.

short legs. It dates from the early part of the seventeenth century, and round the middle are inscribed the letters of the alphabet. Fig. 9 represents a particularly handsome example of the brass mortar of the seventeenth century. Copper mortars when polished have a very elegant appearance, and are somewhat rare. A specimen is depicted in Fig. 10. A very fine bell-shaped mortar of brass was found in Chester about two years ago, and is now deposited in the museum of that city. It stands nearly two feet high, and dates from the early part of the eighteenth century.

Small brass mortars were also formerly used by housewives in the stillroom, and for other domestic purposes, and may often yet be found ornamenting the kitchen mantelshelf in old country houses.

FIG. 9.

During the last and the early part of this century Italian marble was largely employed for making mortars, but with the introduction of wedgewood and composition ware, which is lighter, more durable, and less liable to be acted on by chemicals,

FIG 10.

marble mortars have now almost gone out of use with pharmacists.

Small antique mortars of bronze are still to be found in many French pharmacies, often bearing some symbol or device, such as St. Michael and the dragon.

PART II.

CHAPTER I.

CHAUCER.

CHAUCER's *Canterbury Tales* present one of the most interesting pictures of life and manners in the fourteenth century we have in English literature. The father of English poetry was born in 1328, and London is generally believed to have been his birthplace. It was his fortune to live under the wing of that chivalrous and high-spirited king, Edward III., a time when gallantry, prowess, and courage were counted in the highest esteem. In his *Canterbury Tales* he embodies some vivid sketches of the times and characters among which he lived. A physician of course forms one of his motley crew of pilgrims, who beguile the monotony of their ride to Canterbury, to pay homage at the shrine of Thomas à Becket, by the quaint stories related.

The pilgrim doctor is thus described:—

> "With us there was a doctor of physic,
> In all this world there was none him like
> To speak of physic and of surgery,
> For he was grounded in astronomy,
> He kept his patient in a full great deal,
> In houres by his magic natural.
> Well could he fortune the ascendant,
> Of his images for his patient
> He knew the cause of every malady,
> Were it of cold, or hot, or moist, or dry,
> And where engendered and of what humour,
> He was a very perfect practisour.
> The cause-y-know and of his harm the root
> Anon he gave to the sick man his boot.
> Full ready had he his apothecaries,
> To send his drugges and his lectuaries
> For each of them made other for to win
> Their friendship was not newe to begin.
> Well knew he the old Æsculapius,
> And Dioscorides, and eke Rufus,
> Old Hippocras, Hali, and Gallien,
> Serapion, Rasis, and Avicen
> Averrois, Damascene, and Constantin,
> Bernard, and Gatisden, and Gilbertin.
> Of his diet measurable was he,
> For it was of no superfluity,
> But of great nourishing and digestable;
> His study was but little on the Bible,

In sanguine and in perse he clad was, all
Lined with taffata and with sendall,
And yet he was but easy of dispence,
He kept that he won in the pestilence.
For gold in physic is a cordial,
Therefore he loved gold in special."

One can thus picture the ancient physician riding his steady jennet, clad in doublet and hose of red and blue, with cloak of sendall, a fine silk material, all lined with taffata. In telling the stars and casting horoscopes he would be learned, as astrology entered very largely into his practice, and brought many big fees. So learned a leech would doubtless have a large practice, and the apothecaries evidently vied with one another in preparing his prescriptions. The names of ancient philosophers with whom he was familiar is quite formidable, nearly all the old authors being enumerated. It is satisfactory to know he was no glutton, and had an easy conscience. That he was a wise and careful man is evident from the fact that when an epidemic came he lived but moderately, and saved extra money that flowed in during the plague time.

The closing couplet is a pretty bit of wit, and alludes to the frequent use of gold in medicine in ancient times.

Among the pilgrims also was a cook—

"To boil the chickens and the marrow bones,
And powder marchant tart and garlingale".

The former ingredient, probably a kind of baking powder, is now unknown, and the use of galingal in cookery has been quite forgotten. This aromatic condiment was commonly used as a culinary spice in the middle ages. Reference is made to the drug in the writings of Ibn Khurdadbah, the Arabian geographer, in the year 869. It was used mixed with cloves and cardamoms, and also employed in medical practice as early as the ninth century.

In the course of the knight's romantic tale, Palamon, a gallant young knight, escapes from a prison in which he has been immured for seven years, by drugging the jailer:—

> "Soon after the midnight, Palamon
> By helping of a friend brake his prison
> And fled the city, fast as he might go,
> For he had given drink his gaoler so,
> Of a clary made of a certain wine
> With narcotise and opie of Thebes fine,
> That all the night through that men would him shake,
> The gaoler slept he mighte not wake".

Clary was Hippocras wine made with spices, probably chosen in order to mask the taste of the opium and other narcotics, of which it was evident Palamon must have given the unfortunate jailer a large dose if he slept through the vigorous shaking which is said to have been administered. The opium of Thebes was much used in the thirteenth and fourteenth centuries. Prosper Alpinus, who visited Egypt in 1580-83, states that opium or meconium was in his time prepared in the Thebäid from the expressed juice of poppy-heads, and it was called *Opium Thebaïcum*. Later in the story a sharp encounter occurs between two bands of knights, in which:—

> "All were they sorely hurt and namely one,
> That with a spear was thirled his breast bone,
> To other wounds and to broken arms,
> Some hadden salves and some hadden charms,
> And pharmacies of herbs eke sage,
> They dranken, for they would their lives have."

The carrying of salves by knights to battle probably originated with the Crusaders, who carried, prepared and blessed, unguents to dress their wounds. Other warriors scorned to encumber themselves with the healing medicines, and relied on the charm or talisman which almost every knight carried on going to war. Some would trust to the simple herb or decoction, and sage which is here mentioned was supposed to have special healing virtue.

In the Miller's tale we are introduced to one Hendy Nicholas, a poor scholar or tutor who lived at Oxford, and

> "Had learned art, but all his fantasy
> Was turned for to learn astrology".

Nicholas was a sly fellow to boot, and somewhat of a beau or a fop of his time and evidently having a turn for science, he practised it in his leisure, and was consulted by the farmers of the neighbourhood as to the state of the weather, or in prognosticating the future for their wives. He had a laboratory at his lodgings, which is described in the following words:—

> "A chamber had he in that hostelry,
> Alone withouten any company,
> Full fetisly-y-dight with herbs swoot,
> And he himself was sweet as is the root
> Of liquorice or any setewale.
> His almagest, and books great and small,

> His astrolobe belonging to his art,
> His augrim stones layed fair apart,
> On shelves couched at his beddes head.
> His press-y-covered with a falding red,
> And above all them lay a gay psaltry,
> On which he made at nightes melody
> So sweetely that all the chamber rang,
> And Angelus a virginem he sang;
> And after that he sung the Knight's note;
> Full often blessed was his merry throat.
> And thus this sweete clerk his time spent,
> After his friendes finding, and his rent."

One can easily imagine from this sketch the astrologer sitting arrayed in his laboratory, the room filled with the perfume of fragrant herbs, with a manner that vied with the sweetness of liquorice or valerian root. Prominent among the many books with which he is surrounded is the *Almagest*, the book of Ptolomy, which formed the canon of astrological science in the middle ages. In one corner his bed, and above on a shelf his astrolobe, with which he told the stars, and the augrim stones, probably pieces of slate marked with figures used by astrologers in their art. Then there was the press or chest covered with a red cloth, and hanging above it his psaltery gaily decked with ribbons, on which he accompanied himself when he sang, at which he was evidently an adept. Later in the story the astrologer and man of science becomes smitten by Cupid, and one fine morning goes forth at an early hour to serenade a comely maid (unfortunately for him, married) of whom he is enamoured, and we are told—

> "When that the first cock hath crowed, anon
> Up rose this jolly lover Absolon,
> And him arrayed gay at point devise,
> But first he chewed grains and liquorice,
> To smelle sweet ere he combed his hair.
> Under his tongue a true love he bear,
> For thereby thought he to be gracious."

Like unto other votaries at the shrine of Venus, our astrologer took pains to make himself look to the best advantage, and evidently bestowed the greatest care on his dress. To perfume his breath and make himself acceptable to his lady love, he chewed grains of paradise and liquorice. The former was a favourite spice in early times, but now rarely used. It has a strong aromatic taste, which is imparted by an essential oil it contains. The "true love" is thought to mean some charm or sweetmeat in the form of a "true lover's knot," which he placed under his tongue for the same purpose, and thus this ancient gallant went forth to woo.

That belladonna was used in Chaucer's time as a narcotic may be gathered from a passage in the Reeve's tale, which runs:—

> "To bedde went the daughter right anon,

> To bedde went Alein and also John.
> There was no more, needed them no dwale."

Dwale was an old name for the nightshade, and we may infer its properties were known, as it was used to produce sleep at this period.

In the Nun's Priest's tale we are given a receipt for bad dreams and melancholy, which gives an example of the housewife's knowledge of the herbs and simples which grew in her garden:—

> "Through in this town is no apothecary,
> I shall myself two herbes teache you,
> That shall be for your health and for your prow,
> And in our yard the herbs shall I find,
> The which have of their property by kind,
> To purge you beneath and eke above,
> Sire, forget not this for Godde's love.
> Ye be full coleric of complexion,
> Ware that the sun in his ascension,
> You finde not replete of humours hot,
> And if it do I dare well lay a groat,
> That ye shall have a fever tertiane,
> Or else an ague that may be your bane.
> A day or two ye shall have digestives,
> Of wormes, ere ye take your laxatives
> Of laurel, centaury, and fumetére,
> Or else of elderberry that groweth there,
> Of catapuce, or of the gaitre berries,
> Or herb ivy growing in our yard that merry is.
> Pick them right as they grow and eat them in,
> Be merry husband for your father's kin.
> Dreade no dream. I can say you no more."

The patient seems threatened with a fever, and the good-wife, after some wholesome advice, doses him with digestives for a day or two, and afterwards with aperients. Laurel would doubtless refer to the leaves of the cherry laurel, which, infused with wine, was an old digestive tonic. Centaury, common in our fields, enjoyed a very early reputation. The herb was so called because it is said that by its virtue the centaur Chiron was healed when the poisoned arrow of Hercules had accidentally wounded his foot. Fumitory, too, was grown by the housewives, and was used as a tonic and a remedy for jaundice.

The curative properties of the elder-berry are still recognised as astringent and sudorific, and take a place in domestic remedies.

Catapuce is the old name for spurge, a common herb formerly used for its purgative properties; while the gaitre or dogwood-berries, and the herb ivy, were also used as laxative medicines and liver stimulants.

In the Canon's Yeoman's tale we are introduced to a canon who practises alchemy, and whom Chaucer makes the butt for some keen satire against the followers of that science. "It seems," says Tyrwhitt, "that some sudden resentment had determined Chaucer to interrupt the regular course of his work in order to insert a satire against the alchemists. That their pretended science was much cultivated about this time, and produced its usual evils, may fairly be inferred from the Act that was passed soon after, whereas it was made a felony to multiply gold or silver above the art of multiplication." The description of the canon as he joined the procession is somewhat amusing:—

> "His hat hung at his back down by a lace,
> For he had ridden more than trot or pace,
> He hadde pricked like as he were wood.
> A clote leaf he had laid under his hood,
> For sweat and to keep his head from heat,
> But it was joye for to see him sweat.
> His forehead dropped as a stillatory
> Were full of plantain or of paritory."

To keep his head cool while riding hard he had placed a clote or burdock leaf, which was formerly used as a poultice, in his hat or hood, a common custom in some parts of the country at the present time. To show the tone of the poet's mind when he wrote this tale, it may be noted how early the chemical hyperbole is introduced, in comparing the canon's perspiring forehead to a still which is in operation, filled with plantain, or paritory, an old name for the wallflower. The former plant had a large, thick, juicy leaf, and was formerly used as an astringent, while the wallflower once enjoyed a reputation as an anodyne. The yeoman, in proceeding with the story of his master's practises, first describes his duties as the philosopher's man:—

> "I will speak of our work,
> When we be there as we shall exercise
> Our elvion craft, we seeme wonder wise,
> Our termes be so clergial and quaint,
> I blow the fire till that mine hearte faint.
> Why should I tellen each proportion
> Of things whiche that we work upon,
> As on five or six ounces may well be
> Of silver, or some other quantity?
> And busy me to tell you the names,
> As orpiment, burnt bones, iron squames,
> That into powder grounden be full small,
> And in an earthen pot how put is all."

The poet here describes an old amalgam used in alchemy composed of red lead, bone ash, and iron scales:—

> "Of the care and woe
> That we had in our matters subliming,
> And in amalgaming, and calcining
> Of quicksilver, called mercury crude,
> For all our sleightes we can not conclude".

The subliming of mercury was considered a most important process, and was performed with much care.

The yeoman then goes on to enumerate other articles and apparatus used by the craft, in a somewhat disjointed manner:—

> "Yet I will tell them as they come to mind,
> As bol armoniac, verdigris, borace,
> And sundry vessels made of earth and glass,
> Our urinals, and our descensories;
> Phials, and croslets, and sublimatories,
> Cucurbites and alembikes eke,
> And other suche dear enough a leek".

The descensorie was a kind of flask used in distilling *per descensum*, while the croslet was an old name for the crucible. The cucurbite was the retort used in distilling, and the alembike was the still itself.

The yeoman then continues:—

> "Waters rubifying and bulle's gall,
> Arsenic, sal-ammoniac, and brimstone,
> And herbs could I tell eke many a one,
> As egremonie, valerian, and lunary;
> And other such if that me list to tarry,
> Our lampes burning both night and day,
> To bring about our craft if that we may,
> Our furnace eke of calcination,
> And of waters albification".

Egremonoine or agrimony, commonly called liverwort, was used in early medical practice as an astringent tonic, lunary or moonwort (*Botrychium Lunaria*) being possessed of similar medicinal properties:—

> "Clay made with horse and mannes hair, and oil
> Of tartar. Alum, glass, barm, wort, and argoil,
> Rosalgar and other matters imbibing,
> And eke of our matters encorporing;
> And of our silver citrination,
> Our cementing and fermentation,
> Our ingots, tests, and many things mo'."

Among the other strange articles named, argoil was the potters' clay used as a luting to close the joints, seal the flasks, and exclude the air. Rosalgar was the ancient name for flowers of antimony, much esteemed by the philosophers. The term citrination refers to the yellow colour, which, when it occurred through chemical action, proved the philosopher's stone.

We next have the alchemist's creed, and the fundamental principles of the old philosophy:—

> "I will tell you as was one taught also,
> The foure spirits and the bodies seven.
> By order as oft I heard my lord them neven,
> The first spirit quicksilver called is;
> The second orpiment, the third y-wis
> Sal-ammoniac, and the fourth brimstone,
> The bodies sion eke lo them here anon;

Sol gold is, and Luna silver was threpe,
Mars iron, Mercury quicksilver, we clepe.
Saturnus is lead, and Jupiter is tin,
And Venus copper by my father's kin."

The metallic bodies were described in the works of alchemists by the planet under whose influence they were supposed to operate, and known by the alchemical symbol of that planet. Thus gold is called Sol, represented by the symbol ☉ and copper is termed Venus, represented by the symbol ♀. It appears to have been a custom of the apothecaries from very early times to fill bottles with coloured solutions which were marked with these symbols; thus, a bottle containing a yellow solution signifying gold would be marked , and a red one would be marked ♁, signifying iron. These gradually became a kind of trade sign, and are probably the origin of the coloured globes used as the insignia of the pharmacist or compounder of medicines at the present time.

CHAPTER II.

SHAKESPEARE.

THE bard of Avon, in the wide and general knowledge he displays of the manners, ways, and customs of his own and other countries in his plays, makes many allusions to drugs and herbs, and their use. In his references to drugs, there is none perhaps on which greater difference of opinion exists than that alluded to in the speech of the Ghost in *Hamlet*, in which the apparition says:—

"Sleeping within mine orchard,
My custom always in the afternoon,
Upon my secure hour thy uncle stole,
With juice of cursèd hebenon in a vial,
And in the porches of mine ear did pour
The leprous distilment; whose effect
Holds such an enmity with blood of man,
That, swift as quicksilver, it courses through
The natural gates and alleys of the body;
And, with a sudden vigour, it doth posset
And curd, like eager droppings into milk,
The thin and wholesome blood: so did it mine".[9]

It has always been a matter of individual speculation and dispute as to the juice of what plant Shakespeare alludes to here as the "cursed hebenon". The meaning of the word hebenon is ebony-coloured, or black, so that it might apply to any dark liquid. Most writers and commentators seem to be of opinion that henbane is alluded to, but judging from the rapid effect of the liquid, it would appear that some more powerful poison is intended. The juice of henbane is not a powerful poison, and it is but a feeble narcotic whose effects are mainly sedative and soothing. It acts also as a neurotic, affecting the brain and producing delirium. It will be seen that there is little similitude between the actual effect of henbane and that of the poison described by the poet. Others think it more probable that hemlock, an ancient poison of the Greeks, is intended. Its action is much more rapid and powerful, the spinal cord being chiefly affected, and paralysis caused, ending in death. The drug is a powerful narcotic and anodyne, and is also a paralysant. It was well known to the apothecaries of Shakespeare's day, its poisonous properties having been observed from very early times. It should be taken into account, that as a matter of fact the pouring of any poisonous liquid of vegetable origin into the ear would have little or no immediate effect; and unless the tympanum had been ruptured it would be almost impossible for it to be absorbed into the system and at once prove fatal.

Paris says: "Might not the juice of cursed hebenon by which, according to Shakespeare, the King of Denmark was poisoned, have been the essential oil of tobacco?" In the first place, the learned commentator Dr. Grey observes, that the word here used—hebenon—was more probably designated by a metathesis, either of the poet or transcriber, for henebon, *i.e.*, henbane. Now, it appears from Gerade, the "tobaco" was commonly called henbane of Peru —*Hyoscyamus Peruvianus*; and when we consider how high the public prejudice ran against this herb in the reign of James, it seems not unlikely that Shakespeare should have selected it as an agent of extraordinary malignity. No preparation of *hyoscyamus* with which we are acquainted would produce death by application to the ear, whereas the essential oil of tobacco might possibly have such an effect.

The term "distilment," says Stevens, "is calculated to support this conjecture. Surely the expression signifies that the preparation was the result of a distillation." It is a singular fact that the essential oil of tobacco differs considerably in its physiological action from an infusion made from the leaves, the former affecting the brain, and the latter the heart.[10]

Ellacombe states: "Before, and in the time of Shakespeare, other writers had spoken of the narcotic and poisonous effects of heben, hebenon, or hebona."

Spenser says:—

"Faire Venus sonne,...
Lay now thy deadly heben bow apart".

Gower and Marlowe also wrote of the juice of hebon. It may be taken for granted that all these authors allude to the same tree.

Nicholson and Harrison, after a very exhaustive investigation of the subject, agree that the true reading is hebona, and that hebona is the yew. Their main arguments are based on the following three facts:—

1. That in nearly all the northern nations the name of the yew is more or less like heben.

2. That all the effects attributed by Shakespeare to the action of hebona are described by different medical writers as arising from yew poisoning.

3. That the *post-mortem* appearances after yew poisoning and snake poisoning are similar.

Later on, in the play performed before the King, Lucianus thus speaks of the poisonous medicine he uses:—

> "Thoughts break, hands apt, drugs fit, and time agreeing,
> Confederate season, else no creature seeing,
> Thou mixture rank, of midnight weeds collected,
> With Hecate's ban thrice blasted, thrice infected,
> Thy natural magic and dire property
> On wholesome life usurp immediately".

Here allusion is made to a mixture of poisonous herbs gathered at midnight, probably hemlock among others, as mentioned in the witches' incantation in *Macbeth*, to which we shall refer later. With regard to the gathering of herbs at night, the practice was common, it being supposed that the properties of the plant collected at night were stronger than in the daytime. That there is a certain amount of truth in this is proved by the researches of Sachs and Brown, who have found from their investigations that starch is formed in the leaves of plants during the day, and is consumed during the night, so that the old superstition of the increased activity of the midnight gathered herb was not mythical.

Shakespeare's well-known description of the poor apothecary of his time, which he introduces in *Romeo and Juliet*, presents an excellent picture of the needy practitioner in the sixteenth century:—

> "I do remember an apothecary,
> And hereabouts he dwells, whom late I noted
> In tatter'd weeds, with overwhelming brows,
> Culling of simples; meagre were his looks,
> Sharp misery had worn him to the bones:
> And in his needy shop a tortoise hung,
> An alligator stuff'd, and other skins
> Of ill-shaped fishes; and about his shelves
> A beggarly account of empty boxes,
> Green earthen pots, bladders, and musty seeds;
> Remnants of packthread and old cakes of roses,
> Were thinly scattered to make up a show".[11]

One can readily picture the poverty-stricken appearance of the dark little shop, littered and crowded with the stuffed skins of curious fishes and alligators. One can almost smell the close musty odour blended with the aromatic perfume of drugs and the old cakes of pressed rose leaves, the manner in which they were formerly preserved for medicinal purposes.

The fashionably-dressed Romeo enters, after having made a considerable noise to rouse the attention of the old apothecary from his perchance much-needed repose, and offers his bribe for the poison. Of the purpose for which he requires it he makes little secret.

"ROMEO.

    Come hither, man. I see that thou art poor;
    Hold, there is forty ducats; let me have
    A dram of poison, such soon-speeding gear
    As will disperse itself through all the veins,
    That the life-weary taker may fall dead;
    And that the trunk may be discharged of breath
    As violently as hasty powder fir'd
    Doth hurry from the fatal cannon's mouth."

The Apothecary's reply:—

"Such mortal drugs I have; but Mantua's law
Is death to any he that utters them,"

would show that Shakspeare's idea of the law respecting the sale of poisons was a severe one, and much before his time. The law in England at that time as regards the selling of poisons was very lax. But for the poor apothecary the bribe was too tempting. Perchance he was hungry, and there is something pathetic in his rejoinder,

"My poverty, but not my will, consents".

And giving Romeo the poison:—

"Put this in any liquid thing you will,
And drink it off; and, if you had the strength
Of twenty men, it would despatch you straight".

The poet gives no indication of the nature of the poison beyond that its effect was very rapid, as when the distracted lover drinks to his lady love in the deadly draught he exclaims:—

"O true apothecary!
Thy drugs are quick. Thus with a kiss I die."

In the early part of the sixteenth century the practice of the black art was carried on throughout England, mostly by old women, who also sold charms and love philtres. Shakespeare's description of the witches' incantations in *Macbeth* presents some idea of a seance, and the gruesome articles in which they dealt. To know the properties of the most poisonous herbs (often quite fictitious) was part of their trade.

"Round about the cauldron go;
In the poison'd entrails throw.
Toad, that under coldest stone,
Days and nights hast thirty-one
Swelter'd venom sleeping got,
Boil thou first i' the charmed pot.
    Double, double, toil and trouble;
    Fire burn, and cauldron bubble.
"Fillet of a fenny snake,
In the cauldron boil and bake;
Eye of newt and toe of frog,
Wool of bat and tongue of dog,
Adder's fork, and blind-worm's sting,
Lizard's leg, and owlet's wing,
For a charm of powerful trouble;
Like a hell-broth boil and bubble.
    Double, double, toil and trouble;
    Fire burn, and cauldron bubble.
"Scale of dragon, tooth of wolf,
Witch's mummy, maw and gulf
Of the ravin'd salt-sea shark;
Root of hemlock, digg'd i' the dark,
Liver of blaspheming Jew;
Gall of goat, and slips of yew,
Sliver'd in the moon's eclipse;
Nose of Turk and Tartar's lips;
Finger of birth-strangled babe,
Ditch-delivered by a drab,
Make the gruel thick and slab;
Add thereto a tiger's chaudron,
For the ingredients of our cauldron.
    Double, double, toil and trouble;
    Fire burn, and cauldron bubble."

The method here used by the witches to measure the time that the cauldron should boil by singing their incantation is, according to Dr. Lauder Brunton, an ancient mode of calculating time still used in some parts of the country at the present day. By thus repeating several verses they could regulate the time of boiling fairly well. The old apothecaries used the moon as a method of calculating the time certain processes should take, and the word "menstruum," still commonly used, was employed because certain drugs were allowed to macerate a month in the liquid to extract the active constituents.

In the toad that had been lying under a stone for thirty-one days and nights, we have another curious instance how the empirical practitioners of mediæval times acted on a certain traditional knowledge, which modern science has since proved to be correct.

We have again in the toad which has lain dormant for a month, the idea that it was the best time for his use, when his venom would be most active, besides the advantage also of catching him napping, when he would have no opportunity of getting rid of the poisonous principle contained in his skin. Dr. Lauder Brunton remarks with respect to this practice: "I remember reading as a child a story of how King John was poisoned by a friar who dropped a toad into his wine, but some books of natural history forty or fifty years ago scouted the idea of toads being poisonous at all. A little while ago, however, Dr. Leonard Guthie sent me an interesting account of a wicked Italian woman whose husband was dying of dropsy. He took so long about it that his wife became tired of the process, and thought that she would help him on. She accordingly caught a toad and put it in his wine, so that he should drink the liquid and die, but instead of dying he, to her astonishment and disgust, completely recovered. Forty years ago this story would have been scouted as equally mythical with that of King John, but now we know that it is precisely what the woman would have expected if she had only been acquainted with the researches of modern pharmacology. For the skin of a toad secretes a poison, the active principle of which, phrynin, has an action very much resembling that of digitalis, which is the remedy *par excellence* for dropsy depending on heart disease."

Not less curious are the directions for gathering the poisonous hemlock at night, which has recently been shown to be the time of its greatest activity. These few instances show that the ancient apothecaries had often much greater knowledge than we give them credit for, and that some of the modern discoveries in modern science were well known to them, even if they could not account for them.

In the *Taming of the Shrew* allusion is made to the simples in vogue at the time for hurts and bruises. The lord's directions for the treatment of Christopher Sly, who is found sleeping in the road on a cold night after a drinking bout, are curious:—

> "Balm his foul head with warm distilled waters,
> And burn sweet wood to make the lodging sweet".

The distilled aromatic waters, of which the apothecary manufactured a considerable number, were much used in the middle ages for the purpose of fomentation. The burning of sweet woods, such as aloe or sandal, to take away evil smells, was a very ancient practice.

An old cure for melancholy is embodied in the following lines:—

> "Your honour's players, hearing your amendment,
> Are come to play a pleasant comedy,
> For so your doctors hold it very meet:
> Seeing too much sadness hath congeal'd your blood,
> And melancholy is the nurse of frenzy,
> Therefore they thought it good you hear a play,

And frame your mind to mirth and merriment,
Which bars a thousand harms, and lengthens life".

In *Measure for Measure*, the poet had evidently the dulcamara or bitter-sweet in mind when he penned the lines:—

"I should not think it strange, for 'tis a physic
That's bitter to sweet end".

The dulcamara or bitter-sweet has the peculiar property, when first taken into the mouth, of imparting a bitter flavour which gradually changes to a sweet one, hence its name.

The knowledge of drugs and herbs possessed by the noble dames and housewives is frequently mentioned by Shakespeare. The chatelaine of his time was well acquainted with the medicinal properties of all the simples and herbs, which she cultivated in her own garden. Her skill and experience were always at the service of her household and of dependants for miles around.

The Queen, wife of Cymbeline, gives evidence of this in her conversation with Cornelius the physician:—

"QUEEN.

Whiles yet the dew's on ground, gather those flowers;
Make haste: who has the note of them?

. . . .

Now, master doctor, have you brought those drugs?

"CORNELIUS.

Pleaseth your highness, ay: here they are, madam

(*presenting a small box*),

But I beseech your grace, without offence—
My conscience bids me ask—wherefore you have
Commanded of me these most poisonous compounds,
Which are the movers of a languishing death;
But, though slow, deadly?

"QUEEN.

I do wonder, doctor,
Thou ask'st me such a question. Have I not been
Thy pupil long? Hast thou not learned me how
To make perfumes, distil, preserve? yea, so,
That our great king himself doth woo me oft
For my confections? Having thus far proceeded
(Unless thou think'st me devilish), is't not meet
That I did amplify my judgment in
Other conclusions? I will try the forces

Of these thy compounds on such creatures as

We count not worth the hanging, but none human,

To try the vigour of them, and apply

Allayments to their act, and by them gather

Their several virtues, and effects.

"Cornelius.

Your highness

Shall from this practice but make hard your heart:

Besides, the seeing these effects will be

Both noisome and infectious.

"Queen.

Oh content thee.

    Enter Pisanio.

(*aside*) Here comes a flattering rascal; upon him

Will I first work: he's for his master,

And enemy to my son. How now, Pisanio?

Doctor, your service for this time is ended;

Take your own way.

"Cornelius.

(*aside*) I do suspect you, madam,

But you shall do no harm.

I do not like her. She doth think she has

Strange lingering poisons. I do not know her spirit,

And will not trust one of her malice with

A drug of such damn'd nature. Those she has

Will stupify and dull the sense a while:

Which first, perchance, she'll prove on cats and dogs,

Then afterwards up higher, but there is

No danger in what show of death it makes,

More than the locking up the spirits a time

To be more fresh reviving. She is fool'd

With a most false effect; and I the truer

So to be false with her."[12]

The caution of the physician is well described, and his resort to subterfuge in order to checkmate the evil design of his wily mistress and old pupil, whom he evidently distrusts.

The Queen is supposed to have possessed considerable knowledge and skill in the use of drugs, and her conserves had evidently a great reputation. Her scientific ideas were in advance of the age she lived in when she states her desire to make physiological experiments on animals to advance her knowledge; but the clear acumen of Cornelius saw through the apparently laudable spirit of research that imbued his pupil, and he supplied her with drugs of less potency.

The following allusions are made to the apothecary:—

> "Cardinal Beaufort. Bid the apothecary
>   Bring the strong poison that I bought of him."[13]

And again, in *Pericles, Prince of Tyre*, Cerimon says:—

> "Your master will be dead ere you return;
> There's nothing can be minister'd to nature,
> That can recover him. Give this to the apothecary,
> And tell me how it works."[14]

This lord of Ephesus was evidently something of an amateur physician, as he tells us later that

> "'Tis known I ever
> Have studied physic, through which secret art,
> By turning o'er authorities, I have
> (Together with my practice) made familiar
> To me and to my aid the blest infusions
> That dwell in vegetives, in metals, stones;
> And can speak of the disturbances that nature
> Works, and of the cures; which doth give me
> A more content in course of true delight
> Than to be thirsty after tottering honour".

The lines—

> "One whose subdu'd eyes,
> Albeit unused to the melting mood,
> Drop tears as fast as the Arabian trees
> Their medicinal gum,"[15]

spoken by Othello, refer to the manner in which many of the medicinal gums are collected in the East. Small slits or punctures are made in the bark of the tree, through which the semi-liquid gum slowly oozes. It then coagulates in the form of a tear, and is at length scraped off and collected.

> "Set ratsbane by his porridge."[16]

> "I had as lief they would put ratsbane in my mouth as offer to stop it with security."[17]

> "I would the milk
> Thy mother gave thee, when thou suck'dst her breast,
> Had been a little ratsbane for my sake."[18]

Ratsbane, mentioned in the three preceding quotations, was an old name for arsenic, which in Shakespeare's time was commonly used for poisoning rats, hence the name.

> "I have bought the oil, the balsamum, and aqua vitæ,"[19]

says Dromio of Syracuse. These were the medical comforts for the barque of Epidamnum, and show that sailing vessels in those days carried a certain amount of medicine. The oil may have been one of the many panaceas of the time for "purging the body of bile or humour," while balsams there were by the score, of Hungary, and aromatics for "wind and pain". The *aqua vitæ* alluded to was probably brandy, which would serve to keep the courage of the voyagers up and the cold out.

Proteus, in the *Two Gentlemen of Verona*, exclaims:—

> "When I was sick you gave me bitter pills;
> And I must minister like to you".[20]

In *Lucrece* the bard shows he knew something of the counteracting effects of certain drugs from the following lines:—

> "The poisonous simple sometimes is compacted
> In a pure compound; being so applied,
> His venom in effect is purified".[21]

"KING HENRY.

The united vessel of their blood,

Mingled with venom of suggestion,

As, for a purpose, the age will pour it in,

Shall never leak, though it do work as strong

As aconitum or rash gunpowder."[22]

The aconite or monkshood, formerly called wolf's bane, gives us one of the most powerful vegetable poisons, its properties having long been known and employed in medical practice. It was used by the early Greeks and Romans, and is probably even of still greater antiquity. On account of its rapid and deadly action, Shakespeare compares it to gunpowder. Some commentators are of the opinion that aconite was the poison sold by the apothecary to the lovesick Romeo.

A curious old tradition is alluded to by Falstaff when speaking of the chamomile, in the following sentence:—

"Though the camomile, the more it is trodden on the faster it grows, yet youth, the more it is wasted the sooner it wears".[23]

The chamomile has an ancient reputation for its medicinal properties as a stomachic and febrifuge.

Its growth is said to be improved by being pressed or trampled into the earth.

"SHALLOW. Nay, you shall see my orchard, where, in an arbour, we will eat a last year's pippin of my own graffing, with a dish of caraways and so forth."[24]

Carraway seeds were very largely used in Shakespeare's time as a spice and condiment. The essential oil they yield has carminative properties. The seeds were often served with roast apples, a custom still said to be kept up at Trinity College, Cambridge.

"IAGO. The food that to him now is as luscious as locusts, shall be to him shortly as bitter as coloquintida."[25]

The coloquintida mentioned, is the old name for colocynth, a drug largely used in medicine at the present time. It was employed by the Greek and Roman physicians as a purgative, and was known in Britain as early as the eleventh century. It has a drastic, bitter taste, and is commonly known as bitter apple.

Shakespeare makes several allusions to the elder, a tree concerning which there are many old traditions. One of them will suffice.

"HOLOFERNES.

Begin, sir, you are my elder.

"BIRON.

Well followed; Judas was hanged on an elder."[26]

The *sambucus nigra*, or black elder, has long been used in medicine as a discutient, yet tradition gives it an evil name. Judas was supposed to have hanged himself on an elder tree, which doubtless brought it into disrepute, although its flowers distilled with water make an excellent cosmetic.

"OPHELIA.

There's fennel for you and columbines."[27]

This herb was greatly valued by the old apothecaries, and was known also to the ancients. There was an old belief that the fennel in flower predicted an early summer. Its chief use now is as a flavouring agent.

Several allusions are also made to ginger.

"CLOWN. I must have saffron to colour the warden pies; mace; dates—none, that's out of my note; nutmegs, seven; a race or two of ginger, but that I beg."[28]

Ginger was known and used by the Greeks and Romans as a spice, and was esteemed by physicians in England at the time of the Norman Conquest. Its hot, burning taste is due to a resinous principle contained in the root, and is still used in medicine.

The mandrake or mandragora is frequently mentioned in the plays. Thus says

"IAGO.

Not poppy, nor mandragora,

Nor all the drowsy syrup of the world,

Shall ever medicine thee to that sweet sleep

Which thou owedst yesterday."[29]

Also—

"JULIET.

And shrieks like mandrakes torn out of the earth,

That living mortals, hearing them, run mad,"[30]

alluding to the old tradition that the mandrake groaned when pulled up by the roots, and the person who did it would surely die soon. The mandragora, to which wonderful properties were ascribed by the ancients, is not now used in medicine.

"LAFEU. Go to, sir, you were beaten in Italy for picking a kernel out of a pomegranate."[31]

The medicinal properties of the pomegranate have been known from very ancient times, frequent mention of it being made in the Bible. A decoction of the root is recommended by Celsus, Dioscorides, and Pliny for tapeworm; and it is still used as an astringent.

The poppy is mentioned by Iago in the quotation previously given, as being known for its narcotic properties.

"MACBETH.

What rhubarb, senna, or what purgative drug

Would scour these English hence?"[32]

Rhubarb was known to the Chinese 2700 B.C., and has been used for its purgative properties from the earliest times. It is said to take its name from the river Rhu, now the Volga, on whose banks it grows.

> "PERDITA.
>
> > For you there's rosemary and rue; these keep
> >
> > Seeming and savour all the winter long;
> >
> > Grace and remembrance be to you both."[33]

Rosemary has been esteemed for centuries for its refreshing and aromatic perfume, due to the essential oil it contains, and which even now has a reputation as an application for the hair. It is mentioned by Pliny, and has been cultivated in Britain since the time of the Norman Conquest. On account of its evergreen leaves it was considered an emblem of constancy, and was frequently carried at wedding and funeral ceremonies. It was customary in France at one time, to place a bunch of rosemary in the hands of the dead. The old apothecaries had great faith in the oil as an embrocation, and it was largely used to place among clothes as a preventive of moths.

> "OPHELIA. There's rue for you; and here's some for me: we may call it herb grace o' Sundays: O, you must wear your rue with a difference."[34]

Some curious traditions are attached to rue, or, as it was formerly called, the herb of grace, probably on account of its being often worn as an amulet to ward off disease, and also used by the old Romanists in the exorcisms. It has ever been regarded as a symbol of sorrow or pity, as its name implies. The word is probably derived from the same root as Ruth, meaning sorrow and remorse, while "to rue" was to be sorry for.

In ancient times it was supposed to be useful for almost every disease, its properties being due to an essential oil still used in pharmacy.

It was largely employed in affections of the eye and for its antiseptic properties as a preservative to ward off decay.

The plant is not a native of England, but has been cultivated in this country for more than 800 years, and was extensively grown in the old herb gardens.

Euphrasie and rue were often used together as a curative application for the eyes. In *Paradise Lost* Milton says:—

> "Then purged with euphrasie and rue
> The visual nerve, for he has much to see".

Rue was employed also to take away warts, the freshly cut stem being rubbed over the excrescence, and the following couplet repeated:—

> "Ashen true, ashen tree,
> Pray bury these warts of me".

Another old rhyme runs:—

> "What savour is better, if physicke be true

For places infected than wormwood or rue".

"C_{LOWN}. I must have saffron to colour the warden pies."[35]

Saffron was formerly much prized as a medicine, a condiment, and a dye. It is said to have been introduced into England in the reign of Edward III., and was cultivated in the neighbourhood of Walden, in Essex, to which it gave its name. The quality of English saffron was renowned in Shakspeare's time. It was used by the monks in mediæval days in illuminating their missals, and dyeing materials, as well as being esteemed as a febrifuge and cordial.

"M_{ACBETH}.

What rhubarb, senna, or what purgative drug

Would scour these English hence?"[36]

The well-known purgative properties of senna leaves were held in great repute by the old apothecaries. The drug was introduced into Europe about the ninth or tenth century by the Arabs, and it soon attained a reputable position in medical practice. The best variety was originally supposed to have been brought from Mecca.

"R_{OSALINE}. To weed this wormwood from your fruitful brain."[37]

Wormwood has always had a high reputation as a medicine, and was chiefly used as a tonic. It yields an essential oil with an extremely bitter taste, which is yet largely used in France in the manufacture of absinthe.

In one of his Sonnets, Shakespeare alludes to the old alembic of the alchemist in the following lines:—

"What potions have I drunk of Syren tears,
Distill'd from limbecks foul as hell within".

And in the following verse he deals with some theories of medical treatment:—

"Like as to make our appetites more keen,
With eager compounds we our palate urge;
As, to prevent our maladies unseen,
We sicken to shun sickness when we purge:
Even so, being full of your ne'er-cloying sweetness,
To bitter sauces did I frame my feeding,
And, sick of welfare, found a kind of meetness
To be diseas'd, ere that there was true needing.
Thus policy in love, to anticipate
The ills that were not, grew to faults assur'd,
And brought to medicine a healthful state
Which, rank of goodness, would by ill be cur'd.
    But thence I learn, and find the lesson true,
    Drugs poison him that so fell sick of you."[38]

CHAPTER III.

SPENSER.

EDMUND SPENSER was born in London towards the close of the year 1552, and in his after career, added lustre to an age which for brilliancy in literature has never been equalled in the history of this country. He lived for some time in Lancashire in his early days, but in 1578 quitted the country for the court. It was probably his friend Sir Walter Raleigh who introduced him to court-favour and Queen Elizabeth. In 1589 he published the *Faerie Queen*, a poem which will ever live in English literature.

There are few allusions in the works of Edmund Spenser to medicinal plants, although he frequently mentions salves and other methods of administration used in the leechcraft of his time, as instanced in the following quotations:—

> "Eftsoons he gan apply relief
> Of salves and med'cines which has passing prefe".[39]

> "With wholesome read of sad sobriety,
> To rule the stubborn rage of passion blind,
> Give salves to every sore, but counsel to the mind."[40]

In the first book of the *Faerie Queen* Spenser makes an interesting allusion to trees and their uses in his time, in the following lines:—

> "Much gave they praise the trees so straight and high:
> The sailing pine; the cedar proud and tall;
> The vine-prop elm; the poplar never dry;
> The builder oak, sole king of forests all;
> The aspen good for staves; the cypress funeral;
> The laurel, meed of mighty conquerors
> And poets sage; the fir that weepeth still;
> The willow, worn of forlorn paramours;
> The yew, obedient to the binder's will;
> The birch for shafts; the sallow for the mill;
> The myrrh sweet bleeding in the bitter wound;
> The warlike beech; the ash for nothing ill;
> The fruitful olive, and the plantane round;
> The carver holm; the maple, seldom inward sound".[41]

The sailing pine was doubtless so called on account of it being so largely used for the masts of ships. The wood of the aspen tree was often used for making staves on account of its toughness. He alludes also to the ancient use of the cypress at funeral rites, and the wearing of the willow as a badge of the unfortunate; the yew, chiefly employed for making the long bows; the birch, for the strongest arrows; and the sallow, which when plaited formed the sails of the windmills.

Incisions are cut in the bark of the myrrh tree in order that the gum should exude as from an open wound.

Beech was used for the shafts of spears and axes, and the carver holm or cutting holly was so called from its prickles.

In the sixth canto we have mention of the flower-de-luce:—

"The lily, lady of the flowering field,
The flow'r-de-luce her lovely paramour".[42]

Flower-de-luce was the old name for the iris, and is also the French *fleur-de-lis*, and the origin of that symbol. The roots of many of the iris species have long been used in medicine for their cathartic and emetic properties. That of the *I. florentina* is well known for its sweet violet smell, and from early times has been employed to sweeten the breath and as an ingredient in tooth powders. Another old name for this plant was "The flower of delights".

In the seventh canto the poet shows he was well acquainted with some medicinal plants, and gives us quite a group of "herbs of ill favour".

"There mournful cypress grew in greatest store;
And trees of bitter gall; and ebon sad;
Dead sleeping poppy, and black hellebore;
Cold coloquintida, and tetra mad;
Mortal samnitis; and cicuta bad,
With which th' unjust Athenians made to die
Wise Socrates, who, thereof quaffing glad,
Pour'd out his life and last philosophy
To the fair Critias, his dearest belamy!"[43]

Here we have mention of the narcotic poppy and the black hellebore, a drastic purgative with which tradition states Melampus, the great soothsayer and physician, cured the daughters of Prœtus, King of Argos, of madness. Also the colocynth or bitter apple; tetra mad, an old name for the belladonna or deadly nightshade; savin, here called mortal samnitis, a plant possessing powerful properties, used in medicine from the time of the Romans; and the cicuta or hemlock, which formed the active ingredient in the poison cup of the Greeks.

In the *Shepherd's Calendar* we have another allusion to the black hellebore:—

"Here grows melampode ev'rywhere,
And terebinth, good for goats;
The one my madding kids to smear,
The next to heal their throats".[44]

The ancient name for hellebore was melampus root, hence the name melampode, which doubtless arose from the old tradition. By terebinth the poet probably means one of the species of pine from which turpentine is obtained.

CHAPTER IV

GOETHE.

T<small>HE</small> Faust-legend around which Goethe wove his great tragedy, was one of those floating traditions which were common in the romantic lore of many countries during the fifteenth and sixteenth centuries, and which seem to have originated in the general belief in occult forces. The Johann Faust of the popular stories was undoubtedly an individual of that name, born towards the close of the fifteenth century in the little town of Knittlingen, near Maulbronn, in Würtemberg. His parents were poor, but he was enabled by the bequest of a rich uncle to study medicine. He attended the University of Cracow (where he probably received his doctor's degree), studied magic which was there taught as an accepted branch of knowledge, and appears to have afterwards travelled for many years through Europe. Manlius, the disciple of Melancthon, quotes the latter as having said: "This fellow Faust escaped from our town of Wittenberg, after our Duke John had given the order to have him imprisoned. He also escaped from Nuremberg under the like circumstances. This sorcerer Faust, an abominable beast, a common sewer of many devils, boasted that he, by his magic arts had enabled the Imperial armies to win their victories in Italy." It was probably the famous battle of Pavia fought in 1525 of which Faust spoke, as the time of his visit to Wittenberg appears to have been about the year 1530. Further evidence of the existence of such a character is to be found in the *Index Sanitatis* of the physician, Philip Begardi, published at Worms in 1539, and in the *Sermones Conviviales* of Johann Gast, who gives an account of a dinner given by Faust at Basle at which he was present. The original form of the legend is contained in a work published by Spiess in Frankfurt in 1587, entitled the *History of Dr. Joh. Faust, the Notorious Sorcerer and Black-artist, etc., etc.* This book was first translated into English in 1590, and from it Marlowe doubtless obtained the material for his tragedy of "Dr. Faustus," which appears to have been first performed in London in 1593, the year of his death.

In the first act of Goethe's tragedy we are introduced to Faust, who is sitting in his lofty-arched Gothic chamber or laboratory, his desk piled high with the works of noted writers on magic and astrology.

> "And this one Book of Mystery
> From Nostradamus' very hand,
> Is't not sufficient company?"

Nostradamus, the famous astrologer, was born at St. Remy, in Provence, in the year 1503. His real name was Michel de Notre Dame. For some time he practised as a physician, but finally devoted himself to astrology, and published in 1555 a collection of prophecies in rhymed quatrains, entitled *Les*

Prophecies de Michel Nostradamus, which created an immediate sensation, and found many believers, especially as the death of Henry II. of France seemed to verify one of his mystical predictions. He was appointed physician to Charles IX., and continued the publication of his prophecies, asserting, however, that the study of the planetary aspects was not alone sufficient, but that the gift of second sight, which God grants only to a few chosen persons, is also necessary.

He died in the year 1566.

In the following lines allusion is made to two popular forms of divination.

> "CITIZEN'S DAUGHTER. Come, Agatha! I shun the witch's sight
> Before folks, lest there be misgiving!
> 'Tis true, she showed me, on Saint Andrew's Night,
> My future sweetheart, just as he were living.
> "THE OTHER. She showed me mine, in crystal clear,
> With several wild young blades, a soldier-lover".

St. Andrew's Night is celebrated in some parts of Germany by forms of divination very similar to those which are practised in Scotland on Hallow E'en. The maidens believe that by calling upon St. Andrew, undressed, before getting into bed, their future sweetheart will appear to them in a dream. Another charm is practised by pouring melted lead through the wards of a key, wherein there is the form of a cross, into a basin of water brought between eleven o'clock and midnight: the cooling lead will then take the form of tools which indicate the trade of the destined lover.

Crystal gazing, which we have described in a previous chapter, was also a common method of foretelling future events, and young maidens were supposed to be specially successful in its practise.

Faust's description of the preparation of a panacea is a good illustration of the fantastic language employed by the alchemists:—

> "Who, in his dusky work-shop bending,
> With proved adepts in company,
> Made, from his recipes unending,
> Opposing substances agree.
> There was a Lion red, a wooer daring,
> Within the Lily's tepid bath espoused,
> And both, tormented then by flame unsparing,
> By turns in either bridal chamber housed.
> If then appeared, with colours splendid,
> The young Queen in her crystal shell,
> This was the medicine—the patient's woes soon ended,
> And none demanded—who got well?"

Goethe is said to have drawn this description partly from Paracelsus, and partly from Welling's *Opus Mago Cabbalisticum*. The "Lion red" is cinnabar, called a "wooer daring" on account of its action in rushing to an intimate union with other bodies. "The Lily" is a preparation of antimony, which bore the name of Lilium Paracelsi. Red, moreover, is the masculine, and white the feminine colour. The retort containing these substances was first placed in a "tepid bath" and gradually heated, then "tormented by flame unsparing," the two were driven from one "bridal chamber" to another, that is, their wedded fumes were forced by the heat into an alembic. If then the "Young Queen," the sublimated compound, appeared with a brilliant colour in the alembic the proper result was obtained and this signified the true medicine.

In scene iii. Mephistopheles says:—

"My steps by one slight obstacle controlled,—
The wizard's foot, that on your threshold is".

The wizard's foot or pentagram, was supposed to possess an especial potency against evil spirits, and was often chalked on the door-steps to protect the household from their influence. It consisted of a five-rayed star, thus:—

The belief in its efficacy doubtless sprang from the circumstance that it resolves itself into three triangles, and thus a triple symbol of the Trinity. Paracelsus ascribes a similar, though a lesser degree of virtue to the hexagram. Another peculiarity of the pentagram is, that it may be drawn complete from one point, without lifting the pen, and therefore belongs to those *involuntary* hieroglyphics which we sometimes make in moments of abstraction. In scene xiii. where Margaret plucks a star-flower, and pulls off the leaves one after the other, murmuring—

"He loves me—loves me not"

we have an illustration of a favourite mode of amorous divination by means of flowers still practised by country maidens.

The custom is of great antiquity and is mentioned by Theocritus. The single daisy is a favourite flower for the purpose.

The following allusion to the red mouse refers to an ancient superstition concerning one of the many forms of diabolical possession. The "evil one" was supposed to enter the body in the form of a red mouse.

"MEPHISTOPHELES.

Wherefore forsakest thou the lovely maiden,
That in the dance so sweetly sang?

"FAUST.

Ah! in the midst of it there sprang

A red mouse from her mouth—sufficient reason."

In the second part of the work we are introduced to an astrologer who, prompted by Mephistopheles, delivers himself as follows:—

"The Sun himself is gold of purest ray;
The herald, Mercury, serves for love and pay;
Dame Venus has bewitched you all, for she,
Early and late, looks on you lovingly;
Chaste Luna has her whims, no two alike;
Mars threatens you, although he may not strike,
And Jupiter is still the splendid star.
Saturn is great, though seeming small and far;
As metal, him we don't much venerate,
Of value slight, though heavy in his weight.
Now, when of Sol and Luna unions had,—
Silver with gold,—then is the world made glad:
All else, with them, is easy to attain,—
Palaces, gardens, cheeks of rosy stain;
And thus procures this highly learned man,
Who that can do which none of us e'er can."

The astrologer here alludes to the seven principal metals, to which the early alchemists attached the names of seven planets. The Sun was gold, the Moon silver, Mercury quicksilver, Venus copper, Mars iron, Jupiter tin, and Saturn lead.

In the same act, reference is made to an old tradition that is still believed in some parts of Germany.

"Lo! at hand there
Is ancient juice of strength divine.
Yet trust to him who's knowledge gotten,
The wood o' the staves has long been rotten,
A cask of tartar holds the wine."

It is a general belief in the wine districts, that when a cask of wine has been kept for centuries, the crust of argol or crude cream of tartar which is gradually deposited, may acquire such a consistency as to hold the liquid when the staves have rotted away. The wine thus becomes its own cask, and preserves itself in a thick oily state. It is then said to possess wonderful medicinal virtues.

Later on Mephistopheles is asked by a blonde beauty for a cure for her complexion.

"One word, sir! Here you see a visage fair,—
In sorry summer I another wear!
There sprout a hundred brown and reddish freckles,
And vex my lily skin with ugly speckles.
A cure!

"MEPHISTOPHELES. 'Tis pity! shining fair, yet smitten,—
Spotted, when May comes, like a panther-kitten!
Take frog's spawn, tongues of toads, which contribute,

Under the full moon deftly distillate,
And when it wanes, apply the mixture:
Next spring, the spots will be no more a fixture.

"A B<small>RUNETTE</small>. To sponge upon you, what a crowd's advancing!
I beg a remedy: a frozen foot
Annoys me much, in walking as in dancing;
And awkwardly I manage to salute.

"M<small>EPHISTOPHELES</small>. A gentle kick permit, then, from my foot!

"T<small>HE</small> B<small>RUNETTE</small>. Well,—that might happen when the two are lovers.

"M<small>EPHISTOPHELES</small>. My kick a more important meaning covers;
Similia similibus, when one is sick,
The foot cures foot, each limb its hurt can palliate;
Come near! Take heed! and pray you don't retaliate!"

Frog's spawn and toad's tongues formed an old remedy for spots on the skin, and in the "gentle kick" we have a satire on the homœopathic theory of medicine.

CHAPTER V.

LE SAGE.

L<small>E</small> Sage draws a vivid picture of the medical practitioner of his day in his well-known work *Gil Blas*. Doctor Sangrado, bigoted, obstinate, and dominated by one idea, was doubtless very true to nature, and a type of physician not unfrequently met with even later than the seventeenth century. The character is supposed to have been drawn from that of Doctor Hecquet, Dean of the Faculty of Medicine at Paris, a man extremely thin and spare in body, and who is said never to have drank anything but water.

Le Sage describes his physician as "a tall, meagre, pale man, who had kept the shears of Clotho employed during forty years. He had a very solemn appearance, weighed his discourse, and gave an emphasis to his expressions: his reason was geometrical, and his opinions extremely singular." All the city looked upon him as another Hippocrates. The licentiate Sedillo, a fat clerical epicurean, having fallen sick with the fever and gout, this great physician was called in, and after examining his patient delivered himself of the following diagnosis: "The business here is to supply the defect of obstructed perspiration; others in my place would doubtless prescribe saline draughts, diuretics, diaphoretics, and such medicines as abound with mercury and sulphur; but cathartics and sudorifics are pernicious drugs invented by quacks, and all the preparations of chemistry are only calculated to do mischief," said this disciple of Æsculapius.

"You must renounce all palatable food; and do you drink wine?"

"Yes," said the poor canon; "wine and water."

"Oh! watered as much as you please," replied the physician: "what an irregularity is here! what a frightful regimen! You ought to have been dead long ago. If you had drunk nothing but pure water all your life, and had been satisfied with simple nourishment, such as, for example, boiled apples, peas, and beans, you would not now be tormented with gout, and all your limbs would perform their functions with ease."

The poor canon promised to obey in all these things, but the doctor hadn't finished yet, for he sent for a surgeon, and ordered him to let "six good porringers of blood as the first effort" to supply the want of perspiration.

"And return in three hours, and take as much more, and repeat the same to-morrow," said this veritable leech to the surgeon, "for a patient cannot be bled too much."

Besides this, the unfortunate patient was dosed incessantly with warm water, two or three pints in as many draughts, "for," said the physician, "water is the true specific in all distempers what-ever".

Little wonder that in less than two days, Gil Blas tells us, the old canon was reduced to the last extremity, and soon after breathed his last, much to the regret of the physician, who declared it was because he had not lost blood enough, nor drank a sufficient quantity of water.

The mercurial Gil Blas shortly after took service with this learned medico, and kept his books, which he declares might have been with great justice styled a register of the dead; for almost all the people whose names it contained died soon afterwards.

But after being about a week with the physician, Gil Blas was seized with a cramp which he attributed to the quantity of the "universal dissolvent" he was compelled to imbibe, and had to consult his master.

"Why, truly, Gil Blas, I am not at all surprised that thou dost not enjoy good health," said the hydropathist. "Thou dost not drink enough, my friend. Water taken in small quantities serves only to disentangle the particles of the bile, and give them more activity, whereas they should be drowned in a copious dilution. I will warrant the consequence, and if thou wilt not take my word, Celsus himself shall be thy security."

It need hardly be wondered at that Gil Blas soon came to believe that he also had a natural talent for the medical profession, which was so easy to acquire and lucrative to practise, and was rapidly promoted as assistant to his master.

"Listen, my child," said the doctor one day, "I will immediately disclose to thee the whole extent of that salutary art which I have professed so many years. Know, my friend, all that is required is to bleed thy patients and make them drink warm water. This is the secret of curing all the distempers incident to man. I have nothing more to impart; thou knowest physic to the very bottom."

Thus the *ci-devant* valet soon robed himself in a physician's gown and long *perruque*, then went forth to practise, but resolved to drink wine every day, of which he said he drank huge draughts, and (no disparagement to the Roman oracle) "the more I filled my stomach, the less did that organ complain of the injury it received". So he bled and watered the community. But the time soon came when this young practitioner met with a reverse. When called in to consultation with a Spanish doctor of another school, a dispute arose on the subject of the water-cure, which ended in a pitched battle being fought between the rival medicos over the unfortunate patient, and they were not separated until each had lost a handful of hair. This ended in the discharge of Gil Blas, who immediately took the opportunity of imbibing a considerable quantity of wine at the first tavern he came across, and returned to his patron in a condition of considerable elevation.

The wine having made him thirsty, he consumed a large quantity of water while telling his story.

"I see, Gil Blas, thou hast no longer an aversion to water," said the physician. "Heaven be praised! thou drinkest it now like nectar! a change that does not at all surprise me, my friend."

"Sir," replied Gil Blas, "there's a time for all things; I would not at present give a pint of water for a hogshead of wine."

That Le Sage had a very poor opinion of the professors of the art of medicine in his time may be gathered from the following conversation which Gil Blas holds with his employer: "Scarcely a day passed in which we did not visit eight or ten patients each, from whence it may be easily conceived what a quantity of blood was spilt and water drank. But I do not know how it happened, all our sick died. We very seldom had occasion to make three visits to one patient; at the second we were either told that he had just been buried, or we found them at the last gasp; and as I was but a young physician who had not yet had time to be inured to murder, I began to be very uneasy at the fatal events which might be laid to my charge." And so he at last gave it up, after being threatened with his life by a gallant, whose wife had succumbed to his drastic treatment.

Towards the close of the story Gil Blas has an interview with his former master, who describes to his old pupil the change that had taken place in the practice of medicine in a few years, which forms an interesting account of the transition through which the medical art was passing towards the end of the seventeenth century.

"Ah, my son," says the worthy doctor, "what a change has happened in physic within these few years. There are in this city, physicians, or such as call themselves so, who are yoked to the triumphal car of antimony—*currus triumphalis antimonii.* Truants from the school of Paracelsus, adorers of kermes, accidental curers who make the whole science of medicine consist in knowing how to prepare chymical drugs. What shall I tell you! Everything is turned topsy-turvey in their method. Bleeding at the foot, for example, hitherto so seldom practised, is now almost the only bleeding in use. Those purgatives which were formerly gentle and benign are now changed for emetics and kermes.

"I published a book against this brigandage of medicine, but it was no use. The surgeons, mad with ambition of acting as physicians, think themselves sufficiently qualified when there is nothing to be done but to give kermes and emetics, to which they add bleeding at the foot, according to their own fancy. They even proceed so far as to mix kermes in apozems and cordial potions; and so they are on a par with your celebrated prescribers. This contagion has spread also among the cloisters. There are some monks who act both as apothecaries and surgeons. These apes of medicine apply themselves to chemistry, and compose pernicious drugs, with which they abridge the lives of the reverend fathers."

The doctor describes the dawn of pharmacy in France and Spain, which was first practised by the surgeons who became surgeon-apothecaries. The use of emetics in medical treatment came largely into vogue in 1658. It is said that the life of Louis XIV. was saved by an emetic administered by Dusausoi, in opposition to the opinion of Vallot, the chief physician to the king.

CHAPTER VI.

BEN JONSON.

Ben Jonson gives a description of the itinerant doctor in Queen Elizabeth's time, who travelled the country, usually accompanied by a jester or zany, as he was called, who carried the box or chest containing his remedies. We see the professor with his copper rings, shining chain, better than gold but not quite so valuable, his yellow jewel, his dirty feather-embroidered suit, grave look, and starched beard.[45] Hush! he begins:—

"Most noble gentlemen and my worthy patrons!—I have nothing to sell, little or nothing to sell, though I protest, I and my six servants are not able to make of my precious balsam so fast as it is fetched away from my lodging by the worthy men of the town. O health! health! the blessing of the rich, the riches of the poor, who can buy thee at too dear a rate? And since there is no enjoying the world without thee, for when a humid flux or catarrh, by the mutability of air, falls from your head into an arm or shoulder, take you a rose noble or an angel of gold and apply to the place affected; see what good effect it can work. No, no; to this blessed unguent, this rare extraction, that hath only power to dispose all malignant humours that proceed either of hot, cold, moist, or windy causes; to fortify the most indigest and crude stomach—aye, were it one that through extreme weakness vomited blood, applying only a warm napkin to the place after the unction and fricace; for the vertigoe in the head, putting out a drop into your nostrils, likewise behind the ears, a most sovereign and approved remedy; the *mal caduco*, cramps, convulsions, paralysies, epilepsies, tremor cordia, retind nerves, ill vapours of the spleen, and stoppings of the liver, or stops a dysentery, immediately cureth poison of the small guts, and cures melancholia, being taken and applied according to my printed recipe (shows his bill and vial, and the zany sings a song). It will cost you eight crowns, and has cured all the kings in Christendom. Many have attempted to make this oil, wasting thousands of crowns in the ingredients (for there go to it sixty several simples, besides some quantity of human fat for conglutination, which we buy of the anatomists); but when these practitioners come to the last decoction, blow, blow! puff, puff! it flies in fumes, poor wretches.

"Gentlemen, honourable gentlemen, I will undertake by virtue of chemical art, out of the honourable hat that covers your head, to extract the four elements—that is to say, the fire, air, water, and earth, and return you your felt without burn or stain. You all know, honourable gentlemen, I never valued this ampulla or vial at less than eight crowns, but for this time I am content to be deprived of it for six; six crowns, then, is the price in courtesy. I know you cannot offer me less; take it or leave it, howsoever, both it and I are at your service (zany sings another song).

"Well, I am in a humour at this time to make a present of the small quantity my coffer contains to the rich in courtesy, and to the poor for God's sake; wherefore now mark, I asked you six crowns, and six crowns at other times you have paid me: you shall not give me six crowns, nor five, nor four, nor three, nor two, nor one, nor half a one, nor a shilling; sixpence it will cost you or £60. Expect no lower price, for I will not bate a jot; and this I take away as a pledge of your love, to carry something from amongst you to show I am not condemned."

CHAPTER VII.

SIR WALTER SCOTT.

T<small>HAT</small> picturesque period when the astrologer formed part of the *entourage* of almost every European court, and was petted by emperors and kings, is graphically described by Sir Walter Scott in *Quentin Durward* in the following words:—

"Louis XI. of France had retired to the castle of Plessis, where he received an ambassador from the Duke of Burgundy, with whom his relations were somewhat strained. Attached to the court of the king, we are told, and lodged in magnificent apartments, was the celebrated astrologer, poet, and philosopher, Galeotti Martius, author of the famous treatise *De Vulgo Incognitis*. He had long flourished at the court of the King of Hungary, from whom, it is said, he was in some measure decoyed by Louis, who grudged the Hungarian monarch the counsels of a sage accounted so skilful in reading the decrees of Heaven. Martius was none of those ascetic, withered, pale professors of mystic learning of those days, who bleared their eyes over the midnight furnace, and macerated their bodies by outmatching the polar bear. He was trained in arms, and renowned as a wrestler. His apartment was splendidly furnished, and on a large oaken table lay a variety of mathematical and astrological instruments, all of the most rich materials and curious workmanship. His astrolabe of silver was the gift of the Emperor of Germany, and his Jacob's staff of ebony, jointed with gold, was a mark of esteem from the reigning Pope. In person the astrologer was a tall, bulky, yet stately man. His features, though rather overgrown, were dignified and noble, and a Santon might have envied the dark and downward sweep of his long descending beard. His dress was a chamber robe of the richest Genoa velvet, with ample sleeves clasped with frogs of gold, and lined with sables. It was fastened round his middle by a broad belt of virgin parchment, round which were represented in crimson characters the signs of the zodiac.

"Such was the astrologer of Louis XI., who was consulted in matters of state policy and intrigue, and exercised a considerable influence over that weak monarch.

"The costly nature of such a courtier is well illustrated in an interview which the king has with his astrologer, and leaves on his table a purse of gold as a reward for some special service. But the contents did not by any means satisfy the man of science.

"He emptied the purse, which contained neither more nor less than ten gold pieces.

"The indignation of the astrologer was extreme.

152

"'Thinks he that for such paltry rate of hire I will practice that celestial science which I have studied with the Armenian Abbot of Istrahoff, who had not seen the sun for forty years; with the Greek Dubravius, who is said to have raised the dead; and have even visited the Scheik Ebn Hali in his cave in the desert of Thebais? No, by Heaven! He that contemns art shall perish through his ignorance. Ten pieces!—a pittance which I am half-ashamed to offer to Toinette to buy her new breast laces.'"

CHAPTER VIII.

DUMAS.

P<small>HARMACY</small>, pure and simple, occupies but a small space in literature, although the disciples of the sister arts of medicine and alchemy have often formed interesting studies for many great writers of fiction.

Unfortunately the scientific knowledge of the average novelist is, as a rule, extremely limited, and the effects they attribute to certain drugs are usually as fabulous as those believed in the dark ages. They tell us of mysterious poisons of untold power, an infinitesimal quantity of which will cause instantaneous death without leaving a trace behind. They also describe anæsthetics so powerful that a whiff from a bottle or the wave of a handkerchief will at once produce insensibility for any period desired. In fact the writer of romance has a *pharmacopœia* of his own.

But why should we cavil at it or try to analyse it in the prosaic test-tube of modern science.

Exclude the marvellous and mysterious, and you kill romance. It performs its mission if it succeeds in interesting and amusing us, so we should be lenient if it errs in mere matters of science.

The art of the romancer reaches its height when it succeeds in mixing the possible with the impossible so that we can scarce perceive it.

There are few characters in the realm of romantic fiction more fascinating than the Count Monte Christo. As a work of imaginative power and absorbing interest, this masterpiece of Dumas stands unique. Nothing is impossible to this extraordinary individual, and incident after incident of the most dramatic and exciting nature crowd one upon another.

The count, who is supposed to have studied the art of medicine in the East, has always a remedy ready for every ill; from his hashis, in which he is a profound believer, to his mysterious stimulating elixir, a liquid, we are told, of the colour of blood, which he always kept in a phial composed of Bohemian glass.

A single drop of this vital fluid, if allowed to fall on the lips, almost before it reaches them, restores the marble and inanimate form to life. His pill-boxes were composed of emeralds and precious stones of huge size, and their contents were composed of drugs whose effect was almost beyond comprehension.

In the *Memoirs of a Physician*, Dumas describes an alchemist of the last century, a time when the seekers after the philosopher's stone and the *elixir vitæ* had almost died out. Joseph Balsamo, the hero of the story, drawn from the life of the notorious Cagliostro, is a necromancer of the modern kind, who works his marvels by what is now known as hypnotism or mesmerism, a condition little understood in those days. Althotas, an alchemist of renown, lives with Balsamo, and aids him in his researches.

He is described as "an old man of over a hundred years, with grey eyes, hooked nose, and trembling bony hands, and he sits half-buried in his chair. Clad in a long silk robe, now nothing but a shapeless, colourless ragged covering, he grumbled as he drew over his ears his cap of velvet, from under which a few locks of silver hair peeped out.

"The dwelling of the alchemist," says the novelist, "might be about eight or nine feet high and sixteen in diameter; it was lighted from the top like a well, and hermetically closed on the four sides."

"Besides the phials, boxes, books, and papers strewed around, copper pincers were seen, and pieces of charcoal which had been dipped in various liquids; there was also a large vase half full of water, and from the roof, hung by threads, were bundles of herbs, some apparently gathered the night before, others a hundred years ago. A keen odour prevailed in this laboratory, which in one less strange would have been called a perfume.

"The old man was seated in his armchair on wheels, in the centre of a marble table formed like a horseshoe, and heaped up with a whole world, or rather whole chaos, of plants, phials, tools, books, instruments, and papers covered with cabalistic characters.

"He was so absorbed that he never raised his head when Balsamo appeared.

"The light of an astral lamp, suspended from the culminating point of the window in the roof, fell on his bald, shining head.

"He was turning to and fro in his fingers a small white bottle, the transparency of which he was trying before his eye, as a good housekeeper tries the eggs which she buys at market.

"Balsamo gazed on him at first in silence; then, after a moment's pause:—

"'Well,' said he, 'have you any news?'

"'Yes, yes; come hither, Acharat, you see me enchanted—transported with joy! I have found—I have found——'

"'What?'

"'Pardieu! what I sought.'

"'Gold?'

"'Gold, indeed! I am surprised at you!'

"'The diamond?'

"'Gold? diamonds? The man raves! A fine discovery, forsooth, to be rejoiced at!'

"'Then what you have found is your elixir?'

"'Yes, my son, yes!—the elixir of life! Life?—what do I say?—the eternity of life!'

"'Oh!' said Balsamo in a dejected voice (for he looked on this pursuit as mere insanity), 'so it is that dream which occupies you still?'

"But Althotas, without listening, continued to gaze delightedly at his phial.

"'At last,' said he, 'the combination is complete: the elixir of Aristæus, twenty grains; balm of mercury, fifteen grains; precipitate of gold, fifteen grains; essence of the cedar of Lebanon, twenty-five grains.'

"'But it seems to me that, with the exception of the elixir of Aristæus, this is precisely your last combination, master?'

"'Yes, but I had not then discovered one more ingredient, without which all the rest are as nothing.'

"'And have you discovered it now?'

"'Yes.'

"'Can you procure it?'

"'I should think so!'

"'What is it?'

"'We must add to the several ingredients already combined in this phial, the three last drops of the life-blood of an infant.'

"'Well, but where will you procure this infant?' said Balsamo horror-struck.

"'I trust to you for that.'

"'To me? You are mad, master!'

"'Mad? And why?' asked the old man, perfectly unmoved at this charge, and licking with the utmost delight a drop of the fluid which had escaped from the cork of the phial and was trickling down the side.

"'Why, for that purpose you must kill the child.'

"'Of course we must kill him; and the handsomer he is the better.'"

But in the end the old man falls a victim to his own infatuation, and at length dies incontinently without discovering the long-looked-for arcana.

CHAPTER IX.

READE.

A_N excellent picture of a physician of the fifteenth century is drawn by that master in the art of fiction, Charles Reade, in his work *The Cloister and the Hearth*, a story of much historic interest and beauty.

The hero, Gerard, wounded in an encounter with a bear, lies sick at Düsseldorf, and is visited by a physician.

"It was an imposing figure that entered the sick room; an old gentleman in a long sober gown trimmed with rich fur, cherry-coloured hose, and pointed shoes, with a sword by his side in a morocco scabbard, a ruff round his neck, not only starched severely, but treacherously stiffened in furrows by rebatoes, or a little hidden framework of wood; and on his head a four-cornered cap with a fur border; on his chin and bosom, a majestic white beard. This was the full dress of a physician. A boy followed at his heels with a basket, where phials, lint, and surgical tools rather courted than shunned observation."

The old doctor, on learning that his patient suffered from a wound, exclaimed, "This must be cauterised forthwith," and immediately called for his urchin to heat his iron. Gerard, who didn't like the look of things, informed the leech the wound was caused by the bear's paw, and not his jaw.

"And why did'st not tell me that at once?"

"Because you kept telling me instead."

"Never conceal aught from your leech, young man," continued the senior, who was a good talker, but one of the worst listeners in Europe. "Well, it is an ill business. All the horny excrescences of animals—to wit, claws of tigers, panthers, badgers, cats, bears, and the like, and horn of deer, and nails of humans, especially children, are imbued with direst poison. I had better have been bitten by a cur, *whatever you may say*, than gored by a bull or stag, or scratched by bear. However, shalt have a good biting cataplasm for thy leg; meantime keep we the body cool: put out thy tongue!—good!—fever. Let me feel thy pulse: good!—fever! I ordain flebotomy, and on the instant. Hans, go fetch the things needful, and I will entertain the patient meantime with reasons."

The man of art then entered into a learned disquisition on pathology and the healthful practice of blood-letting. Time was evidently no object, neither the extremity of his patient. "Think not," said he warmly, "that it suffices to bleed; any paltry barber can open a vein. The art is to know what vein to empty, and for what disease. T'other day they brought me one tormented with earache. I let him blood in the right thigh, and away flew his earache. By-the-bye, he has died since then. Another came with the toothache. I bleed him behind the ear, and relieved him in a jiffey. He is also since dead as it happens."

After thus reciting his powers in venesection, the worthy doctor thought he could not do better than back it up with a show of knowledge, and recommenced on a new theme.

"Know, young man, that two schools of art contend at this moment throughout Europe. The Arabian, whose ancient oracles are Avicenna, Rhazes, Allricazis; and its revivers are Chauliac and Lanfranc; and the Greek school, whose modern champions are Bessarion, Platinus, and Marsilius Ficinus, but whose pristine doctors were medicine's very oracles—Phœbus, Chiron, Æsculapius, and his sons Podalinus and Machaon, Pythagoras, Democritus; Praxagoras, who invented the arteries, and Dioctes, *qui primus urinæ animum dedit*. All these taught orally. Then came Hippocrates, the eighteenth from Æsculapius, and of him we have manuscripts, to him we owe 'the vital principle'. He also invented the bandage, and tapped for water on the chest; and above all, he dissected, yet only quadrupeds, for the brutal prejudices of the pagan vulgar withheld the human body from the knife of science. Him followed Aristotle, who gave us the aorta, the largest blood- vessel in the human body."

"Surely, sir, the Almighty gave us all that is in our bodies, and not Aristotle nor any Grecian man," objected Gerard humbly.

"Child! of course He gave us the thing; but Aristotle did more—he gave us the name of the thing. But young men will still be talking. The next great light was Galen; he studied at Alexandria, then the home of science. He, justly malcontent with quadrupeds, dissected apes, as coming nearer to man, and bled like a Trojan. Then came Theophilus, who gave us the nerves, the lacteal vessels, and the *pia mater*."

"I am put to silence, sir."

"And that is better still, for garrulous patients are ill to cure, especially in fever. I say, then, that Eristratus gave us the cerebral nerves and the milk vessels; nay, more, he was the inventor of lithotomy, whatever you may say. Then came another whom I forget; you do somewhat perturb me with your petty exceptions. Then came Ammonius, the author of lithotrity, and here comes Hans with the basin to stay your volubility. Blow thy chafer, boy, and hand me the basin; 'tis well. Arabians, quotha! What are they but a sect of yesterday, who about the year 1000 did fall in with the writings of those very Greeks, and read them awry, having no concurrent light of their own? for their demi-god and camel-driver, Mahomed, impostor in science as in religion, had strictly forbidden them anatomy, even of the lower animals, the which he who severeth from medicine, *tollit solem e mundo*, as Tully quoth. Nay, wonder not at my fervour, good youth; where the general weal stands in jeopardy a little warmth is civic, humane, and honourable. Now, there is settled of late in this town a pestilent Arabist, a mere empiric, who, despising anatomy, and scarce knowing Greek from Hebrew, hath yet spirited away half my patients, and I tremble for the rest. Put forth thine ankle; and thou, Hans, breathe on the chafer."

At the end of this tirade Gerard's friend and fellow-traveller Denys appears on the scene, and will not hear of the bleeding being carried out. The blustering but good-tempered soldier soon comes to hot words with the old physician on the subject, and a wordy battle ensues, which ends by the doctor being offended, and decides to beat a dignified retreat. The concluding scene is too good to omit, and we will give it in the author's own words.

"Ah! you reject my skill, you scorn my art. My revenge shall be to leave you to yourself; lost idiot, take your last look at me, and at the sun. Your blood be on your head!" And away he stamped.

But on reaching the door he whirled and came back, his wicker tail twirling round after him like a cat's.

"In twelve hours at furthest you will be in the secondary stage of fever. Your head will split. Your carotids will thump. Aha! And let but a pin fall, you will jump to the ceiling. Then send for me, and *I'll not come*." He departed. But at the door-handle gathered fury, wheeled and came flying, with pale, terror-stricken boy and wicker tail whisking after him. "Next will come —*Cramps of the stomach*. Aha! "Then—

Bilious vomit. Aha! "Then—*Cold*

sweat and deadly stupor. "Then—

Confusion of all the senses. "Then—

Bloody vomit.

"And after that nothing can save you, not even I; and if I could I would not, and so farewell."

Even Denys changed colour at threats so fervent and precise; but Gerard only gnashed his teeth with rage at the noise, and seized his hard bolster with kindling eye.

This added fuel to the fire, and brought the insulted ancient back from the impassable door, with his whisking train.

"And after that—*Madness!*

"And after that—*Black vomit!*

"And then—*Convulsions!*

"And then—*That cessation of all vital functions the vulgar call 'death,'* for which thank your own Satanic folly and insolence. Farewell." He went. He came. He roared: "And think not to be buried in any Christian churchyard, for the bailiff is my good friend, and I shall tell him how and why you died: *felo de se! felo de se!* Farewell."

Gerard sprang to his feet on the bed by some supernatural gymnastic power excitement lent him, and, seeing him so moved, the vindictive orator came back at him fiercer than ever, to launch some master-threat the world has unhappily lost, for as he came with his whisking train and shaking his fist, Gerard hurled the bolster furiously in his face and knocked him down like a shot, the boy's head cracked under his falling master's, and crash went the dumb-stricken orator into the basket, and there sat, wedged in an inverted angle, crushing phial after phial. The boy, being light, was strewed afar, but in a squatting posture, so that they sat in a sequence, like graduated specimens, the smaller howling. But soon the doctor's face filled with horror, and he uttered a far louder and unearthly screech, and kicked and struggled with wonderful agility for one of his age.

He was sitting on the hot coals.

They had singed the cloth, and were now biting the man. Struggling wildly but vainly to get out of the basket, he rolled over with it sideways, and lo! a great hissing; then the humane Gerard ran and wrenched off the tight basket, not without a struggle. The doctor lay on his face groaning, handsomely singed with his own chafer, and slaked a moment too late by his own villainous compounds, which, however, being as various and even beautiful in colour as they were odious in taste, had strangely diversified his grey robe, and painted it more gaudy than neat.

Gerard and Denys raised him up and consoled him. "Courage, man, 'tis but cautery; balm of Gilead—why, you recommended it but now to my comrade here."

A curious specimen of medical treatment came to light when Philip, Duke of Burgundy, lay sick at Bruges. He was a doughty warrior this Earl of Holland, as he was sometimes called, and wealthy withal, so the best advice was secured.

"Now, paupers got sick and got well as Nature pleased, but woe betided the rich," says the novelist, "in an age when for one Mr. Malady killed, three fell by Dr. Remedy.

160

"The duke's complaint, nameless then, is now called diphtheria. He was old and weak, so Dr. Remedy bled him.

"The duke turned cold—wonderful!

"Then Dr. Remedy had recourse to the arcana of science.

"Ho! This is grave. Flay me an ape incontinent, to clap him to the duke's breast! Officers of state ran septemvious, seeking an ape to counteract the blood-thirsty tomfoolery of the human species.

"But an ape could not be found.

"Then Dr. Remedy grew impatient, and bade flay a dog.

"A dog is next best to an ape; only it must be a dog all of one colour.

"So they flayed a liver-coloured dog and clapped it, yet palpitating, to their sovereign's breast; and he died."

Thus ended Philip the Good.

CHAPTER X.

DICKENS.

THE apothecary of romance is almost invariably pale and lean, with head nearly destitute of hirsute covering, and a man of retiring habits and sad demeanour. This is perhaps because he gets little chance to make the wherewithal to make him fat, and has few opportunities to seek enjoyment and recreation.

Dickens' chemist, whom he describes in his pathetic little story *The Haunted Man*, is no exception to this rule. "Who could have seen his hollow cheek, his sunken, brilliant eye; his black-attired figure, indefinably grim, although well knit and well proportioned; his grizzled hair hanging like tangled seaweed about his face,—as if he had been through his whole life a lonely mark for the chafing and beating of the great deep of humanity—but might have said he looked like a haunted man?

"Who could have observed his manner—taciturn, thoughtful, gloomy, shadowed by habitual reserve, retiring always and jocund never, with a distraught air of reverting to a bygone place and time, or of listening to some old echoes in his mind—but might have said it was the manner of a haunted man?

"Who could have heard his voice—slow-speaking, deep and grave, with a natural fulness and melody in it which he seemed to set himself against and stop—but might have said it was the voice of a haunted man?

"Who that had seen him in his inner chamber, part library and part laboratory,—for he was, as the world knew far and wide, a learned man in chemistry, and a teacher on whose lips and hands a crowd of aspiring ears and eyes hung daily,—who that had seen him there, upon a winter night, alone, surrounded by his drugs and instruments and books; the shadow of his shaded lamp, a monstrous beetle on the wall, motionless among a crowd of spectral shapes raised there by the flickering of the fire upon the quaint objects around him; some of these phantoms (the reflection of glass vessels that held liquids) trembling at heart like things that knew his power to uncombine them, and to give back their component parts to fire and vapour;—who that had seen him then, his work done and he pondering in his chair before the rusted grate and red flame, moving his thin mouth as if in speech, but silent as the dead, would not have said that the man seemed haunted and the chamber too?"

In the *Pickwick Papers* the author describes in one of his happiest veins, the troubles of a chemist who is suddenly called to serve on a common jury— to try indeed the celebrated case of "Bardell *versus* Pickwick".

"'Answer to your names, gentlemen, that you may be sworn,' said the gentleman in black.

"'Richard Upwitch.'

"'Here,' said the greengrocer.

"'Thomas Groffin.'

"'Here,' said the chemist.

"'Take the book, gentlemen. You shall well and truly try——'

"'I beg this court's pardon,' said the chemist, who was a tall, thin, yellow-visaged man, 'but I hope this court will excuse my attendance.'

"'On what grounds, sir?' said Mr. Justice Stareleigh.

"'I have no assistant, my lord,' said the chemist.

"'Then you ought to be able to afford it, sir,' said the judge reddening, for Mr. Justice Stareleigh's temper bordered on the irritable, and brooked not contradiction.

"'I know I *ought* to do, if I got on as well as I desired, but I don't, my lord,' answered the chemist.

"'Swear the gentlemen,' said the judge peremptorily.

"The officer had got no further than the 'You shall well and truly try' when he was again interrupted by the chemist.

"'I am to be sworn, my lord, am I?' said the chemist.

"'Certainly, sir,' replied the testy little judge.

"'Very well, my lord,' replied the chemist in a resigned manner. 'Then there'll be murder before this trial's over: that's all. Swear me if you please, sir.' And sworn the chemist was before the judge could find words to utter.

"'I merely wanted to observe, my lord,' said the chemist, taking his seat with great deliberation, 'that I've left nobody but an errand boy in my shop. He is a very nice boy, my lord, but he is not acquainted with drugs; and I know that the prevailing impression in his mind is, that Epsom salts means oxalic acid, and syrup of senna, laudanum. That's all, my lord.' With this, the tall chemist composed himself into a comfortable attitude, and, assuming a pleasant expression of countenance, appeared to have prepared himself for the worst."

This little sketch shows the disabilities the chemist laboured under before he was exempted from jury service, and the intimate knowledge Dickens had of almost every phase of life on which he wrote.

In *Oliver Twist* he gives us an instance of prompt prescribing on the part of the parochial doctor's assistant and dispenser, related by Bumble.

Mr. Bumble betakes himself to the undertaker's shop to arrange for the funeral.

"'Bayton,' said the undertaker looking from the scrap of paper to Mr. Bumble; 'I never heard the name before.'

"Bumble shook his head as he replied, 'Obstinate people, Mr. Sowerberry —very obstinate. Proud, too, I'm afraid, sir.'

"'Proud, eh?' exclaimed Mr. Sowerberry with a sneer. 'Come, that's too much.'

"'Oh, its sickening,' replied the beadle; 'antimonial, Mr. Sowerberry!'

"'So it is,' acquiesced the undertaker.

"'We only heard of the family the night before last,' said the beadle; 'and we shouldn't have known anything about them then, only a woman who lodges in the same house made an application to the parochial committee for them to send the parochial surgeon to see a woman as was very bad. He had gone out to dinner, but his 'prentice (which is a very clever lad) sent 'em some medicine in a blacking bottle off hand.'

"'Ah, there's promptness,' said the undertaker.

"'Promptness indeed!' replied the beadle. 'But what's the consequence; what's the ungrateful behaviour of these rebels, sir? Why, the husband sends back word that the medicine won't suit his wife's complaint, and so she shan't take it—says she shan't take it, sir! Good, strong, wholesome medicine, as was given with great success to two Irish labourers and a coal-heaver only a week before. Sent 'em for nothing, with a blacking bottle in, and he sends back word that she shan't take it, sir!'"

THACKERAY.

The great satirist, in *Pendennis*, gives us a brief sketch of the apothecary of the Georgian era in the early life of John Pendennis, who in the city of Bath practised as an apothecary and surgeon, "attending gentlemen in their sickrooms, and ladies at the most interesting periods of their lives, and condescending to sell a brown-paper plaister to a farmer's wife across the counter, or to vend tooth-brushes, hair-powder, and London perfumery". How he eventually merged into John Pendennis, Esq., of Fairoaks, Clavering, with a "family pride," is it not described with the pen of inimitable genius in the pages of the story?

CHAPTER XI.

MARRYAT.

IN his novel entitled *Japhet in Search of a Father*, Captain Marryat introduces to us that eccentric apothecary, Mr. Phineas Cophagus; and although the character is doubtless exaggerated to some extent, it forms an amusing picture of the practising apothecary in the early part of this century.

Japhet, who is taken in hand and apprenticed to the worthy practitioner, describes the shop looking upon Smithfield Market, with its usual allowance of green, yellow, and blue bottles. All the patent medicines in the known world were kept in stock, even to the all-sufficient medicine for mankind of Mr. Euony. The shop was large, and at the back part there was a most capacious iron mortar with a pestle to correspond.

The proprietor himself, we are told, might have been forty-five years of age. "He was of middle height, his face was thin, his nose very much hooked, his eyes small and piercing, with a good-humoured twinkle in them. His mouth was large and drawn down at one corner. He was stout in his body, and carried a considerable protuberance before him, which he was in the habit of patting with his left hand complacently. But although stout in his body, his legs were mere spindles, so that in his appearance he reminded you of some bird of the crane genus.

"He dressed in a black coat and waistcoat, white cravat, and high collar to his shirt; blue cotton-net pantaloons and Hessian boots, both fitting so tight that it appeared as if he was proud of his spindle shanks. His hat was broad-brimmed and low, and he carried a stout black cane with a gold top in his right hand, almost always raising the gold top to his nose when he spoke.

"The apothecary's assistant, Brookes, was a tall, fresh-coloured, but hectic-looking young man, and, with the ubiquitous Timothy, who took out the medicine, formed the staff of the establishment."

Japhet's introduction to the rudiments of the profession was to pound up some drugs in the big iron mortar, which he did with a will until the perspiration ran down him in streams. He hadn't been many months in the shop before he was left in charge with Timothy, who, after cudgelling his brains as to how they shall make a little money on their own account, agrees with Japhet to physic any one who comes in the shop.

The story is related by Japhet as follows:—

"An old woman soon came in, and addressing Timothy, said that she 'wanted something for her poor grandchild's sore throat'.

"'I don't mix up the medicines, ma'am,' replied Timothy; 'you must apply to that gentleman, Mr. Newland, who is behind the counter; he understands what is good for everybody's complaints.'

"'Bless his handsome face—and so young, too! Why, be you a doctor, sir?'

"'I should hope so,' replied I. 'What is it you require—a lotion or an embrocation?'

"'I don't understand those hard words, but I want some doctor's stuff.'

"'Very well, my good woman; I know what is proper,' replied I, assuming an important air. 'Here, Timothy, wash out this phial very clean.'

"'Yes, sir,' replied Timothy very respectfully.

"I took one of the measures, and putting in a little green, a little blue, and a little white liquid from the medicine bottles generally used by Mr. Brookes, filled it up with water, poured the mixture into the phial, corked, and labelled it *haustus statim sumendus*, and handed it over to the old woman.

"'Is the poor child to take it, or is it to rub outside?' inquired the old woman.

"'The directions are on the label; but you don't read Latin?'

"'Deary me, no! Latin! and do you understand Latin? What a nice clever boy!'

"'I should not be a good doctor if I did not,' replied I. On second thoughts I considered it advisable and safer that the application should be *external*, so I translated the label to her: *haustus*, rub it in; *statim*, on the throat; *sumendus*, with the palm of the hand.'"

Their next effort at doctoring is humorously described by the novelist in the following words:—

"An Irish labourer, more than half-tipsy, came in one evening and asked whether we had such a thing as was called '*A poor man's plaister*'. 'By the powers, it will be a poor man's plaister when it belongs to me; but they tell me that it is a sure and sartain cure for the thumbago, as they call it, which I've at the small of my back, and which is a hinder to my mounting up the ladder; so as it's Saturday night, and I've just got the money, I'll buy the plaister first, and then try what a little whisky inside will do. The devil is in't if it won't be driven out of me between the two.'

"We had not that plaister in the shop, but we had blister plaisters, and Timothy, handing one to me, I proffered it to him. 'And what may you be after asking for the same?' inquired he.

"The blisters were sold at a shilling each, when spread on paper, so I asked him eighteen-pence, that we might pocket the extra sixpence.

"'By the powers, one would think that you had made a mistake, and handed me the rich man's plaister instead of the poor one's. It's less whisky I'll have to drink, any how; but here's the money, and the top of the morning to ye, seeing as how it's jist getting late.'

"Timothy and I laughed as we divided the sixpence. It appeared that after taking his allowance of whisky the poor fellow fixed the plaister on his back when he went to bed, and the next morning found himself in a condition not to be envied. It was a week before we saw him again, and, much to the horror of Timothy and myself, he walked into the shop when Mr. Brookes was employed behind the counter. Timothy perceived him before he saw us, and pulling me behind the large mortar, we contrived to make our escape into the back parlour, the door of which we held ajar to hear what would take place.

"'Murder and turf!' cried the man, 'but that was the devil's own plaister you gave me here for my back, and it left me as raw as a turnip, taking every bit of my skin off me entirely, forbye my lying in bed for a whole week and losing my day's work.'

"'I really do not recollect supplying you with a plaister, my good man,' replied Mr. Brookes.

"'Then by the piper that played before Moses, if you don't recollect it, I've an idea that I shall never forget it. Sure enough, it cured me, but wasn't I quite kilt before I was cured?'

"'It must have been some other shop,' observed Mr. Brookes. 'You have made a mistake.'

"'Devil a bit of a mistake, except in selling me the plaister. Didn't I get it of a lad in this same shop?'

"'Nobody sells things out of this shop without my knowledge.'

"The Irishman was puzzled—he looked round the shop. 'Well, then, if this a'n't the shop, it was own sister to it.'"

"Like all embryo apothecaries," says Japhet, "I carried in my appearance, if not the look of wisdom, most certainly that of self-sufficiency, which does equally well with the world in general. My forehead was smooth and very white, and my dark locks were combed back systematically and with a regularity that said, as plainly as hair could do, 'The owner of this does everything by prescription, measurement, and rule'. Altogether I cut such a truly medical appearance that even the most guarded would not have hesitated to allow me the sole conduct of a whitlow, from inflammation to suppuration, and from suppuration to cure, or have refused to have confided to me the entire suppression of a gumboil.

"Such were my personal qualifications at the time I was raised to the important office of dispenser of, I may say, life and death."

FOOTNOTES:

[1] Etc. is probably a direction *ad lib.* for the doctor speaking the formulæ.

[2] Hanbury's *Notes on Chinese Materia Medica.*

[3] Lilly's *Autobiography*, 1774.

[4] The Egyptian magical texts show that hair, feathers, the serpent's skin, and *"the blood of the mystic eye,"* were used as charms of protecting or destroying power. This very probably denotes what is known as the charm of dragon's blood, which is still employed as a potent love charm or philtre, the blood being now typified by the red resin of this name.

[5] Bullen's *Governmente of Health.* 1558.

[6] William Coles, *Adam in Eden.* 1657.

[7] Lib. viii., c. ii., 5.

[8] Now in the possession of Mr. E. W. Cox, to whom we are indebted for the sketch.

[9] *Hamlet*, act i., scene v.

[10] Paris, *Pharmacologia*, p. 294.

[11] *Romeo and Juliet*, act v., scene i.

[12] *Cymbeline*, scene vi.

[13] *Henry VI.*, part iii., act ii., scene iii.

[14] *Pericles*, act iii., scene ii.

[15] *Othello*, act v., scene ii.

[16] *King Lear*, act iii., scene iv.

[17] *Henry IV.*, part ii., act i., scene ii.

[18] *Henry VI.*, act v., scene iv.

[19] *Comedy of Errors*, act iv., scene i.

[20] *Two Gentlemen of Verona*, act ii., scene iv.

[21] *Lucrece*, v., 76.

[22] *King Henry IV.*, part ii., act iv., scene iv.

[23] *King Henry IV.*, part i., act ii., scene iv.

[24] *King Henry IV.*, part ii., act v., scene iii.

[25] *Othello*, act i., scene iii.

[26] *Love's Labour's Lost*, act v., scene ii.

[27] *Hamlet*, act iv., scene v.

[28] *Winter's Tale*, act iv., scene iii.

[29] *Othello*, act iii., scene iii.

[30] *Romeo and Juliet*, act iv., scene iii.

[31] *All's Well that Ends Well*, act ii., scene iii.

[32] *Macbeth*, act v., scene iii.

[33] *Winter's Tale*, act iv., scene iv.

[34] *Hamlet*, act iv., scene v.

[35] *Winter's Tale*, act iv., scene iii.

[36] *Macbeth*, act v., scene iii.

[37] *Love's Labour's Lost*, act v., scene ii.

[38] *Sonnets*, verses 118, 119.

[39] *The Faerie Queen*, book i., canto x.

[40] *The Faerie Queen*, book vi., canto vi.

[41] *The Faerie Queen*, book i., canto i.

[42] *The Faerie Queen*, book ii., canto vi.

[43] *The Faerie Queen*, book ii., canto vii.

[44] *Shepherd's Calendar*—July.

[45] Ben Jonson's *Fox*, act ii., scene i.